TIME TO BYRNE

TIMEKEEPER SERIES
BOOK ONE

S.E. REICHERT

5 PRINCE PUBLISHING
5PRINCEBOOKS.COM

Published by:

5 Prince Publishing and Books, LLC

DBA 5 Prince Publishing

PO Box 865

Arvada, Colorado 80001

This is a work of fiction. Names, characters, places, and incidents are the product of the author's imagination or are used fictitiously. Any resemblance to actual persons, living or dead, events, or locales is entirely coincidental.

Digital ISBN: 978-1-63112-421-1

Print ISBN: 978-1-63112-422-8

Cover design by Marianne Nowicki

Interior design by 5 Prince Publishing

First Edition F09192025

For more information about this title, visit: www.5princebooks.com

To Madelyn and Delaney and all the adventures you'll have

ACKNOWLEDGMENTS

Many thanks to Lauren and your never-ending encouragement. I almost believe in myself because of you.

Thank you in the same heart, to Bernadette, who lifts me up and keeps me in her catalog, even when things get weird. I never would have made it this far without your faith in me.

Thank you to Cate Byers, always, and forever. You are an endless well of knowledge and the right amount of tough love to keep me humble and working harder.

Thank you to my family, except you, Penny Dreadful. You're a terrible cat and a chair thief. Your nose is snotty, and you've deleted so many lines with those delicious bean toes (which you never let me touch) that I don't know why I haven't sold you to the gypsies. I suppose it's because I may love you.

Thank you to my critique group and fellow writers. All of whom listen to all of my troubles and joys with unfailing grace and patience.

Thank you to Writing Heights Writers Association, Rocky Mountain Fiction Writers, and Wyoming Writers Inc, whose members and instructors help to inspire and educate me. Even after all these years, you are the support structure for my writing success.

Finally, a huge thank you to Jane Austen, who gave me unrealistic expectations in men and a love of language.

ALSO BY S.E. REICHERT

Timekeeper Series

Time to Byrne

Sweet Valley Series

Raising Elle

Granting Katelyn

Composing Laney

Stand Alone Titles

Back to the 80s

Rewriting Christmas

No Words After I Love You

TIME TO BYRNE

THE DAY LILY FELL

Lillian Byrne fell, face first down the stairs, as was typical of her style.

She might have blamed the Regency dress she'd worn to the 'Afternoon Tea' event, or her general inattentiveness. It could have been her excitement at taking this trip with her mother and brother as a present to herself for graduating from nursing school. It could have been her anticipation to participate in the reenactment of her favorite era in an English manor once owned by her ancestors, or the fact that she'd not slept much on the flight over from Chicago. Whatever the deciding factor, when the toe of her Converse caught the frayed carpet of the stair's precipice, she felt the heart-stopping, weightless abandon just before a horrible pressure closed in over her whole body. When the light returned, she felt her knees knocking like a leggy foal, tumbling and tangled, down the wooden steps. She hadn't been truly concerned until she felt a banister crack her temple rudely, then two balusters after that, smashing against her ribs. Her unfocused gaze made out the lace-lined light from a window above her. Then the world shrunk away, like a porthole getting smaller and smaller until a pinprick of light twinkled out and she was gone.

"Miss, oh heavens, Miss!"

Lillian heard the voice through the suffocating clouds of fluff between her ears. Some attendant must have found her, but her head hurt far too much to try opening her eyes just yet.

"Mom?" she croaked.

"Oh, poor dear. She's calling for her nursemaid."

"No nurses. I'm fine," Lillian mumbled.

"It's quite alright, I know her. I've fetched a doctor," came a muffled voice that felt both familiar and long-forgotten at the same time. The conversation continued on in roughened accents that Lillian was sure were being overdone on account of her being an American tourist. They fussed and fretted; warm hands pressed to her temple.

"It's fine, I'm used to falling," she groaned and tried to rise to her knees but the world spun and pulled her back down.

Lillian's head swam with pain, and she put her forehead to the cold floor. It hurt to breathe, and she muffled a cry against the stone. She tried to rise again but steady hands stilled her and held her down.

"Easy now, easy. Your head has a terrible bleed you need to stay still. We've just now sent young Master Byrne to fetch the doctor," the calm older man whispered. Lillian could not focus to see him.

"Master Byrne?" Lillian scoffed, hating but not surprised that her brother had somehow convinced the staff to call him by a title. The floor pressed against her forehead even harder and she felt blood slowly pooling in a warm ring around her cheek and ear. Mom was going to be worried and wouldn't let her climb any more towers, she thought, before slipping into the darkness.

2

Lillian was dreaming and came to slowly. She kept her eyes closed against the relentless pain in her forehead. She must have been in a hospital, but heard not the raucous machines, nor sensed the flickering and artificial light.

Heard not?

Was she thinking in proper Regency English?

She must have cracked her skull harder than she'd thought, to be postulating in Austen-ese. Lillian snorted a laugh, and cool fingers came to touch her forehead gently. She closed her eyes tighter and relaxed back into the pillows.

"Take ease, my angel." The deep voice was soothing. She must still be dreaming. No one ever called her an angel, and certainly no man. Lillian's brow drew in. She tried to sort out the confusion of cotton and haze in her mind.

Fingers delicately moved to her wounded temple, causing an incredible flash of pain that should have been dulled by the medication they would have given her. Her eyes sprung open and she expected them to be assaulted by the fluorescent lights of a hospital ICU, but only darkness surrounded her. Cool darkness, a canopied bed, and the outline of a golden-haired man coming into focus. He had a strong, dimpled chin and beautifully full lips. His eyes searched hers, blue as the Whitby Sea on a clear and bright day.

Surely these poetic musings were a definite sign of a brain bleed.

"Ah, the angel awakens. Such a shade of eyes I've never been more contented to fall into," he whispered, and his fingers traced her cheek. Lillian's mouth, dry and empty, fumbled, lips moving but no words coming. She wasn't in a hospital; she was certainly dead and this heavenly being was sent to take her to the afterlife.

"You are surely mistaken, good sir, for I am far from celestial and I cannot be awake," her voice was husky with sleep, and slipped into an accent that did not feel unnatural. She'd only been visiting in Britain for a couple of weeks; how could her speech have altered so? Maybe she *was* dead.

"Miss Byrne," he whispered, and they gazed at one another, in profound wonderment. His eyes closed and he shook his head as if to right his thoughts. "You must not speak," he said more seriously, with the morose diction of a professional. As if her being awake and aware had changed his whole demeanor. "You have succumbed to a terrible fainting spell, I'm afraid. You are quite delicate and must not move."

"I did no such thing. I am not delicate, and I did not faint." Lillian's sudden and strong argument took him back and he sat straighter with surprise. "I tripped. I'm a bold and fumbling clod at best."

The smallest of smiles pulled at the corner of his beautiful lips, and she was determined that she needed nothing more in life than to kiss him.

"You fell," he acquiesced.

"I think I'm still falling," she whispered back, and her eyes closed to the confusion and the constant throbbing of her head. When she tried to breathe in, her whole rib cage felt tight and limited. She placed a hand on her torso and felt a secure bandage over the tender ribs. They must have some kind of pain medication to give her, she thought as she fell back into the pillows and tried to sort out the moment. She willed herself to be more pragmatic.

Where was her mom? Why wasn't she here, fretting over her? Why hadn't they taken her to a hospital? Maybe the ambulance was still on its way out to the middle-of-nowhere estate they'd been visiting. This overzealous young actor was probably having a hard time getting out of character. She groaned again and put her fingers up to her head where she found a scratchy bandage secured around it.

"Please, Miss Byrne, please do not touch it, we have managed to staunch the bleeding. And though I don't like to praise my technique, the stitching is quite delicate in order to save you the horror of a permanent scar." His warm hand encircled her wrist. He delicately took her pulse. She opened her eyes and watched him counting the time on his pocket watch to the beat of her heart. The horror of a permanent scar? As if that's the worst thing that could happen to a girl? She tried to focus on the young actor more closely.

"Who are you?" she whispered.

"I'm afraid we have not yet had the pleasure of meeting while you were conscious. I am Doctor Blackwell—Matthew Blackwell," he paused to clear his throat, "The second, of course. My father insists while we practice within the same county that I remind every patient that he is the senior, more experienced physician."

"You?" she paused and looked at the dimple in his chin. "Aren't you a little young to be a doctor?"

The quick twitch of a smile threatened again, and she moved her hand to touch the dimple it made, but he held her wrist fast.

"I am eight and twenty. I'm surprised you would think me youthful." A new expression passed over his face, perturbed and confused.

"I beg your pardon, good sir," she said as quietly as possible, falling into the ridiculous speech play that he seemed insistent to keep up. It felt more natural every moment she spent in what was, she assumed, wakefulness. "I've fallen and hit my head and am not to be trusted in my observations. I meant no disrespect for your position. Indeed, I am most grateful that you are here. It is merely your youthful and divine dimple that confuses my befuddled mind so."

His thick throat swallowed as he looked down into her eyes, falling into them in a way that seemed to cross the lines of good bedside manner into something much more akin to other activities in the bedroom. She arched her eyebrow at him. He looked torn and confused.

"Your compliments are ill-placed, Miss Byrne. I certainly do not deserve such praise from such an—accomplished young lady such as yourself. One who should, by all accounts and in her current state of mental confusion, should be cautious how complimentary she is. While I encourage free thought between the sexes, some proprieties must be maintained. Even in the year of 1812."

Lillian sat up, far too quickly, and nearly startled the good doctor from his bedside perch. She took in a sharp breath and put both hands to her head.

"Oh 1812, huh? Look, I get you're trying for an Oscar here, but my head hurts so you can drop the act. It's 2023 and you damn well know it."

"Miss Byrne, please. Such language from a young woman of your standing is most unbecoming." The use of a swear word seemed to amuse him more than shock him, but he looked around the room to see who else had witnessed her uncommon outburst. They were alone.

"Look, pal, I think you've taken this act far enough," Lillian gasped. The world turned and tipped around her.

"Act? Pal?" the doctor's voice receded as Lillian felt the world go black again.

2

THE ANGEL AWAKES, AND
SHE'S MAD

Lillian was playing a game with herself; a game wherein every time she opened her eyes, she made rationalized odds as to whether or not she'd wake up in her own bed, or at the very least, a hospital, and that the good Doctor Blackwell would retreat back into her subconsciousness' fantasyland. She would take a deep breath in, squeeze her eyes shut tighter, and think of the ridiculous words of Dorothy.

There's no place like home.

The odds changed based on whether she sensed the confining drape of a nightgown around her legs. Or if she felt the warm hand that smelled of bread touching her forehead, from the housekeeper who had been faithfully in the room on every occasion she'd opened her eyes. Or if she smelled the lavender and pipe tobacco scent of the doctor, heard his even breathing, felt his warm fingers on her wrist. Her in-between dreams were plagued with the vast swirling dark, and the sound of a voice somewhere in the shadows calling to her. Sometimes it sounded like her mother, sometimes it sounded like her own voice echoing back.

The clearest one she heard, however, sounded like her father's voice. A man that had been absent from her life for years. He seemed worried and called to her, as if from a long hallway. Sometimes he was close to her bedside, speaking to her all of his sorrys and should-haves. Sometimes the voice spoke to the doctor. Sometimes the doctor was alone at her side, whispering the words *Lily*, and *Angel*, and *Darling*.

This time, the light felt different. Her eyes fluttered open to a blurry vision of a room. She knew that the head trauma and pain must have been a concussion. She'd studied enough of them when she interned in the ER to know the signs. She hadn't known how confused it would leave her though. When the fog cleared and she was again staring at the red velvet curtains of the ostentatious bed, she sighed. The room was empty.

The longer she kept her eyes open, the more the throbbing in her head intensified. But before she could close her eyes again, she received the greatest shock of her consciousness. Her father stepped from behind the bed's draperies, in full costume, his face concerned and hands holding a piece of parchment nervously. Though still blurry, she thought for sure that this was the moment that she'd finally woken up in her own time. Even though he'd been in and out of her life since childhood, at least his was a familiar face. Her chest flooded with relief.

"Dad?" she whispered and moved to sit up. But even as she did, he rushed to the side of her bed and spoke lowly.

"Listen to me Lily, you are in danger. I don't have time to explain, but you must play along."

"Play along?" Lillian asked. "What are you talking about? How did you even get here?"

"I know you want more answers, but please, you must trust me. You must pretend that you were born in this era, and are merely confused by the fall."

"But I am confused. What are you doing here? Where's Mom? Where's Will?" Lillian peppered him with questions but he shook his head quickly and held out his hands.

"Please, Lily, just listen!" He sighed and sat on her bed. He studied her face with a nostalgic sense of sadness. "I can't explain it all right now. But you are in the year 1812." Lillian inhaled to speak but he held up his hand. "I am working on getting you home, but until I do, you must pretend that you are from here, and that I am Colonel Mayfield, your uncle."

"I don't understand what this is about! How can I be in a different time, and how are you here?"

"I promise I will tell you everything, but for now, play along, Lily, just like when we used to host our Queen's tea parties, you remember?"

"But I—" her father leaned down and kissed her tender head and left the room.

Queen's tea parties? Her vision flashed back to one of the few times he was home. Always with some stories of his far away travels. He brought her pretty dresses, and they would put on their best royal British accents and be as proper as possible.

Play along?

The housekeeper entered the room, with the doctor and another man. Lillian took a deep breath when the other man's face came into view. He looked almost exactly like her brother, but with strange differences. A freckle on his cheek that hadn't been there before. A slightly narrower nose, not like their father's. Darker hair, like hers. He spoke nervously.

"Thank goodness, you're awake. We've all been terribly worried! I hope I am not disturbing you. The housemaid said you had called for me, and Doctor Blackwell thought it might help to bring back some memories if we were to converse. Colonel Mayfield seemed to agree. I hope I am not intruding."

"Will?" Lillian stuttered and shook her head. "What's happened to you?"

"I'm not sure what you mean, dear lady. When the Colonel said his niece was visiting, I was eager to meet you, but you had that nasty fall and thus we have not yet been acquainted. I am sorry this is how we are to first meet," the man said. He could have been Will; it could have been the concussion. Lillian remembered her father's words. He was the Colonel. Her uncle. She must pretend.

"I'm sorry," she said, befuddled and grasping at her bandaged head, "But who are you?"

"Oh! I apologize, I'm Fitzwilliam Byrne, and I believe we are distant cousins. And though I have only just learned of your existence from the Colonel, I am ever so happy to have another Byrne at Westbury," he responded kindly.

"Fitzwilliam?" she said. Her brain sorted through a deck of a thousand facts and remembered the diaries and family journals that her mother and she had pored over ever since she was a little girl. It was the reason she'd gone on the trip to begin with; to trace her family line.

The diaries of Fitzwilliam Byrne and his wife. Fitzwilliam held a key role in her family's history through his pristine and detailed diaries. His own mother had passed away, and he had moved to live with his aunt and uncle at Westbury Manor. The names and stories blurred in her mind and she groaned. Fitzwilliam lived in the 1800's. Lillian stared at his clothing, the room, and put her hand to her head. Before she could tear the scratchy fabric of the bandage away, warm fingers were there, capturing her wrist and reading her pulse. She looked up to see the doctor, silent and attentive as always beside her, keeping his eyes demurely turned away and studying her stats with a detached and professional manner. He cleared his throat.

"It is common for people who have sustained severe trauma to the head to forget the things they went through before the accident, or to formulate connections not yet forged," he said calmly to not-Will who nodded in understanding. Lillian glared at him. She could pretend.

"I am not formulating! This gentleman merely reminds me of

my brother. That we are distant cousins, it is not such a stretch of the imagination, given my state."

She took off the bandage then and laid back once more. She looked at Fitzwilliam, uncomfortable and so refined. Not at all like her brother. But if the drawings and paintings she'd seen could be believed, he was Fitzwilliam.

Her father had been so serious in his claim. The evidence was supporting it so far.

Lillian put a hand to her forehead, and her fingers touched the stitches. The possibility that she was somehow lost in a different era seemed to make the pounding headache worse and she felt sick to her stomach. She wanted to see how badly she was hurt, to see her own face, to know this was real.

"May I ..." she began the question but wondered if she really wanted the answer.

"Yes, anything, Miss Byrne," The doctor said from her other side.

"May I please," she stopped to word it correctly. "Trouble you for a looking glass so that I may see the extent of the damage?"

"Miss Byrne, it is quite a disturbing wound and I would not wish to distress you further," Doctor Blackwell argued.

"I am quite well enough to handle the sight," she said stubbornly and glared at him. "Or are you afraid that your stitching is subpar?" The grating insult seemed to take him back and Fitzwilliam laughed beside her.

"Miss Byrne! Such terrible manners for a Byrne," he laughed. "She must not be herself and I apologize, Doctor Blackwell."

The doctor smiled and shook his head. As if her rudeness were a ruse he saw through and thought it quite charming that she should put up such a brave front in the face of such trauma.

"It is quite all right." He turned to Lillian. "And I was not referring to my impeccable work, I was referring to the alteration of her rather plain appearance. I'll allow you to decide if that is for the better or worse," he retorted. Lillian gasped.

"You ass—assumptive cad," she stopped short of using a profanity and the doctor chuckled. Fitzwilliam at first looked horrified but then laughed along.

"He is indeed a match to your wit and most dark mood, cousin."

"My *lady*," the doctor smiled and handed her a silver handled mirror from the vanity table beside the bed.

It seemed, in all of the time suffering through her mother's obsession with the history and cultural norms of the era, that a true gentleman would not be so brash or rude. But perhaps the Austens and Brontës of the time were not so unlike the romantic idiots of the modern world, who tended to sugar-coat the affections and behaviors of the opposite sex. She snatched the mirror away from him with a glare.

The glass was milky and dusted, and for a moment Lillian feared that her vision had been impacted by the fall. She had gotten far too used to the modern world's minor conveniences. Like mirrors. Cameras with their fancy filters and effects. The face she found was her own, right down to the lavender eyes and the scar on her chin from a fall off a bike at the age of twelve. Her hair was frightful, even in its raven color and tangled length, and barely hid the large gash on the side of her head, now outlined with bruises. It was actually a wonder she'd survived. She gently prodded at the stitches and saw no sign of infection. They were fine stitches for something done by hand. In low light.

"Do not fear, dear cousin, I'm sure the ladies of the house can help you right your hair again when you are feeling better. You mustn't think it's unbecoming, you are, after all convalescing." She looked back at Fitzwilliam. He thought she was upset at the state of her hair, out of its proper complicated updo?

Doctor Blackwell smiled. "I actually prefer it," he paused and blushed.

"Down and wild from days in bed?" Lillian asked with a scowl. The words stopped Doctor Blackwell's movement and he stared at her for an uncomfortable moment in a way that made her wonder if he was imagining days in bed with her. Both men cleared their throats. Lillian scowled. That level of propriety seemed hard to fake. It was another point in support of her truly being in a different time, as her father had said.

"Yes, well, in any case, we can see to it that someone comes this afternoon to help you, if you wish," Fitzwilliam offered. "Mrs. Shaw," he said addressing the housekeeper. "Do you think we could send an invitation to the charming Miss Darlingwood? I know she is eager for new friends and since she heard news of your visit, she has asked after your health repeatedly." Fitzwilliam mentioned this woman, Miss Darlingwood, with a warmth and a blush. The world tumbled in her head.

Lillian closed her eyes and the mirror fell to the bed beside her, still clasped in her hand. More people she had to perform for, more people that knew her as someone she was not. She sighed and felt tears sting the corners of her eyes. How had this happened? When would her father come back? Would she ever get home again?

She sniffed and opened her eyes. She needed to move. To get up. She wouldn't gain understanding by lying in bed, stuck in a horrible dream state. She dried her eyes quickly and sat straighter. "My hair does not matter. What I would greatly like, is to get up and walk."

"It is not recommended, Miss Byrne," Doctor Blackwell said and looked into her eyes. "If you should fall again—"

"I will be careful," she interrupted. He gave her a disbelieving stare. "I assure you Doctor Blackwell, I am quite well enough to stand on my own."

"Oh? Will you be as careful as when you decided to take the stairs, eight at a time?" Doctor Blackwell argued. Fitzwilliam burst out in a beautiful, room-lighting laugh and in it, Lillian found the comfort of her own brother's laughter. She scowled at the man, like she would her brother.

"It wasn't the preferred method but it got me there with some haste," she countered and jutted her chin at the doctor in defiance. He looked down at her, eyes falling to her mouth, and his expression softened, his smile grew.

"If it were up to judgement on your spirit alone, I would think you are healed all but in the severity of the cut." His warm fingers went up to delicately touch the healing wound. She shied away until the contact against her skin seemed to draw the whole room into focus once more and she leaned in.

"You may walk," he said and pulled away. "In short increments and only when accompanied by someone else."

"Oh, well," she scoffed and sat back against her pillows, still pouting. "Thank you for your professional permission." Both men raised their eyebrows at her tone. Matthew leaned in to Fitzwilliam.

"I wonder if she's always this obstinate," he whispered though not so quietly that she wouldn't be assured to hear him.

"The Colonel assures me that she's usually much more so. She must be tired." Fitzwilliam nodded looking directly at Lillian.

"Oh you!" she took a small pillow and threw it at her cousin, connecting it squarely with his buttoned-up chest. Her new cousin laughed.

"I shall send someone to help you bathe and dress," he said softly and came closer to gently press a kiss to her hand. Doctor Blackwell watched and Lillian swore he had the look of envy on his face, as though he wished he could leave her with such warmth. Or maybe he wished he could be the one to bathe and dress her. She blushed.

"I can do that myse—"

"Please, Miss Byrne," Doctor Blackwell interjected. "I know you are quite ready to be healed and understand your frustrations, but waves of dizziness can catch one unaware after such a wound. Be you a grown man or a—" he stopped, seeming to battle with improper thoughts, "delicate, young woman."

"I am not delicate."

"So you keep insisting. Please," he sighed with frustration, "I ask that you take the opportunity to allow others to help you."

He gathered his navy-blue coat from the chair beside the bed and she noticed the dark circles beneath his eyes. Lillian wondered how long he'd been there, with her, beside her bed, no doubt sleeping in the chair in order to be close to her in the hours of her need. She had seen him in almost all of the moments she'd opened her eyes. Her heart warmed and built walls simultaneously, and she didn't know which reaction was the right one.

Lillian wasn't good at letting people help her. When her father had spent so many years disappearing and reappearing again, she'd learned that women couldn't count on anyone but themselves to make sure they survived and thrived in life. And here she was, stuck in an era where women had little choice but to be taken care of by men.

"Do you know when the Colonel will return?" she asked.

Doctor Blackwell paused, "I do not know, he passed us in the hall and asked that I keep watch over you. That he had business in Westbury to attend to."

"Does keeping watch over me mean you will return to walk with me?" she asked him, and then felt a hot flash warm her cheeks. She knew from the movies and books she'd been inundated with by her mother, that it was not proper for her, an unmarried young lady to ask an unmarried man for such a thing. She was not pretending well.

But the fact remained that Matthew Blackwell was the one person she was most familiar with, and it seemed that her father trusted him enough to be her caretaker. He'd been with her since she'd found herself in this strange and impossible set of circumstances. Fitzwilliam raised his eyebrows and looked at the young doctor in anticipation of his answer to such a strange and forward question.

"I—I must go and see to my own business, which I've been kept from these last three days."

"Three days?" Lillian stuttered. Had she been out that long?

"My father is expecting me as soon as my work here is concluded as I have much to catch up on in his clinic and with our personal affairs. I'm sure that your cousin, Miss Darlingwood, or the Colonel when he returns, would be more than happy to accompany you," he said softly, and donned his coat.

"You've been here for three days?" she reiterated the question as if reminding him that he hadn't sufficiently answered her.

"Quite so! He's a credit to his profession." Fitzwilliam jumped back into the conversation. "The good doctor even slept in the chair by your bedside in the event you should need anything at any time of day or night."

Lillian blushed and looked up at Doctor Blackwell who avoided her gaze with deliberate effort while he adjusted his collar and gathered up the medical journals he'd been reading by her side.

"It is merely my duty."

"Mr. Byrne," she said without taking her eyes off the doctor. "Could you please excuse us for just a small moment?"

"My dear cousin, I could not—"

"I will be here with the two of them," the housekeeper said from the other side of the bed, where she was folding fresh linens. Lillian looked at her and smiled. The older woman winked and Lillian felt like maybe they were already friends.

"Thank you, Mrs.—"

"Mrs. Shaw, Miriam Shaw," the housekeeper said and gave a small curtsey.

"Mrs. Shaw, thank you," Lillian said and nodded.

"Yes, of course." Fitzwilliam looked between the doctor and his cousin, still with an air of uncertainty.

"Now?" she asked and stared at Fitzwilliam with the universal look of someone who was dropping a huge hint.

"Of course, Miss Byrne," he said and nodded to the doctor and Mrs. Shaw before taking his leave.

"I shall take my leave as well," Doctor Blackwell said lowly. Miriam turned to put the linens away and busied herself tidying the bureau at the farthest side of the room,

"Wait, please," Lillian whispered and sat up to uncover her pale legs. They seemed longer and even more ungainly than normal. She stood on them, wobbly and unsure. The doctor's eyes lit with surprise and he moved to catch her if she fell.

"Miss Byrne, please."

"Don't go yet. Allow me to stand." She adjusted the twisted and overly long fabric of her bedgown. It pulled tight across her chest. Matthew looked away quickly.

"Miss Byrne you are not," he looked skyward. "Properly dressed."

"Did you or did you not spend the last three days beside my bed?"

"I did."

"And in that time, did you ever behave inappropriately?"

He scowled at her. "Of course I did not."

"Then why are you worried that your moral compass will suddenly falter?" She walked over to him and he clenched his jaw tightly, his hands tightened around his hat. He tried to look away but his eyes fell to hers and he sighed. His voice was low when he spoke.

"I am trying, Miss Byrne. But the needle seems to wobble in your presence. If you knew the thoughts that have transpired, uninhibited—" Lillian walked closer, curious about his flustered state, the deep blue of his eyes, the small dimple in his chin. "Do not, please." he held out his hands and stepped back.

She wanted to run to his arms and tell him not to leave. To stay with her until her father returned. To stay with her until she had to leave. That he felt like the only comfort she had. But he looked so uncomfortable and so worried that she merely held her cold and shaking hands out to his.

"Thank you," she whispered. "I do not know what I would have done without your generous offering of time and talent."

He sighed, looked at her fingers, and took them into the warm and strong expanse of his hand.

Doctor Blackwell bent low and kissed her hand with warm lips that Lillian wished would travel to the rest of her body.

"It was my pleasure, Miss Byrne," he whispered and looked up at her. "Now, please return to bed and rest until the Colonel returns. I would like to see you up and back to your normal life as soon as possible."

"That is my wish as well," she said softly as he rose from his bow, let go of her hand, and turned away. After he'd gone, she collapsed into the chair where he'd spent three days, watching over her. She pinched her skin. It hurt and it did not startle her. It was clear she wouldn't be able to simply wake up from this dream. She was really here.

3

RATIONALITY AND ROMANTIC
MUSINGS

Matthew paced in thoughtful contemplation in front of the parlor windows, pausing to gently touch the top of the pianoforte. He had been so sure of his plans. So certain he would not stay in this county, near his father and the idea that he would one day take over his role as the town's physician. He had no reason to stay.

Until three days ago.

It wasn't just that she was exceedingly beautiful. And strong, to sustain such an injury and still have her wits about her. Matthew could tell that she had a brilliant mind, even if it was still trying to sort itself out after the contusion. Lillian Byrne was a lot of things he didn't know a woman could be. Definitely a few things she shouldn't be. He thought of her direct and improper English and the strange things she'd muttered while coming in and out of consciousness in his three days of watching over her. What was Advil? A cell phone?

He'd seen patients with similar injuries, and it altered their personalities. Perhaps that was what was responsible for her impropriety? As she healed, he hoped that she would remember her position, her manners, and that she was probably already slated to marry someone in an advantageous arrangement. After all, her Uncle was the Colonel, and he assumed Lady Mayfield would want to see her properly engaged soon. Matthew was only a lowly doctor who preferred to administer to the poor. If she were to even consider him worthy, he would only have his heart broken when her family declined the match.

He flushed beneath his collar and adjusted it, hating the tight and confining nature of being back home. He missed his work in the south of Wales. There he could loosen his collar and his own sense of propriety. There he could be more himself, practice medicine, and have the community respect and care for him instead of always living in the shadow of his father's profound reputation. There, in the rural hamlets, where he stayed in sublimely unfettered accommodations and even at times cozy and warm barns, his smile was easy and he breathed freer out from under the tight thumb of his father and the expectations of his station.

He'd been on his way to this freedom. He had been on his way to tell his father he'd be relocating permanently, when the Colonel had summoned him on the road and begged him to make haste towards Westbury Manor. Upon arrival he encountered a flurry of activity at the gate. The housekeeper, Mrs. Shaw had beckoned him inside.

Was it serendipitous to cross paths with Miss Byrne in her time of medical need? Or was it just a test of his willpower, he thought, as he replayed every aching moment of carrying her to the bed. He had kept the maids within the room as each limb in turn was inspected, and kept his cool aloofness even as his heart hammered at the sight of her slender ankles, long legs bruised but not broken, and scraped and scuffed arms and shoulders.

He'd been careful as he'd draped her to inspect the ribs which had been struck rather hard. He remembered the slightness of them as he ran his thumbs over each in turn with great care. She'd moaned and shifted away and he declared two of them, indeed, bruised if not broken. Together he and Mrs. Shaw carefully wrapped Lillian's torso tightly in order to immobilize the area. Bleeding, from the cut that stretched into the hairline of her raven tresses, was staunched as he carefully washed and stitched the delicate skin together. He touched his lips without thinking when memories of her skin came to his mind.

She had affected him in ways he wasn't prepared for, and that was before she'd even opened those lovely eyes. He'd never seen such a shade of soft and heather blue. Never seen such a wide and full mouth on a woman. Never such a delicate and pert nose. The small beauty spot below the corner of her right eye, long and thick black lashes that fluttered over her cheeks as she fell in and out of an unsettled sleep.

At first, he had placed his fingers alongside her beautifully long and graceful neck to find the flutter of pulse until the old housekeeper had cleared her throat from the improper touch. In the country, he could use the most efficient and accurate means necessary and was not questioned. Perhaps it was the way he'd inadvertently grazed his fingers over her statuesque collarbones or the pleased gasp she'd let out at his touch.

Saints help him, he was nothing more than a cad! He surely would burn in hell for the thoughts and desires that had plagued him since first laying hands and eyes on Lillian Byrne. He leaned against the windowsill and stared out at the grand gardens outside. He must do his best to remember that she was not a woman. She was a patient, one who was above his station.

The sooner he could acquire his father's blessing to move back to Wales to begin his own practice, the better for him. Perhaps he would find a quiet and humble wife whose eyes weren't the captivating hue of dusk, one that was full of sunshine and brightness, not impropriety and stubbornness. Matthew's brow gathered in a scowl. Such a woman may have suited another man. Perhaps even himself years ago. But now, he thought and stared up to the ceiling where she lay resting in the bedroom above, now he wasn't sure any woman would suit him the same way again.

~

Lillian was not, in fact, resting in the bedroom above. She was pacing, her legs confounded by the narrow skirt and ridiculous undergarments that Miriam insisted she put on and which seemed to dissuade too much movement. They were, no doubt, designed as such to keep the fairer sex, unfairly bound. What she'd give for a pair of pants! Or a hot shower. Or an Advil. The bath she'd gotten from Miriam was an influx of boiling water that cooled far too quickly in the drafty room, in a copper tub where the maid scrubbed her down without the gentleness she had grown accustomed to from the sad, blue-eyed doctor. A shower would have been much preferred.

If she wanted to see or have any of the modern amenities that she desperately craved again and not be sent to a loony bin for acting like an emancipated, modern woman, she needed to concentrate on and practice the propriety that her father had begged she uphold.

"Come on, Dad," she said and nibbled at her thumbnail. She'd asked Miriam, after the bath, if her 'uncle' had come back or sent word. The old maid was sad when she shook her head.

"No miss, I'm afraid he hasn't."

She paced and thought. Her father was a scientist, and maybe it had been what had spurred her to become a nurse. But it was really in helping people, and being dependable that she found her passion. Both of those things were unlike her father. He would disappear for months at a time. To such a degree that her mother could never get him to sign divorce papers. Was she really hanging all her hopes on the idea that he knew what was going on? He was never dependable. He hadn't waited by her bedside for her to wake up.

Matthew's long straight nose and high cheekbones, his teasing smile, all flashed in her mind and she sighed.

Focus, Lil, he's the least of our worries.

How did one just stumble across an anomaly in the universe? Did such a thing happen to a lot of people? Was it only her and possibly her father? He'd said as much.

"So, what then? I fell down a magical staircase and ended up in a different time?" she asked the empty room.

She stopped in front of the windows in her room and her heart rate steadily climbed. The pulsing in her wounded body increased, amplifying the horrendous headache. She faltered and sagged against the desk beside the window; it rattled beneath her hand and her weight.

It was clear, be it some kind of hole in the space-time continuum, or from some other magical source, she was, trapped in a different time. Lillian sat down and closed her eyes. She tried to will her brain to remember the journals. Had there been a great cousin Lillian? Had Fitzwilliam written about her?

She seemed to recall something. A barely-known girl, the daughter of a nobleman. Taken in by the Colonel and Lady Mayfield, who had arrived just before Fitzwilliam's engagement. It was there, but her brain protested. Something had happened to that girl.

Movement outside the window caught her eye and she watched as Fitzwilliam and Doctor Blackwell came out from the parlor doors below her window and meandered through the back garden. The doctor's hands were clasped behind his broad back, holding on to his hat and gloves and he nodded and spoke as Fitzwilliam asked him questions. She loved watching the way the sunlight lit on his hair and the serious gathering of his brow at the glare of it.

She could not recall reading about Matthew Blackwell from the journals. But as she studied his shoulders, and watched him nod to Fitzwilliam before departing, she wondered if her fall into time hadn't been purposeful. She would like to believe they were meant to meet. She hoped he'd return to check in on her, she missed his presence already. Just as she thought it, Matthew turned to look back up at her window. Lillian blushed and felt her body heat rising, just from his smile alone.

That's when Kitty Darlingwood stepped into her room, unannounced, and squawked with surprise and dismay.

4

MISS DARLINGWOOD: SPLENDID
AT UPDOS AND SPILLING TEA

"Oh Miss Byrne, the horror of such an injury I could not have expected!" The blonde woman came in like a flurry of pink propriety, a flush of indignation and twitters. "And your hair is simply dreadful! When your dear, er—that is to say Mr. Byrne requested that I help you, he was not asking in jest. It looks as though someone has put a pitchfork to it."

Lillian backed away with her hands out, only barely piecing together that this must be the Miss Kitty Darlingwood that Fitzwilliam had spoken of. His blushing stammering wasn't misplaced at the sprite of a woman, petite and blonde, curls perfectly coiffed and lips a delicate pink bow, now turned down in dismay at the state of Lillian's appearance. No wonder her cousin was smitten by this woman. She was a hurricane of cuteness.

"Miss Darlingwood?" Lillian said and felt her knees hit the chair behind her as she continued to back away.

"Please do sit, Miss Byrne. And please, now that we are in safe quarters, do call me Kitty. The doctor was not wrong; you are exceedingly lovely."

"The doctor said I was lovely?"

"He asked that I inform you to take ease and not tear out your stitches."

"I would expect he still thinks he can tell me what to do." Lillian's voice was tight. Kitty studied her with some worry. "Forgive me, Kitty, I am still having some confusion."

"It is no wonder! But you are safe here and in good hands. Sit, and I will see to this monstrosity." Lillian fumbled at the chair, pulled it out and plopped down rather ungracefully, to Kitty's eye raise of disapproval. When Lillian stared into the mirror, she saw Kitty's horror as she took a comb through the long and unfettered locks and pulled them away to reveal the wound, still red and angry though much less swollen. They both stared at the gash. Kitty's brown eyes filled with tears.

"My dearest," she sniffed. "When I think of how we almost lost you, just as you were finding us, it vexes me. Your dear cousin, myself, two hearts would have been broken so irrevocably." Tears began to fall and Lillian felt a warmth fill her chest. For not having known this woman more than a few minutes, she still felt the sincerity of her words. Lillian never had a close friend, not one that would have cared so much about something so silly as the state of her hair, let alone to tell her they cared about her being alive. She turned in the chair and took Kitty's cold and small hand in her own.

"Please do not be vexed, dear Kitty. I am quite alright. I was lucky to have the best of care in the perilous first moments. I will heal, and all will be well again soon," she said, and Kitty dried her eyes on a kerchief from the desk. Lillian wondered what had happened to Kitty in history. Lillian's head swam trying to recapture the fading details of the journals. Who had Fitzwilliam married? Bethany Caterina something-or-other. Was Kitty short for Caterina? Lillian realized she'd been staring too long in thought and now Kitty looked into her eyes, worried.

"Are you about to faint? Have you lost your faculties?" Kitty asked, with her pouting mouth serious.

"I will be much better if you could just help me with the awful state of my hair," Lillian said, trying to feign normality.

"Of course, my darling," Kitty sniffed and began to untangle the long strands. While she worked, she filled Lillian in on all of the news and gossip that had transpired since she'd arrived but had been bedridden. There was a surprising amount for such a short time, and though Lillian didn't know any of the families or people that Kitty spoke of, it was amusing, nonetheless. Like having someone read you a gossip blog.

John Worthington from the county over the river had lost a prize bull that had jumped the fence in every field and impregnated several heifers, which was so scandalous that the mere mention of it caused Kitty to blush profusely and giggle behind her hand. Some nobleman from London was said to have driven his carriage through their county and had stopped at a neighboring hamlet to spend the night. It was overheard at the pub that he'd exclaimed Westbury Manor to have some of the prettiest lands he'd seen, but that their gardens failed to impress. Kitty talked of Lady Mayfield's dismay at this news.

Lady Rachel Mayfield, who had reluctantly taken in her nephew Fitzwilliam at the request of his brother on her deathbed, was married to the Colonel, and none too pleased, Kitty said in hushed tones, that he seemed adamant to also take Lillian in. But presently, she was most horrified that the passing dandy from London had called her gardens subpar. Lillian blew a curl from her forehead and rolled her eyes. A sudden and sharp stabbing pain caused her to flinch and cry out.

"Oh dearest, I'm so sorry!" Kitty squealed, after pulling the hair around the delicate stitches.

"It is fine," Lillian gritted her teeth. "I am not hurt," she lied.

"These stitches! How I hate that you will be scarred."

"I am lucky to have had the young doctor's assistance," Lillian said. Kitty took in a sharp breath and released it in a whoosh of giggles.

"Miss Byrne! I am beyond amused by your teasing of Doctor Blackwell by calling him 'young'. He is quite the aged bachelor."

"Ah yes, at the ripe old age of eight and twenty," Lillian smirked. Matthew was not married. Her heart clapped with joy; she shut it down. "Is not being a doctor a profession sought after by potential wives? Why should he still be a bachelor?" she asked and only wondered afterwards if it were scandalous to do so. Miss Darlingwood looked around the deserted room.

"Well, yes, one would normally think so, but 'young' Doctor Blackwell," she giggled at repeating the name, "appears to be fallen from his social grace by practicing medicine in rural bumpkin-filled hovels in Wales. He teeters on disgrace and it would be most shocking were he to find himself a willing bride, unbothered by his recent escapades."

"Escapades?" That sounded juicy and now it was Lillian who leaned forward to stare at Kitty in the mirror. "Whatever do you mean?"

"I mean that he is treating the poor with so much regularity that he has become quite poor himself and has assuredly upset his father's plans to be the successor of the family's highly respected hospital and board position in Bath! While we are all very grateful for his continued attention to your care, we were in part shocked that the good Colonel would allow him such access, with his reputation." She responded as if this was all very new information, and shockingly so. Lillian contemplated it all while Kitty continued.

"With all his work in the poor houses, one wonders if he could really call himself by the title of 'Doctor' at all. He makes barely more than even his stipend and does not seem bothered to live below his means."

"But isn't it noble and kind to give of one's talent and time so selflessly?" The words drifted between her lips and Lillian's blush returned. Miss Darlingwood watched her face in curiosity before her eyes lit with mischief.

"True nobility and kindness do not often mix, dearest Lillian. He should have joined the clergy if he was so inclined, at least there is some honor in that. But in treating boils for trades of eggs and shelter in barns does not make for good husband material."

Lillian sat back and frowned. Beautiful to look at was one thing. But that Matthew was also honorable and kind made him even more attractive. Rebelliousness, smarts, nice hands, long legs and broad chest… the warmth in the room intensified, the heat spread from her body, up her neck and lit her cheeks. She needed to stay focused and try to learn what she could about her new situation so she could play along until a solution to take her back home was found.

"It should be of little consequence to you in any case," Kitty continued, interrupting Lillian's thoughts.

"Whatever can you mean?"

Kitty leaned in closer to her ear and smiled. "I've heard a rumor from Sarah Jane in the kitchens that Lady Mayfield has already been speaking to Mr. Frederick Sutton about a possible match."

"Who is Mr. Sutton? A match to whom?"

Kitty laughed and hid it behind her hand. "Why Lillian! I know you are recovering but surely you understand it is you."

"Me? But I've only just arrived."

"Mr. Sutton has been looking for a bride for quite some time."

"Who is Mr. Sutton?"

"As luck would have it, he is the close cousin of Doctor Blackwood."

Lillian stared blankly at Kitty through the mirror. "Doctor Matthew Blackwood's cousin?"

"Yes."

"Wants to marry me? But we've not even met."

"It is not set in stone, but you would be lucky if it were. He is a well-bred gentleman with a fine estate and a whole fleet of ships."

"But I do not know him."

"I imagine that will come with time," Kitty smiled and pinned another curl in place.

"Lady Mayfield, being exceptionally efficient in her business dealings might very well have the whole matter settled by the end of this week. You shall be very well taken care of," she said and nodded curtly.

"Well taken care of?" Lillian whispered back and thought to the man who had been by her side, for three days, taking actual care of her. "But surely my ... uncle, must agree to such a thing?"

"I suppose."

Lillian tried to take in a deep breath and reassure herself that her father would be back, he would have a plan and know how to get her home. Preferably before she got married off to the first available stranger. Would she be panicking if Matthew had instead asked for her hand? Perhaps less.

When Kitty had finished, Lillian turned her head this way and that, admiring the elegant pinned updo that had been secured with a ribbon which hid the gash.

"Kitty," she breathed, admiring the length of her neck and the attractive line of her light cream dress' bodice in contrast to the dark pile of styled hair. "Thank you. It's simply stunning."

"This?" Kitty frowned in the mirror behind her. "Why it is just a simple style for your convalescence."

"You should not downplay your skills," Lillian tried to cover. "You've made me feel pretty enough to go to a ball."

"Oh Lillian!" Kitty giggled. "You are indeed touched with good humor. Think nothing of it. Perhaps you would like to accompany me to the parlor? It is no ball, but the light in there is perfect this time in the morning and will still be sufficient for embroidery before the afternoon rain we're to receive."

Thinking only of getting out of the stuffy room and taking any chance to explore more of the house for clues to help her return home, including a close inspection of the stairway she'd fallen down, Lillian readily agreed.

"I would very much like that." Lillian looked out the window again, but the gentlemen had disappeared. Had Matthew taken his leave permanently, now that she was on the mend? Had he disclosed to her cousin what a strange and disagreeable girl she was? Would he return to walk with her before she found her way home?

None of it really mattered, she reminded herself as she followed Kitty from the room and out into the dim hallway. Matthew Blackwell was nothing more than another piece on the board where she must play the game of belonging. She hoped her father would come back soon.

5

THE RAINSTORM

Kitty had not led her to the same staircase she'd fallen down. She felt no strange, great pressure in her head, only the dark, subtle creaks of the main stairway, and the incessant twittering of Kitty as she talked about her artistic endeavors and how she hoped they would impress her latest admirer. Lillian listened with only half a mind, while the other half tried to get her bearings and look, on the off chance, for any sign this was just some elaborate scheme. No outlets, no switches, no modern-day humming or exit signs. She sighed and put her head down as they turned into the spacious entertaining room.

Once she entered the parlor, she took a moment to study the fine artworks on the walls, the soft rugs beneath various settees, and armchairs. A short wall of books across from a fireplace on the other wall, the furniture for entertaining between. A piano sat in the corner, with a vase of fresh flowers from the garden atop a doily of finely tatted lace. Behind the instrument was a window that looked out on the garden.

Kitty took out an orderly basket filled with fine linens, embroidery floss in hand-dyed colors, and a whisper thin needle. She set it beside her on the couch and beckoned for

Lillian to sit as well. Lillian looked at the materials suspiciously. She'd failed Home Econ, knew nothing about stitches except for sutures, and did not have an eye for fashion. She picked up one of the pieces of cloth and watched Kitty for signs of where to begin.

Kitty barely noticed, but set about her work, stitching the most delicate and beautiful yellow flowers, with bright orange centers. Not all the stitches were done the same, some made lines, some made perfect little dots, some made fanned out patterns.

"These are his favorite," Kitty whispered to herself as she worked, and Lillian glanced over to see her complete a bouquet of the yellow daisies. She looked back at the piano and saw the vase was full of yellow daisies.

"Whose favorite?" Lillian asked. Kitty's face lit up with pink and she laughed and sighed.

"No one at all! Wouldn't you be excited for an engagement?"

"Ugh," Lillian picked up a needle and a bright green piece of thread. She sat back into her side of the couch. "I do not wish to speak of it," was all she could think to say.

"Certainly you have imagined it? How your beloved would look? The sweet things he would say? I admit I do not think Mr. Sutton a fan of poetry, but wouldn't you say it would be romantic? Arranged or not, when your engagement party comes to pass you must have something to tell the circle of women who will no doubt be dying to know how you captured the attention of such a man."

Lillian felt sick to her stomach. She didn't want to capture the interest of any man; she just wanted to go home. Kitty went on.

"So my suggestion is this. Even if it is not what comes to pass, we will say he proposed beneath the large willow tree on the edge of his favorite grouse field, rifle in hand, and the mist making him all the more impressive of a man. You hesitated, as all good and proper young women do when faced with such a delicate and intimate decision, and he chanced a kiss upon your cheek to persuade—"

"He would not kiss me," Lillian said it so loudly and adamantly that it startled them both. "Forgive me. I mean to say, I would not—allow it."

"Well, it is a better thing to say than 'I do not wish to speak of it,'" Kitty argued. Lillian sighed.

"I do not wish to lie about a proposal. I would not accept one that wasn't heartfelt, from someone I knew and trusted." Lillian touched the tender gash on her head.

"Perhaps it is something he will do when you meet."

"I hope to be gone by then," Lillian said distractedly and counted the tight and perfect stitches with her fingers, placed so carefully by such skilled hands. Miss Darlingwood looked at her strangely.

"But your uncle has said you will be staying with us for the summer?"

"The summer? What do you mean? Have you spoken to him?"

"Lady Mayfield said that he had to leave on a very important trip and that you were to stay here until he returned, that it may be weeks to months."

Lillian's stomach turned. He'd lied again to her! Only this time it wasn't a birthday or a play he was missing. Her father was dooming her to a very real engagement. "I see. That is news to me." She took a deep breath and continued. "In any case, I have not even met Mr. Sutton so I do not think the likelihood of our engagement is imminent," she grumbled at the tangled mess of thread between her fingers. It was strange. If a man wanted to be engaged to a woman, advantageously or otherwise, would he not come to see her in the event of her injury? Then again, a man who made a marriage based solely on the agreement with the county's busybody, Lady Mayfield, probably did not care about her well-being. "Hopefully Mr. Sutton is busy having second thoughts of even asking me."

"I assure you, he is merely otherwise occupied," came a deep voice from the hall causing both women to turn. Miss Darlingwood rose immediately and bowed to Doctor Blackwell and then looked down at Lillian in horror as she had stayed seated and only glared at him. Kitty nudged Lillian with her knee to remind her. Lillian made an annoyed sound and rolled her eyes at the ritual of 'rise and curtsey'. She moved to stand but he stopped her with an outstretched hand and a sly grin.

"You needn't get up, Miss Byrne, if you are feeling faint."

She stared at him and seethed, "I assure you I am quite fine." She stood and bowed demurely.

Matthew's eyes narrowed on hers and the heat rose in the room. Miss Darlingwood looked between them and cleared her throat.

"Good day, Mister Blackwell. I was just doing my very best to help Miss Byrne dream up the details of her engagement to your cousin."

"*Doctor* Blackwell," Lillian corrected, ignoring the preposterous idea of her getting engaged.

"*Doctor* Blackwell," Kitty echoed with a scrunch of her nose towards Lillian.

"You needn't worry with titles, Miss Darlingwood. It is not necessa—"

"It is absolutely necessary. Yours is a title that has been earned through hours of meticulous work which you have accomplished on your own merit." Lillian interrupted boldly. Her voice quieted as he stared at her through the speech with a strange look on his face. She remembered the way he'd introduced himself, even with her aching head, how doubt was cast on his ability in the shadow of his father.

She blushed at the overflow of startled affection that she'd felt for him after Kitty had unwittingly bestowed in her gossip details of his good heart but empty pockets.

"Miss Byrne," his eyes fell and he clasped his hands behind his back quickly.

"I would not have survived, if it hadn't been for your calm manner and assured skill. I don't believe I have thanked you nearly enough, and I hope you will not think me ungrateful." She stumbled as she came around the settee to stand before him. Kitty watched. "I am so very grateful." Lillian finished and bowed demurely before him offering her hand.

Matthew's eyes fell to her hair, hiding the neat stitches, and then to the bodice of her dress. Lillian watched his reserve falter. He took her hand in his, warm fingers around cool. He pressed his lips to her skin a moment longer than proper. Lillian's lip trembled.

Kitty cleared her throat.

"Doctor Blackwell, as Mr. Sutton's cousin you surely have heard the story of how your cousin came to desire to be Miss Byrne's husband. Perhaps you would like to tell her more about him." Miss Darlingwood said pointedly. Lillian blushed and stepped away.

"I'm sure all will be revealed in time," he said gruffly.

"You might hasten her happiness by telling her now," Kitty said with a smile.

Lillian studied her. Kitty was trying to keep the status quo, and she must have sensed Matthew's attraction to her, and knew he was not rich enough to warrant her affections. People in this era were much more astute at reading body language and probably could feel the uncomfortable play of emotion and physical response between Doctor Blackwell and herself.

"It is not necessary," Lillian said softly. "I'm sure he's most agreeable."

Doctor Blackwell cleared his throat and paced to the fireplace.

"A great many things have been said of Frederick but I cannot attest that 'agreeable' was one."

Kitty giggled. "Oh Doctor Blackwell, you tease us so!"

Lillian did not giggle. She did not want him to continue. She did not want to know how awful the stranger, perhaps soon to be her fiancé, was. Perhaps he was merely jealous. Maybe Frederick Sutton was a typically upstanding man of the time, and Matthew didn't like the competition.

"As I have barely heard from him, I do not know his intentions on asking you. I would presume he would like to make his official offer in person." Matthew paused and looked back from the fireplace, a resigned aloofness in his features. "You can be sure it will be done with his usual forthright manner. I imagine much as he would if asking to use someone's grounds for hunting." He said the last bit under his breath and with a roll of his eyes. "If it helps you to imagine, I suppose he will hold his hands to his back and rock on his heels in a proper amount of embarrassment and concern for your answer. Surely it will not be memorable, as men do not bother themselves with details in the same way women do."

"Perhaps he will make it memorable with a kiss," Kitty giggled and covered her mouth quickly as she looked back at Lillian, who blanched. She wanted to put her finger down her throat pantomiming utter disgust, but somehow, she contained the urge with pursed lips. She leaned against the piano.

"Perhaps," Matthew said with a smile and turned away before Lillian could read his face. "But, as I've known my cousin since I was but a lad, he rarely crosses the boundaries of propriety for the sake of affection."

"Oh, he is of a decent and excellent character. You see, dear Miss Byrne?" Kitty said and came to her and took Lillian's cold fingers in her hand. "You've nothing to worry about."

"Stoic, unaffectionate, proper, decent? Fantastic. What more could a girl hope for in a life partner?" she said quietly and the air around her grew heavy. What if she didn't get out in time? What if she spent the rest of her life married to such a man? Which would be worse? She felt stifled. She took her hand from Kitty's and deftly lifted her skirts before bowing quickly.

"Please excuse me, Doctor Blackwell, Miss Darlingwood. I think I should like to take some fresh air." Lillian darted from the room, raising her skirts enough so that she was able to make a quick exit that surprised both Doctor Blackwell and Kitty.

"But isn't it raining dreadfully?" Kitty squeaked behind her.

Matthew watched her run out of the room and down the hall before darting to the left for the staircase. Her feet made soft and even taps on the stairs.

"What if she falls?" Doctor Blackwell said and moved to follow but Miss Darlingwood stepped coyly between him and the door.

"I assure you good sir, she shall be safe on the grounds. Perhaps we shall leave her space with which to think. After all, I heard Lady Mayfield is already planning the engagement party for a couple of weeks' time and she may need the solitary moments alone to ruminate over the lovely details."

Matthew looked down at Miss Darlingwood, petite and in pink cotton that illuminated the flush of both cheeks. He looked away quickly as she stared up at him through her eyelashes with a smile. He knew very well that she was a beautiful woman, one that had no shortage of suitors due in part to her soft and sweet countenance and part due to her father's, Lady Mayfield's brother-in-law, good fortune. He also knew that she had captured the heart of Lillian's cousin Fitzwilliam, but the young man was never clear on her feelings towards him as she always came across so indifferent.

"Will you not stay for tea? Lady Mayfield would be pleased to have you. I'm sure she would love to hear stories of our coarse neighbors in Wales," Kitty chirped.

Matthew cringed and his lip drew back. Such were the prevailing attitudes. Certainly, a woman of Miss Darlingwood's upbringing and constitution would not be able to survive such a 'primitive' lifestyle. A woman would have to be adventurous, physically able-bodied, and stubborn. Matthew looked once more to the empty hallway.

"Perhaps some other time. I am running late for meeting with my father and should not linger further." He politely bowed, careful to lean farther away in stiff disinterest. She curtseyed and Doctor Blackwell rushed from the room.

He did have a meeting with his father that afternoon, to talk over his plans. So, it was not a complete falsehood that allowed him to escape. But it was not his only reasoning. Acquiring his hat and gloves from the porter at the door, he stepped outside to the sight of thunderous clouds and the quickening rain drops that fell from a massive system above. He looked in both directions, knowing that he should merely get his horse and go back to his father's estate. He should, as Miss Darlingwood had advised, give Lillian the space she needed to ruminate over her anticipated happiness.

Only, everything about her behavior indicated that she was not in the slightest way anticipating the impending nuptials with happiness. Marriage was not always a cause for bliss, but it certainly should not have been something upsetting enough to physically run away from. The arrangement with his cousin would secure her future and she should not feel so passionately against such an advantageous situation.

Matthew should not care if she was contrary to the idea of marrying his cousin. Except that from the moment he had taken charge of her care at the base of the stairs, he felt, deep in his soul, that he was responsible for her safety. She was his patient. She was, to some extent, his responsibility. And she had just run, headfirst and unaccompanied, into a storm.

"Ridiculous," he grumbled under his breath. How could he

take care of a woman who so blatantly went against his sound advice? There was only so much he could control and she, with her strong will and stubborn countenance, did not make anything easy. The rain began to fall in earnest then, soaking his coat and hat and making it difficult to see much past the gates of the estate.

"Blast," he cursed. Nodding to the stable hand who had brought his horse around, he mounted quickly and rode in an expanding circular path, spiraling out from the house to the surrounding property.

She would be soaked through and cold. Perhaps damaging her stitches. Perhaps she had slipped and fallen in a gully. Bones broken, head split open, any number of horrifying injuries. He had a mind to give her a stern talking to, for the worry she'd created in his poor heart.

His poor heart.

Matthew scowled and pushed the horse faster. His heart should have nothing to do with wanting her to maintain her health and the status of her reputation. If anything, it was paramount that she stay in respectable graces with society for his cousin's—and therefore, his—family's name. Through the rain and wind, the rushing growl of thunder above, and the distant echo of it in the hills surrounding Westbury Manor, he listened for a cry for help.

His eyes scanned the horizon and his heart sped up with every moment she eluded him. True worry, real and hard, seized hold of his good sense. "My god, Lily, where are you?" he gasped and wiped the rain from his eyes, discarding his hat to the ground.

Why would a young girl run away when faced with marriage? Matthew's thoughts circled around in his head, just as his path circled through the gardens and expansive fields of Westbury. Why would a young doctor refuse a prestigious seat on his father's board?

Some things were simply not meant to be. Could it be that Lillian was not meant to be with Frederick? He hadn't even come to see her. What would his straitlaced cousin think of her conduct now? Knowing his cousin as he did, Matthew knew it would anger Frederick.

While Matthew, on the other hand, could scarcely blame Lillian. He knew what it was to be forced into a life you did not choose, and all the worse for a woman who had so little power. He was not angry at her, but damn it if he wasn't worried. He felt a pit of sadness open in his chest at the very thought of seeing Lillian Byrne become his cousin's wife.

"Blast it all. Damn fool idiot!" he said again, not sure if his words were meant for her, his cousin, or himself. His eyes scanned the horizon.

Then, out of the south pasture, he saw her cresting the hill. A sodden bonnet in one hand, an unused shawl in the other. Her hair, coming down in waves around her shoulders, out of the carefully constructed hairstyle that had hidden her wound. Pale and soaked, she stomped with implacable determination. He urged his steed forward, down the first hill and quickly up to intersect her path. The wind tore between them, swirling the rain round in a cacophony of sound and drenching water.

"Miss Byrne, I demand you stop this foolishness at once!" he yelled from behind her. Lillian, deep in thought, took two more striding steps with her skirt lifted, dropped the drenched and heavy material and spun to face him. She pushed the wet locks from her eyes.

"What are you doing out here?" she said. "You'll catch your death!"

"Oh? Is that a matter of fact? But you are perfectly safe to be out in such a torrent?" He dismounted from his horse in anger.

She scowled up at him.

"Miss Byrne, I insist that you allow me to accompany you back home."

"That is not my home," she sobbed and pointed to the gray manor in the distance that was harder by the moment to see. "Those are not my friends, that is not my life." The wind stole her words and Matthew moved nearer.

"I know that you have arrived suddenly and have had much hardship of late," he said. Lillian stared up at him as the rain fell from his nose in droplets and soaked his hair so it plastered to his head.

He watched the rivulets of it pour down her cheeks, drip off the shelf of her top lip, and its perfect pink peaks. The fullness of her bottom lip, wet and calling to him.

"Please come back," he said softly, unable to take his eyes from her lips. Lillian's fingers lost hold of her bonnet and scarf and they fell in wet heaps beside her drenched and muddied feet. "This is no storm to be walking in. There is scarcely any air to breathe, with all the rain. We are worried over your well-being."

"We?" she asked.

"*I* am worried," he said and hung his head. For all of the desperation to take her back and make her fit in the space and place a woman should, he did not try to touch her, nor did he force her.

"You are?" she said softly and tried to peer into his downcast eyes.

"I was much concerned," he said softly, and a relieved breath whooshed from his lips. He knelt to pick up her belongings. When he looked up, her hands were knotted in front of her and she bit her lip.

God but he would stay on his knees for her. His heart hammered and he noticed that the stitches on her temple had come loose, and a small trail of blood was now joining the rain to trace her cheek. He grunted and stood up, quickly pressing his thumb and her shawl to the cut and causing her to take in a quick breath. His fingers felt warm against her cold skin as he put pressure to stop the bleeding.

"See now. You should have listened to me. Look what has happened," he said, feeling relieved for having changed the subject and was now able to reprimand her again, instead of admitting to her effect on him. He took the fabric away briefly and she stared at the blood spiraling around the lace.

"Perhaps your stitches were faulty," she said, nose turned up at him. He scowled down at her and began to formulate an argument from his shock at her suggestion until he saw her smile.

"You ungrateful child," he said and a reciprocal smile played on his lips. Her smile grew with his. Her breath came out in a gasp.

"I am no child," she argued with a raised eyebrow. His eyes traced down her long neck to the wet, thin fabric across her breasts and the skirt that clung to the fullness of her hips.

"You certainly are not," he whispered. Lillian swayed closer and he leaned into the gravitational pull of her softness. "But your behavior suggests otherwise."

"Well, perhaps you should have found a switch along your way, so that you could take it to my backside and teach me a good lesson for such immature petulance," she countered, and he felt his body shock with the delicious idea of her backside.

"Miss Byrne!" he said. "I would do no such thing! I would never strike a woman."

"I know you would not," she whispered and took his other hand in her cold fingers and led it to her face, sinking her cheek into his palm. He took in a deep breath as she looked up at him, into his eyes, showing the dark depths of her own desire as the rain continued around them in waves.

"I do not believe in violence. Especially not towards women. My oath is only to heal, not to hurt," he reminded, his hand stayed for a moment and he looked as though he wanted to pull her in for a kiss. She leaned forward.

"Doctor Blackwell, I wish that you would—"

"And that being as such," he interrupted immediately. "You must come back with me so that I may mend the stitches before you bleed out or catch your death of cold. I shall write my cousin this afternoon to let him know that you are in need of his company."

"I am not."

"Do not—" he sighed, exasperated, and reached out. "Please do not argue with me, Lillian." He took her hand and pulled her to the patient steed.

"Lillian? What happened to Miss Byrne?"

"If you are determined to act like a spoilt child, then you shall be addressed as one," he said, determined to put space between them even as they bumped against one another. "Does my cousin even know what kind of trouble he has set himself up to inherit?"

"Perhaps it is best if he should not ask me," she growled back, but did not struggle in his hands.

"The arrangement is all but made, do not jest so boldly to undermine your guardian's promissory words. It is most unbecoming on a young lady and will only serve to ruin both of our families' good names, and your reputation."

He put his hands around her waist, not allowing himself to make the movement last any longer than necessary, and lifted her to the back of the steed. When she settled, not having ridden a horse since sometime in high school, she looked down to see him staring at the bare leg that her hiked skirt had exposed. She scowled.

"I can walk, damn it!"

Her words snapped him out of his transfixed gaze. "I will not have you falling down a damn hill as well!" he yelled back and with an assured grace, he swung up on the horse behind her. A pause, a breath, when the heat of their two bodies met, and Matthew closed his eyes to her back against his chest, the curve of her hips against his.

"You are being ridiculous," she argued quietly even as she

shivered inside his arms. He gently tightened his grip and his chin sunk down into the crook of her neck and shoulder. To spread as much warmth to her as he could, he told himself, but really, it was for selfish reasons. He inhaled the scent of her neck, and spoke softly.

"Please, Lily, I only want to protect you. Even a simple rainstorm has been known to cause great and life-ending fevers. Especially for those who have been exposed to great trauma. Please, for the sake of my heart, come home." His voice turned desperate and he placed a delicate kiss to the wet skin of her neck just below her ear. She shook in his arms and pressed closer to him, which made him want to do it again, and again, and again, until she begged him to stop. The warmth of her and the way his hands found spaces in the dip of her waist gave him pause. He kissed her softly again, as if trying to apologize for his behavior.

"I do not blame you for being upset. And I'm sorry if I was forceful. I am unaccustomed to being responsible for someone else. You've quite befuddled me, in ways I don't know how to recover from."

Lillian sobbed, and wrapped her arms around his, leaned her softness into the warmth of his chest and allowed him to guide the horse back to the manor.

What were the chances he could find a way to leave before Lily was forced to marry Frederick Sutton? What were the chances he would be able to stay away from her until then?

Both seemed very bad odds.

6

AN OATH OF HONESTY IS MADE

Having returned from the storm, sodden and cold, both were escorted into the small kitchen where Miriam placed a warm blanket over her young charge and scowled at the doctor.

"I suppose I should be thanking you for saving her life."

Lillian snorted. "He did no such thing. He merely manhandled me and forced me to come back." Matthew's face went pale.

"I did no such thing, you…intolerable brat!" he sputtered. Miriam tugged the blanket around Lillian.

"Aye, and you're lucky he did! I bet she fought the whole way, such a stubborn mule," Miriam reprimanded under her breath. Matthew smiled then and Lillian choked back a response. Miriam blanched when she saw the blood starting to seep through Lillian's popped stitches. "Best you attend to those as quickly as possible."

Matthew nodded in agreement. "Come, you must accompany me to the parlor where the light is best and I will see what can be done."

Lillian didn't like the idea of having Kitty sit in on the repair of her stupidity, or be so close and waited upon by the doctor. She sighed, crinkled her nose and begrudgingly wrapped the blanket tighter around her shoulders. Being on a horse with him, his hard body pressed so warmly to her back had been an excruciating mixture of madness and comfort.

"Fine then, let's get it over with." She led the way to the parlor. Matthew followed, close enough that she could still smell his wet hair and feel the warmth of him through her skirt. She sat in the chair closest to the window.

"My goodness!" Kitty rose and bowed to the doctor without thinking, but neither of them acknowledged her. "What's happened?"

Matthew sighed. "I found this drowning vagabond on your property on my way back to my father's estate. Her stitches have come undone. May I trouble you for the use of your sewing kit?"

"Of course." Kitty turned to bring him the needed materials. Lillian looked with horror at the fine needles.

"Surely you'll be sanitizing those."

"Sanitizing?" Kitty asked. "Whatever do you mean?" Lillian stared blankly at her and then at the doctor.

"Before you pierce skin, you should clean the instrument fully so as to not transfer germs, er—dirt into the body." Had they not known about the microscopic world that caused disease yet?

Matthew nodded. "Of course." He held the needle above the open flame of a lantern on the mantle and wiped it with a clean cloth from a tray Miriam had brought in with water and clean linen. Kitty took a seat across the room and continued her work, her eyes darting across the room at them nervously.

Lillian held still and was quiet, while he replaced the torn stitches. She had been watching his steady fingers and hard, unflinching eyes as he worked. It only served to make her admire him more for his grace and skill. He glanced down to see her staring at him and his brow fell even as he steadied his hand.

"Does it not bother you to watch? I know this must—" he stopped.

"Hurt like hell?" she asked quietly so Kitty would not hear

from where she sat on the settee. Instead of shock he simply smiled from one corner of his mouth and nodded. She spoke more loudly to dissuade suspicion on Kitty's part of her foul language and her blooming feelings.

"I'm hoping I can learn to improve my embroidery skill by watching you. Kitty tells me I am quite dreadful and wonders who must have been responsible for my instruction."

"Who indeed had that pleasure?" Matthew asked as he cleaned the remaining blood from the wound and her cheek. Miss Darlingwood looked over at Lillian.

"I would very much like to reprimand them," she chimed in. "Surely it was not Lady Mayfield as she is one of the most skilled in all the county."

"I do not recall," Lillian said softly and looked back down at her hands, knowing very well that she had never in fact been taught the art as all respectable young women of this era were.

"Well, failing at one thing, I am sure you can pursue all of your many other talents," he said, tossing the bloodied cloth onto the tray. Miriam collected the first aid materials and left in the stealthy manner of a woman who ran a household, unpraised.

"And how can you be so assured of my talents?"

"The Colonel tells me you are quite accomplished at the pianoforte." Lillian's head was not up to the challenge of puzzling through how she'd pull off living up to such a reputation.

"Oh, that is so! Why I'm certain that since you are related, you must also sing as beautifully as Mr. Byrne." Kitty blushed and fell silent. Lillian wondered if her cousin had been serenading the young debutante.

"Truly? I would very much like to hear that someday," Doctor Blackwell said as he cleaned and put away his instruments, throwing a small glance at her.

"I assure you; rumors of my talent have been greatly exaggerated." Lillian said dryly. While she may have indeed learned and played the piano at the insistence of her mother for most of her life, she hadn't practiced in years.

"Normally, I would praise you for such modesty." He smiled but Lillian did not return it.

"Praise me?" Lillian rose and closed the space between her and the doctor. Kitty looked up from her sewing as Miriam cracked the door.

"Begging your pardon Miss Darlingwood, but Master Byrne has asked if he could join you later for tea and I wanted to ask you about the dishes you would like to be served," she said quietly from the doorway. Kitty rose with a nervous huff. While she hovered at the doorway to talk to Miriam, Matthew caught Lillian by the wrist.

"*Normally*, I said." His finger gently traced an arch over the delicate skin, fluttering over the pulse of her vein beneath. "But we both are aware that you are too strong minded and honest to be concerned with others' opinions."

"I beg your pardon, Doctor Blackwell, since when is honesty an unbecoming trait?" she said beneath her breath as to not gain Kitty's attention even as a fire lit her eyes. She moved to storm away, but he held her by her wrist.

"Feel, the angel's heart beats faster," he whispered and gauged her pulse. Lillian stopped; the world hung on his lips at the endearment. "Honesty is most becoming. As is a strong mind. So then let us agree, Lily, to never be dishonest with one another, nor hide our true strengths. It would do my heart much good and give my soul ease to find such a friend in my small social circle." He looked down and she wondered if he truly had no friends in his life. Certainly not women.

In the strange and misleading world that was always evolving around them, women and men stood in the constant tension of truth and deceit, one always vying for the power over the other. Such an arrangement of honesty would benefit them both.

"I'm sorry that you've found so little honesty from my gender this far into your life. Though do not be misled that men are more upstanding. They have their share of plays for power and blatant falsehoods for gain. Like arranged marriages where the woman is not even asked." She moved to pull her wrist away but he took her other arm in his as Kitty was now quite engrossed in the exact ingredients for the scones that would need to be made precisely in a certain way, despite the fact that Miriam had been making the most scrumptious, light-as-feather scones since the time she was nine.

"Then I will make you the same promise," Matthew said quickly. "To always be honest with you, even when the questions and subjects you bring forth to me are difficult to broach. Even if I am frightened of what I may divulge, I will always allow the truth to win out."

Lillian raised her hand suddenly and offered it out to him. But instead of the customary delicate touch and curtsey, she held his grip fast, as if shaking the hand of an equal and Matthew smiled.

"It is a bargain and a promise, Matthew."

"My name on your lips is sweet torture," he said softly. "Say it again."

"Only if you agree to the terms." Lillian's grip tightened.

"Yes. A bargain and a promise, Lily. To always be honest with you."

"Thank you, Matthew."

He smiled and dropped her hand, just as Kitty turned back to them.

"What a horrifying ordeal!" Kitty said with exhaustion and went back to her needlework, going on to lament how Lillian's cousin, Mr. Byrne had gravely affronted her with a tease last week on her tribulations with baking.

Lillian wanted to tell her it could be much worse. That *her* brother Will used to prank her mercilessly, even going so far as to cut off sections of her hair while she slept the night before school pictures. She opened her mouth to defend the goodness of this alternate Will but closed it again and sighed.

When she looked back, Matthew was staring at her strangely, as if he'd been studying her. He pretended to inspect his new stitches while he stepped closer as Kitty continued in her own conversation of previous vexation, so caught up in the slight and her obvious confused feelings for Fitzwilliam that she barely noticed how close Matthew now stood to Lillian.

He stared at her lips and leaned closer. "In our new arrangement of honesty, I feel it is my place to inform you that I would much rather seal our new contract with a kiss," he whispered.

"Would that not sully both our reputations should we be found out? And were you not quite vexed that I would make a dishonest woman of myself, as you so harshly lectured me on a rainy hillside, not twenty minutes past to be exact," she whispered back.

"Ah, see, your memory is improving already," he teased and moved back and away from her.

"Wonderful! Perhaps I will one day remember why I agreed to an engagement. Oh, that's right, I did not agree." Lillian watched him from the corner of her eye, while Miss Darlingwood sat at the other end of the couch and looked up periodically between them.

"Isn't it the goal of all young women want to be married?" he said, for the room to hear, and went to stand beside the window while he rolled his cuffs back down. Lillian wondered if he was baiting her.

"Yes of course," Kitty chimed in without even thinking. Lillian rolled her eyes. She could think of no way to control her features and now that she'd agreed to be honest with him, she didn't feel it would be right to lie.

"Some women are much in want of adventure instead. We

surely don't want to sail in calm seas all our lives," she said, recalling one of her favorite Austen sayings. Kitty gasped.

"Miss Byrne! What an awful thing to say, indeed!"

Matthew turned his curious gaze on Lillian. "Not at all awful," he said. "Calm seas make for dull years. Storms build character and strength; they even bring surprises and happy stories sometimes."

"Surely you jest, Doctor Blackwell." Kitty said in rising horror.

"The best stories often come from our wildest adventures," Lillian agreed. "We've only one heart. One body, one life. Why would I want to spend it in only one place?" Matthew looked at her with quickening breath.

"Why indeed?" he whispered, unable to take his eyes from hers. Kitty tittered nervously between them.

"But what of safety, security? Home life? Surely you would not want to tempt starvation and death all the days of your life, traipsing around looking for adventures! What kind of woman would the world know you as?" The tone was heavy and judgmental, still Lillian couldn't look away from Matthew.

"To some, marriage is a cage. A starvation of self, a death of soul," she whispered.

"What a horrible thing to say, Miss Byrne!" Kitty struck out suddenly with a sharp reprimand. Matthew smiled at Lillian's uncharacteristic poeticism.

"Perhaps," he interrupted in calming tones, "the right marriage, to the perfect match, would be a feast of adventure, a finding of self, a life made whole," he whispered and looked down at her lips. Lillian nearly stumbled and ached to rush into his arms, his kisses, his bed. She wished Kitty was otherwise occupied in a room far away.

"Well, this is all just nonsense, and nothing you really have to worry about, dear Miss Byrne, as you are as good as happily engaged already." Kitty stood, brushed the stray threads from her skirt and sighed. "Now, I can tell you are exhausted and should be taken from your wet clothes." She nodded towards the door and Lillian scowled. Kitty wasn't wrong; she'd had an eventful morning and was behaving like a tired child. She sighed. Matthew bowed and Lillian curtseyed in response.

"Doctor Blackwell. Thank you for helping me with the stitches, once more."

"It was my absolute pleasure, Miss Byrne. Please take care and keep them clean. And do try to stay out of the rain." He leaned forward. "In return, I will spend the afternoon trying not to think of you being stripped of your wet clothes," he said lowly. Lillian's body responded in an archaic and pleased way. Her knees felt weak, she wanted to regain control.

"I do not suppose you are available to assist?" she whispered with a smile. Matthew's eyes lowered and he opened his mouth to speak.

"Come along, Miss Byrne!" Kitty called from the doorway. Lillian rushed after her, embarrassed, confused, and cold. She spent the rest of the day in bed and wondering what madness had come over her. How easily the man had made her lose focus!

She was so far failing miserably at pretending. At least with Matthew. Perhaps, since her father was nowhere to be found, she should try to meet with Lady Mayfield to find out more about her circumstances, especially to understand why she felt the need to marry her off so quickly. The longer she stayed here, the more certain she would be trapped in a situation much worse than this. If not that, then surely the ruination of Matthew Blackwell's reputation.

7
THE PICNIC

Summer continued its lazy progression into heat and humidity which made the house restless and the confining clothes suffocating. Before Lillian could ask for a meeting with Lady Mayfield, she had Kitty accompany her to see a friend in a neighboring township. So many of Lillian's future depended upon her father's return so she found herself frustrated and stuck.

However, in the absence of the holders of propriety, Lillian had taken to wearing as few layers as was allowed and worked out in the cool dirt of the garden whenever possible. She helped Miriam in the kitchen rather than spend her afternoons frustrated over needle and cloth. In only a couple of days, she had become an adept scullery maid in the absence of her chaperones. Being able to talk with the kitchen and household staff, the manor's true heart, helped her gain insight into her current situation and the countenance of her new 'family', particularly the hawk-like eye of Lady Mayfield.

On this fine afternoon, she had until dinner before she had to return to her more formal self, so she was spending the time she could in the garden. While there, walking the rows of vegetables and herbs she thought of her father. She tried to remember everything he'd said, in their brief meeting. He was supposedly looking for a solution. He did not seem surprised or particularly bothered by the situation except in that it had happened to her. Could it be that her father had been a time traveler? It certainly accounted for his absences. But how did she fall through? She sighed and stared off into the back garden and the fields beyond. She wasn't one to sit for long. If he didn't return soon, she would have to find her own way home.

But she would miss aspects of this temporary life. The quiet, the slower pace, the beautiful lands and Miriam. Most certainly, a certain doctor who she had not seen in days, as he was attending to his father's requests. What would he think of the truth of her situation? He would not believe her and she might get sent to an institution for being 'hysterical'.

Kitty's suggestion at dinner that night that they have a lakeside picnic at the end of the week, as a way to introduce Lillian to the other prominent families in the county, both lightened her mood and worried her. She would have to be exceedingly careful about her behavior. Lillian suspected the picnic was actually an excuse for Kitty to socialize with Fitzwilliam, whom she had secretly missed, which Lillian had no qualms with. It was obvious that her cousin was quite taken with the bubbly young woman. It also meant she might have another chance to see Matthew.

When the morning of the picnic arrived, and Kitty warned Lillian that wearing a bathing suit without her guardian in attendance may be deemed inappropriate, Lillian nearly didn't go. Not only was she not interested in wearing seventy pounds of scratchy, wet, woolen material, but she ached to be inappropriate. Was it only weeks or centuries ago that she'd visited the water park in a two piece? Kitty's insistence and droning lecture nearly made her reconsider attending at all, until she looked down through her bedroom window, and saw Matthew Blackwell arrive with his father via carriage.

"Perhaps you are right, dear Miss Darlingwood, the best option I have is to remain in the shade, enjoying the activities from afar." Her eyes never left the view of Matthew who had shed his coat on the hot day and talked with Fitzwilliam in jovial tones. Would he be swimming? Did men swim without shirts?

"I'm so glad you've come to your senses. You could use the undisturbed time to work on your embroidery."

A shudder of loathing went through Lillian and she frowned. "I suppose you are right."

Now, after helping Miriam with the food baskets and reluctantly packing up her hated project, she was settled on a blanket, listening to the other water revelers enjoy the cool water, even as her skin flushed in the heat. To make matters worse, the senior Doctor Blackwell insisted on setting his blanket next to theirs. Matthew bowed demurely and acknowledged her.

"Miss Byrne, a pleasure as always. I hope the day finds you in good health."

"Doctor Blackwell, the pleasure is all mine. My health seems to be returning even as we speak," she said coyly as the ribbons from her bonnet blew gently across her neck. Matthew smiled at her, beneath the brim of his hat as he settled on the grass near, but not near enough, to her.

"I hope you do not find it disagreeable to share a blanket in the grass?" he whispered and smiled.

"No, good sir. I only find it highly disagreeable that there are so many eagle-eyed chaperones," she retorted with a quirked eyebrow before turning her wayward attention back to the knots.

He settled in, smiling at every frustrated curse Lillian whispered beneath her breath over the task. When Matthew's father left to find relief in the water, Matthew settled back on the blanket, hat over his eyes and nimble hands crossed over his trim middle. She wondered why he hadn't gone in the water with the others. The silence between them felt pensive. Her nervous energy about how to get back to her own time rose into her head. Maybe he'd noticed something about the morning she fell. Maybe, in their oath of honesty, he would give her a clue as to how she'd come through. She spoke without thinking, except to add to her list of possible solutions to get her home should her father not return.

"Can you tell me something?" she asked, her fingers fiddling with the embroidery and the impossibly small knots.

"Hm?" he said, from beneath his hat which shielded eyes from the sun. His breath was deep and measured in his broad chest. She wished she could press her cheek to his beating heart, run her hands down his middle. Lillian felt hot and moved the umbrella to protect her skin as well as to shield the others from noticing their conversation.

"About when we met? More specifically, when you first saw me."

He grunted below the hat and his mouth turn downward. "Why would you care to know such detail?"

"I just—I don't remember anything, except waking in the room with you there and even that is still a bit fuzzy."

"Fuzzy?" he said and peaked one eye beneath the brim of his hat to look at her.

"Unclear? Con—confusing," she stuttered as he caught her staring at him. Matthew removed his hat and sat up.

He watched the children and families playing in the water, squealing in delight and merriment. He turned his face up to the gentle warmth of the sun and Lillian bit her lip between teeth in anticipation. She shifted to fold her legs beneath her and continued the terrible excuse for embroidery knotted on her lap as though the art was frustrated with her and not the other way around.

"I was passing by, on my way to my father's estate when I was called into the house by your guardian, the Colonel. I rushed, as fast as possible, to your side. I must have smelled quite horrible as I'd been on the road for most of the day, a compellingly rank mixture of horse and sweat."

"Well, I think I'd remember such a detail as that," she smiled and quirked an eyebrow at him. He smirked back at her. "Yet, I only remember lavender. Lavender and dust and the sound of your voice as if coming to me in a long hallway. You called me angel." He studied her in a way that made her feel warm and strange. Lillian cleared her throat delicately. "Go on, please."

"You were at the base of the stairs, mumbling, lying face down. I was afraid to move you, for fear the injury had been to your neck. You pushed yourself up and stumbled to your knees, like a newborn foal. Determined and wobbly." He smiled and shook his head, then his brow turned down and his lips frowned. "The blood was so heavy and had soaked through your dress, down your neck, a horrible amount that made my body chill to see. You looked at me and staggered into my arms, a most trusting soul. The weight of you felt warm and—" Matthew now cleared his throat and his eyes fell. "Forgive me," he paused and continued "I carried you up the stairs and the maids helped me to wash away the blood so that I might know and tend to your wounds."

She flushed and bit her lip harder. She didn't remember trying to walk afterwards, she didn't remember much between landing and waking up in the bed. He'd carried her. Suddenly all thoughts of trying to find out more about the moment she time traveled seemed trivial. "Did you—were you—" she stopped and hung her head.

"What is it that you wish to know? Did we not agree to never lie to one another, Miss Byrne?"

Lillian glanced over to where the other people were otherwise occupied. "Did you undress me?" Matthew sat up and looped his strong arms around his bent knees, he studied his hands and pursed his lips.

"One delicious limb at a time, much to the chagrin of the maids in attendance. I had to," he paused to sigh, "inspect every part you see, to check for abrasions, breaks." He swallowed. "Right down to your perfectly beautiful toes. I've never," he shifted on the blanket and Lillian wondered if he was fighting his own arousal. "I've never known a woman to have so little hair on her body," he said, and he smiled with a light in his eyes.

"Well, I have hair in *some* places," Lillian said without thinking and quickly covered her mouth. Matthew's eyes shot to hers. The way he looked like he might burst out with laughter or die of embarrassment at any moment was charming and she melted into a confused puddle of want and giddiness. "I'm so, so sorry," she whispered.

"I imagine it is as soft and raven dark as those maddening curls on your crown. Would that I could be certain myself with either hand or tongue," he whispered. Lillian gasped and her hands fell to her lap. Her breath quickened. "Have I shocked you? Was it too much honesty?" he said with a voice gravelly and needful.

"No," she swallowed, and her hand trailed up her thigh, shaking. "It is in your honesty that I am letting my mind wander."

"What does the angel's hand seek?" he whispered watching her. "Surely it is the heaven where my thoughts lie." He watched her long fingers clench the flesh of her thigh. Matthew growled low in his throat and put his face in his hands. Closing his eyes and measuring his breaths. Lillian watched him.

"I am a horrible excuse for a gentleman," he said softly. "My apologies. The things that I have said to you, on this day and every day, since we were misfortuned to meet, have not been respectable, nor were they acceptable. Please excuse me." He rose to leave.

"You have lied," she said suddenly after him.

He turned back to her. "I beg your pardon?"

"You have lied to me, Doctor Blackwell. When you discussed

with Miss Darlingwood the unfortunate situation of my engagement you lied and said men didn't remember the details of moments as women do, but you—you remembered every detail from the moment we met."

"Miss Byrne," he said, looking like he wanted to protest.

"You remembered my fall, my waking, you remember all of it."

"If you please, Miss Byrne," Matthew interrupted, as the memories played over his face. He looked pained. "I wish to remember you forever, but I should forget you immediately," Matthew sighed and looked to the heavens. "If I recall such details so clearly it is only because you are quite unforgettable. It seems my heart stands little chance of disregarding you even when my head and all demands of social constraint tell me to do so."

"Matthew," Lillian began, and he looked down at her at the sound of his name. He took a deep breath, sighed it out, looked to the crowd of friends and family now coming up from the water in laughing and jovial waves.

"Miss Byrne, I cannot help but wonder if coming to your aid will be the paramount regret of my life."

He pulled his hat on, tipped it out of habit, and left in a hurried walk towards his carriage. Lillian watched him go, her heart seeming to beat out of her chest with every one of his steps, aching to follow after him. Never in her life had a man said something so cutting and so understandably true. She wanted to collapse into a fit of sobs.

"Where on earth is Doctor Blackwell gone in such a hurry? Is there a medical emergency?" Kitty said exhilarated with the cold water and wrapping a blanket demurely over her woolen suit. Lillian was surprised when a tear fell to her thumb and rolled onto her mottled cloth. Her chest felt heavy and thick and she tried to breathe but the air only came in quick gasps. She felt as though she might faint.

"My dear Miss Byrne, you are quite vexed! Whatever could it

be? Has something happened? Is it something concerning Doctor Blackwell? Has he offended you? What has he said? Tell me I must know, so that I may give him adequate reprimand."

"Kitty please, I—" she whispered and shook her head, trying desperately to wipe her eyes before the others could see. "It is of no consequence." Kitty offered her a damp kerchief but she refused. "I'm afraid I'm not feeling well," she paused to sniffle and wondered how she could extract herself from the crowd without seeming rude or arousing suspicion that Doctor Blackwell had anything at all to do with it. She quickly folded her work and stowed it away in the basket. "I beg upon your good mercy, Kitty, but would you please excuse me to Lady Mayfield and Mr. Byrne? The sunlight has become too warm and I need reprieve. I think I shall walk back home."

"Walk?" Kitty shouted in despair. "But my darling, Miss Byrne! We've only just begun the afternoon of merriment. Surely a little sustenance would improve your countenance. Also, a young lady cannot simply walk by herself, all the way to Westbury Manor! That is at least an afternoon's journey. You will surely expire before you reach the gates."

Matthew's words hung in her thoughts. *Coming to your aid will be the paramount regret of my life.*

"Thank you for your concern, Kitty, but I assure you that the exercise will quite calm my nerves," she managed to croak before rising from her seat and climbing out of the picnic area and back to the road. Once free of the view of the lake, she broke into a run back down the pitted dirt road. She lifted her skirts in the heat and the dust, pacing much slower than her high school track time. She ran over the dirt and rock, across the uneven ground, and hot sun-drenched fields, sweating profusely in the heavy cotton gown and undergarments, her slippers torn to shreds before she finally made her way back to the gates of Westbury Manor.

"Miss Lillian!" Miriam exclaimed when Lillian came through

the kitchen door. She must have been a horrific sight, dirty and sweating, pink in the face and her bonnet trailing from her hand as she had torn it from her neck around mile two. "Are you quite alright, what has happened?" The maid stepped up to help her. "Are you running from someone? Are you in need of a doctor?"

Lillian shook her head, too exhausted and dehydrated to cry at the thought of the doctor she truly needed, who may never again come to her aid. She put her hands to her ribs which ached deeply, and she regretted the brash run that had now put her in even greater pain.

"I assure you, Miriam, I am quite fine. I will be set right in a few moments when I have caught my breath." she said, lying as much to herself as to Mrs. Shaw. She was not sure she would ever be set right. Lillian stumbled up the stairs, shedding her ruined shoes behind her and continuing to her quarters on shaking legs and bare feet, until she collapsed onto her bed.

8

A HORRIBLE LADY AND THE TERRIBLE MR. SUTTON

Two days later, Lillian had confined herself to her room. The difficult conversation with Matthew during the picnic, her ridiculous exhausting run, and the lack of any word about her father's plan to help her leave this god-forsaken time, accumulated into what Miriam described as 'a bout of horrible exhaustion'.

While her feelings for Matthew had momentarily distracted her from the desire to return to her own time, knowing now that he despised being around her made Lillian all the more anxious to go. She could not believe that she'd even considered living the rest of her life out in horrible yards of linen, just to be close to him.

As she lay in bed, watching the mid-morning sun climbing past the horizon, she closed her eyes and tried to picture the journals. *Her ancestor, Lillian Byrne had come to Westbury.* She felt a great pressure in her head. *Lillian Byrne had shown up unexpectedly and was quickly engaged.* The thrumming in her skull intensified. *Lillian Byrne had disappeared shortly after her wedding night, her body discovered days later...*

Lillian shot out of bed and hugged her arms closer to her. Lillian Byrne died young. Her mother had romanticized the story. She'd even named her daughter Lillian. Lillian felt a hard sob build up through her chest and she cried.

She was stuck in the past. She had died, in this past.

She rose to pace, worried even more about the whereabouts of her father and if he really intended to save her at all. The longer she stayed, the more chance she would not survive at all. The Lillian of history had drowned, and she needed to figure out when and why that happened.

The door creaked open, even as she was drying her eyes and thinking herself a foolish and stupid girl for not following her father the day he'd left. Miriam poked her round, cheery face in and whispered.

"Pardon me, miss."

Lillian sniffed and quickly blew her nose "I'm awake, I'm sorry. Please don't bring me breakfast, I'll come down soon."

"Miss Byrne, begging your pardon, but Lady Mayfield would like a word."

Lillian's body shivered in response. She hadn't been able to properly speak with the woman yet, but knew from what the maids had said that she was shrewd and cunning. If anyone could see through Lillian's odd circumstances, it would be Lady Mayfield. She must pull her confused head out of her ass and stay focused.

"Yes, Miriam, I'll be ready presently. Thank you." Miriam nodded with a look of sympathy and closed her door. Lillian dressed and put all thoughts of the doctor, her imminent death, and her disappointment in her father out of her head. It was time to get back in the game of finding her way home.

∽

"I see that you are quite recovered." The older woman's words were like daggers and her gaze over the edge of her glasses, past the intricate embroidery work, shot ice down Lillian's spine. "I am glad to see that no time will be lost in proceeding with finding you a suitable husband." Lillian bowed her head as she stood in front of the woman in the light and airy conservatory. It was a strange and very forward way to greet someone. Lillian had the overwhelming sense that she was not liked by the Lady.

"I am most thankful for your kind words and well wishes for my continued recovery," she said. "I apologize if I have caused any worry for you or Colonel Mayfield. I understand the requirement of medical assistance may garner great cost and I am willing to help in any way—"

"Cost?" Lady Rachel said sharply. Lillian looked up from staring at her hands. She had made the assumption that perhaps Lady Mayfield was upset by the cost as she was rumored to be tight in the purse.

"For Doctor Blackwell's assistance?"

"*Young* Doctor Blackwell did not ask for such compensation."

"But he spent so much time—"

"He hardly has the skill of his father. In fact, it was very much a disgrace to have him and his roughneck methods in this very house after spending so much time in the back country. I would have liked to send him away, but the Colonel insisted that he was more than adequate."

Lillian's cheeks burned. For the time, the knowledge, and technology available, she had thought he'd done quite well. That her own father had insisted on him was a curious detail.

"Well, I am well on my way to regaining a normal countenance so he must have been, as Colonel Mayfield attests, more than adequate."

Lady Mayfield stared at her and pierced the cloth with a vicious stab. "Normal? Is that so? You seem far from normal to me. Something is definitely odd about you, girl. I would offer you a friendly warning to mind your behavior and work harder on the refinements of a proper young lady as you have been raised. It is only because of the Colonel that you are here. And I have been working tirelessly to broker a very advantageous arrangement so that you do not have to stay long. You will soon have your engagement to think of."

"My engagement, Lady Mayfield? To whom?"

Lady Mayfield looked at her as though she'd lost every one of her marbles. "Why Mr. Sutton of course!"

"But, begging your pardon, Lady Mayfield, I have never met the man."

"It is no matter. I have been left with the burden of you by the Colonel and he cannot expect me to house another Byrne."

"When will the Colonel return?"

"Whenever he sees fit, it is not for you to question," she said sharply.

"But, I beg of you, if we could only postpone said engagement until the Colonel returns—"

"Silence, child. You are brash and unrefined," Lady Mayfield interrupted with a sigh and reached over, sharply ringing the service bell beside her chair, summoning the house maid. The young girl dashed in looking as though she'd been pushed in front of a firing squad. Lady Mayfield stared at Lillian.

"Well?"

"My lady?" Lillian said, shaken into addressing her with a formality that felt false in her mouth.

"You are excused, girl. I suggest you take your convalescence to improve yourself ahead of your upcoming nuptials. It would be a dire mistake to lose this opportunity through continued behavior most unbecoming of a young lady."

"Yes, Lady Mayfield," Lillian hid her scowl and curtseyed before leaving the room. What she really wanted to tell the lady was to screw off, that she wouldn't be marrying anyone. But she had to pretend. She had to believe her father would be returning soon. Lillian's heart was pounding thickly. She wanted to turn on her heel, tell the old hag what she really felt about her and her judgmental dickery. Knowing she had arranged the quick engagement to a total stranger, made Lillian hate her already. She clenched her fists and headed to the kitchen.

Miriam was there, preparing for the evening meal with a younger maid. She looked up when Lillian entered, concern on her face.

"Miss Lillian, what on earth are you doin' here? You should be resting. Is there something the matter?"

"How did I get here?" she asked.

"Well, you walked in here on your own two feet," Miriam chortled.

"No, to Westbury, do you remember my arrival?" Miriam looked to the servant girl.

"Go on and fetch me them eggs, Sarah Jane."

"Mum?"

"Now, girl! Are you daft?"

Sarah Jane scurried out, drying her hands on her apron as she made for the backyard coop. Miriam sighed and shook her head.

"If you're going be in here, you best put those hands to work." She handed her a knife, handle side first, and nodded to the bowl of potatoes. Lillian may not have been good at much but she knew how to peel a potato. She settled in next to Miriam and immediately felt calmer.

"I tell you it was strange goings on. And I wouldn't be speakin' so bluntly but ye was the one who asked and I've—well I've sort of taken a liking to ye."

"It was strange?" Lillian asked, looking up from her task.

"Aye, I was there, coming through the hall from the parlor to the kitchen when you fell, out of nowhere, in a rush of great light. I was there when you landed. I tried to help, but there was so much blood."

"Did the Colonel say anything to you when you found me?"

"He was quite distraught he was. Calling your name, and worrying over you as if you was his own daughter. When I asked who you were, he told me a dear niece and that he'd been expecting you. Then he ran to fetch help."

"And he found Doctor Blackwell?" Lillian's heart ticked up.

"Aye, and that man did right by you he did," Miriam said continuing to prepare the roast.

"I suppose he did," Lillian said softly and missed Matthew. "Before the Colonel left on his business, did he say anything at all? About where he was headed? Who he'd be with?"

"No Miss Byrne, not to someone the likes of me. But he did say to keep an eye on you. To protect you. I think he's not too pleased about this engagement that Lady Mayfield has been plotting."

"The Colonel is not the only one," Lillian grouched, peeling harshly. While she was busy waiting on a dad who never came through for her in childhood, Lady Mayfield was making decisions about her life, as though she was some prize piece of property. She guessed, in this time, she was. It irked her. Something still didn't fit.

"Could Colonel Mayfield object to this engagement? If he were here?"

"I suppose he may, he and the lady have only been married a few years, but he's still the man of the house."

Lillian stayed quiet, thinking. If her father returned soon, they could leave and she could get back to her time. If he did not return, the engagement would have to proceed. An unwed girl in a home was a financial burden. That she was not one of Lady Mayfield's blood relatives meant she was even more the unnecessary burden.

"Take heart, child. Nothing is set in stone yet," Miriam soothed looking over her shoulder out the window to where Sarah Jane was returning with an apron full of eggs.

Lillian's fingers slipped and she cut her finger, inhaled sharply and stuck the bleeding cut into her mouth.

Miriam tsked at her clumsiness. She reached overhead to a basket of cloth scraps and handed Lillian one. "Saints, child. Would do *you* better to marry a doctor." Lillian's eyes shot up from where she wound the cloth around the cut. She felt her cheeks burn and looked to Sarah Jane who had gone down to the root cellar.

"Do you know Sutton? Is he a kind man?"

Miriam didn't look up from her carrots and celery. She sighed and shook her head. "Oh child. I don't know. All men are a bit touched in the head, ain't they?"

Lillian sighed and her shoulders fell.

"It isn't my place to say, Miss," she checked to see if Sarah Jane had returned and hurriedly went on, "I don't know the depths of your heart. But I do know how your eyes have wandered over other, better men. And I certainly have never heard Mr. Sutton call anyone angel."

Sarah Jane huffed through the door and Lillian looked down to the pile of peeled potatoes and the small splotches of blood on the table. She wiped them way as best she could.

"Well, you did make quick work of those. Can't stitch worth a pile of manure, but at least you won't be useless in a kitchen." Miriam teased. "Now get out of here, and I'll bring you tea in the parlor later."

"Miriam, you needn't trouble yourself, I can make my own."

"Do go on now! Churlish child!" she scoffed and nudged her out of the room. Lillian smiled at her on the way out, feeling much better than she had after meeting with Lady Mayfield. At least she knew she wasn't completely hated in the household. It also gave her much to think about when it came to her current engagement.

She stormed up the stairs as if to run from the thoughts, and sequestered herself in her quarters. She threw herself on her bed with a sob. She didn't know how much time had passed, but a soft knock alerted her to Miriam, in her doorway, looking rather pale and put out.

"Pardon the interruption, miss, but you've a gentleman visitor, waiting down in the parlor."

Lillian's heart leapt, and she shot up from the bed. Her mind and thoughts turned immediately to Matthew and how she ached to be in his calming and honest presence. Perhaps she could ask him for help, at least for advice. Mr. Sutton was, after all, his cousin. It made her wonder, if proposals were being thrown about, why hadn't he offered one. Probably on account of him being penniless.

"Has Doctor Blackwell returned?"

"Begging you, no miss," Miriam interrupted. "'Tis Mr. Sutton. He's asking if you are well enough to be seen?"

Lillian sat back down, deflated. Of course it would be that faceless dolt. Doctor Blackwell had no reason to see her. If any implication could be made from their last meeting, he had officially deemed their patient-and-doctor relationship over. Any relationship they may have held, as friends, as co-conspirators in the dangerously strange game of honesty, was over. Lillian sighed and nodded.

"Of course," she smoothed her wayward hair. "If it would not aggrieve him to wait in the parlor while I freshen up, I shall be down soon."

"I asked Lady Mayfield if you were to have a chaperone but she insisted on you meeting in private. Still keep the door open and if you are not feeling well enough for such a visit, I have no qualms about letting him know you are not yet recovered," Miriam said with her eyebrows raised. Bless Miriam.

Perhaps the privacy was for the proposal.

Lillian rose and walked to the door. She smiled and took the older maid's hands in hers. She felt the callouses of hard work and was filled with appreciation for such loyalty, not just for her as a charge but as a woman forced into a situation against her heart's will.

"I appreciate that, more than you know. I shall make his acquaintance. It cannot hurt to meet the man." She sniffed.

"I will serve the tea and if you are feeling unwell, you may signal me by dropping your spoon. Then I shall make sure to devise a distraction so that you may take your leave." Miriam offered. Lillian smiled and placed a kiss on her cheek.

"Miriam you are a better friend than I could have hoped for."

After Miriam left, Lillian redressed herself in a pale blue, cotton dress, tying it as tightly as possible on her own, and felt the ache in her side from the deep drawing of breath.

She had wished she had found Matthew along the road. Or that he had come after her. But she hadn't. And he hadn't. It appeared, by all accounts, that the universe was reminding her that Doctor Blackwell was not to be hers. Her hair was an absolute horror, but she tamed it with a comb and water and put it back into a simple bun, something Kitty had shown her she could do herself in a pinch.

Taking the stairs and deep breaths very carefully, she descended and thought through all of the possible questions, comments, and conversations she might have with Mr. Sutton. What would he wish to speak of? What if she wasn't able to pretend to be delighted at his offer? What if he found her mentally unsound or worse, an imposter? What if—

She turned the corner of the parlor and saw him standing, stoically against the fireplace. He was a large man, hands clasped behind his back and reserved as he stared over his long and straight nose down at her. The nose was akin to Matthew's but his eyes were cold and brown; disinterested but for the slight shock at how quickly she had rounded the corner. His hair was trimmed neatly, to the edge of the staunchly pressed collar around his thick neck.

She made a small, surprised sound before remembering herself and bowed.

"Mr. Sutton, it is a pleasure to meet, you," she lied. Still, the peace must be kept to buy time. She bowed her head and knee low, curtseying far longer than necessary in order to gather her wits.

"Miss Byrne, the pleasure is all mine," he said in a clipped and authoritative voice and came nearer. "Forgive me for not calling on you sooner," he bowed and she offered her hand. He kissed it with soft, wet lips, quickly in a perfect example of withheld emotion. "I hope I am not interrupting your convalescence. I would have offered to come sooner," he paused and cleared his throat. "But I'm afraid business in London has kept me away."

She could not see this large and reserved man, his jowly face and barrel chest ever sitting at her bedside calling her Angel.

"I am much improved and am happy that you've given me a joyous reason to leave the confines of bed." Now she blushed and turned away as he looked at her. "That is to say, I am rested and anxious to return to my normal tasks."

"I am glad I could inspire you," he said and sniffed. He looked at her forehead, studied the sutures and shook his head. "Tis a shame you shall be scarred from the event." Lillian tried not to scowl and employed great effort to not reply the way she would have with Matthew. She had no such pact of honesty with this man. He was, after all, her soon-to-be husband.

"With some skill, I can learn to arrange my hair to hide much of it, and you can make the effort to always stay on my left," she said. It was the closest thing to polite she could manage. He turned his head to the side and considered her. She wondered if she were about to be found out for the liar she was.

"I suppose you're right. In any case, our sons will not inherit it."

"Sons?" Lillian choked.

"Do you find my assurances too forward?" he said and put his hands behind his back. "But of course our shared future will hold the blessing of many male heirs to the Sutton name!"

Lillian smiled demurely with clenched teeth.

"Wouldn't that be a blessing?" she seethed and forced herself not to throw up in her mouth. The strangest thought of being too forward, and Matthew's intimate comment to her on the day of the picnic flashed in her mind. To be forward in his desire to pleasure her was far different. How she wished he was here with her instead, unchaperoned, tangled on the couch with his warm, strong fingers trailing up her thigh.

"You are quite flushed, my dear. I see you are as impatient for our future nuptials as I." He leaned in and his eyes narrowed. "And the blessing of a marriage bed."

Lillian stepped back suddenly. The gall of the man! It was one thing for Matthew, who knew her best and held genuine affection for her, to make inappropriate comments. This man was a stranger and she felt sick to think of what was running through his mind. He watched her face turn downward. Probably attributing it to the necessary outward propriety of young women in the era.

"How lucky am I to have such an innocent young woman as my future wife? Your blush suits you."

Lillian was enraged and though the original plan was to get her life safely back on course, a new desire hit her strongly in the gut. The way the man leered at her like a pedophile, nearly drooling over a woman much younger than himself, demanding an innocent to sire multiple, large and jowly men, who no doubt would share of his same manners, made her head convulse with pain and rage.

I won't have to marry him if I can figure out how to get back, Lillian thought and walked to the settee, lowered herself with a huff and crossed her arms protectively over the lower cut of her neckline. Mr. Sutton came to sit in the chair beside her. He was studying her now, like a prize he was about to win.

"How has your business been?" she asked suddenly in an effort bring his attention off of her face. "I hope that you are not too weary from your travels." When he merely glared at her, she cleared her throat and tried to fill the awkward silence. "The weather has been quite unpredictable and I fear I do not know enough to understand how that must affect the ships in your care."

He looked at her as if she'd grown a second head and it occurred to Lillian that women were probably not allowed, nor expected to talk of business, even with their husbands. At least not this husband.

"You mustn't worry for the tedious details of running a shipyard, my darling. Let us talk instead of my cousin."

Lillian's eyes shot up at the mention of his name. "I beg your pardon? I'm not sure to whom you are referring."

"Doctor Blackwell!"

She feigned ignorance and shook her head. "I'm not sure there is much to speak of."

"Well, I understand I have him to thank for saving your life? Though he could have used a lighter hand on that stitching," he added. Lillian's mouth turned down in anger.

"His first stitches were quite perfect. I tore out the others accidentally while slipping up a hill in the rain. He aided me in getting back to Westbury Manor and had to repair them with wet and cold fingers," she defended quickly, remembering every detail of the moment and the way he'd found her, wanted her, held her. Her eyes filled anew. Mr. Sutton watched the tears with a glint of something sinister within his eyes.

"I cannot fathom a reason why you'd be out walking in the rain to begin with, especially alone. Nor why you thought it acceptable to resign to such aide from an unmarried man." His voice was thick with disapproval. "When we are married, you must know that kind of behavior will simply not be tolerated. Rest assured, you are to remain at home. I will not have my wife traipsing about the countryside like some common bumpkin. Did anyone see you? Scrambling through the rain like a witless peasant?" Mr. Sutton's voice rose, and darkness took over his features. His rounded cheeks clenched into hard lines and he rose to pace before the fireplace.

"I am quite fond of walking," she said simply and glared up at him.

"I am quite fond of a complacent wife," he said back in a tone that brought a rising of bile into Lillian's throat. The door burst open and Miriam stepped in, unannounced, with a rattling tea service tray and a face quite flushed itself. She looked once at her young charge and her beady, hard eyes landed on Mr. Sutton.

"Begging your pardon, *sir*. Miss Byrne requested serving tea after your long journey."

Lillian loved Miriam for the complete lack of respect in her tone. She smiled at the older woman's audacity and noted that Miriam had not set out her delicious scones for tea with Sutton.

"Fine," he acknowledged with a curt nod, and held his tongue while Miriam, whom he felt far beneath the benefit of his direct attention, set the tea service down in front of Lillian. Miriam began to pour him the first cup and looked up at Lillian's pale face.

"When we are married, you will find everything you need in our family's grounds and shall be quite content," Mr. Sutton said and turned away to the window overlooking the garden.

"As for my cousin, you will no longer cause him the grief of attending to your foolishness as he is leaving in short time to seek his fortunes elsewhere. You, however, shall have no reason to leave when we are happily betrothed. Walking or otherwise." He did not face her, only gave the edict as if talking to a servant about how his dinner should be cooked. Miriam looked at her and gave a small shake of her head in warning.

No reason to leave. Complacently content.

Lillian knew what her proper place was supposed to be, knew

the reaction she should give, when a man, *the man* who was promised to be her husband, the man she was to obey and cherish, spoke to her in such a commanding tone. She knew the decent and right thing to do if she were to keep up the façade long enough to escape.

She knew all of these things and chose to open her mouth anyway.

9

LILLIAN WRITES A LETTER

"I will walk," she began quietly without looking up at Mr. Sutton. "When and where I please, in any and all manner of weather. I will keep the company I choose, especially if it contributes to my happiness."

Mr. Sutton's shoulders tensed to his ears as if he'd been struck in the back. He turned on his heel, spun to confront her, his face red with anger. He breathed heavily out of his flared nostrils and his voice boomed so suddenly that it shocked Miriam into dropping the sugar dish on the carpet, spilling out the perfect brown crystals that scattered like glitter at Lillian's feet.

"I will not tolerate a wife who dares speak back to me or deliberately acts against my wishes!"

Lillian stood. "How dare you speak to me in such a manner." She grabbed a spoon from the tray and pointed it at him. "You, who had not one thread of common decency to visit me in my time of need. You who never even asked me for my hand but instead took the cowardly route of brokering the deal as though I were some horse. Now you stand in my home, issuing commands at me like a common dock worker? I will not be treated with such disrespect."

Mr. Sutton leaned back in shock.

"I had business to attend to, more important than you bumbling down a few stairs. Proof in point that you should not be trusted to walk alone, lest you further mar that beautiful face," he lowered his voice and narrowed his eyes. "And like a horse, perhaps a good belting would help you remember just who is in command."

Lillian let out a growl, held the spoon aloft dramatically and threw it to the floor. He watched with astonishment and she refused to take her eyes from his. Miriam set the sugar dish back on the table, grabbed the dropped spoon, and left the room. Lillian watched from the corner of her eye as she scurried out and felt the fear of being alone with Mr. Sutton. She didn't know if Miriam would indeed go for help or if she had lost her nerve in the face of Mr. Sutton's anger.

"I will not tolerate such childish behavior from a woman who, by all accounts, should be lavish in her gratitude towards me at her great fortune at our soon-to-be union."

Lillian tried to calm her breathing and looked squarely into the eyes that seemed to swallow her hole into their cold darkness.

"You will lower your voice, sir," she said, both commanding and calm. Mr. Sutton took an angry breath and glared at her. Not in the way Doctor Blackwell would, as if he were trying to decide if her obstinance was charming or simply maddening. He looked at her coldly, as if he had no qualms about harming her, and in fact, might feel it was his duty.

He took a deep breath, tucked his anger inside like a grenade that could blow at any given moment and offered her a cruel, sharp toothed smile.

"I beg your pardon, Miss Byrne. I have had a long journey and I forget that you have indeed sustained a serious contusion. Perhaps it is causing you to forget your place in the world as an orphan. While I should permit you more patience as you heal, I think it is only fair for you to be aware that I enjoy the challenge of a strong spirit. In my horses, in my workers...in anything that I own."

Lillian's nostrils flared in anger and her cheeks grew pink. She opened her mouth to speak but he came at her, with brazen and overwhelming speed, threw his arms around her and locked her arms down by her sides. His breath was hot and smelled of onions as it blew across her neck and décolletage. He pressed his flaccid lips against hers and forced his tongue into her mouth. Lillian yelled in outrage and struggled, biting her teeth down just as he pulled back, triumphant.

"I'm not above breaking such a spirit by any means necessary, whether it be by a strong hand or a riding crop," he whispered, into her ear, and pulled away to smile with a foreboding sharpness of his teeth. His gaze fell to her neck hungrily, as though her throat could be torn out with nary a problem.

"You will unhand me," she said though her voice shook and she felt a cold sweat start to seep into her clothing. She wondered if she could push him away or if she stood any chance with a man his size, wearing the layers she did. Before she could chance the idea, Fitzwilliam burst through the doorway of the parlor; her savior delivered by Miriam exactly at the right moment. Mr. Sutton let go of her quickly and backed away to a much more respectable distance.

"Mr. Sutton! Such a wonderful surprise to see you again. I hope I'm not late for tea, I do love tea." Fitzwilliam said charmingly, flashed his dimple and shook Mr. Sutton's hand in a firm grip.

"Hello darling, feeling better?" he asked and looked at Lillian before planting a kiss on her forehead gently. "Why, you look absolutely pale! Don't you think she looks pale, Mr. Sutton? As though she's been through too much excitement in her delicate state?"

"Betrothals are quite exciting," Mr. Sutton blustered, red

faced, and befuddled by the sudden appearance of her brother into their intimate meeting.

"Oh! I'm sure she is quite excited, *but* in her delicate condition —" he sighed and looked at Lillian with a sly wink, "perhaps it best if she retires to her quarters. I'm sure seeing you has given her more than she's quite used to. But after a good rest, I'm sure you'll be much improved, won't you, my darling?"

Never before had Lillian felt such sibling affection. It was more often the case that Will, in her time, had done very little to help her in any way. But she felt warmth spread in her heart at Fitzwilliam's appearance and apt reading of her distress. The sudden relief showed on her face and she promised herself that she would help him gain the courage to ask for Kitty's hand as repayment.

"I think it best I take your good advice, cousin." She bowed first to Fitzwilliam. Mr. Sutton stepped forward and offered to take her hand. She reluctantly slipped her hand into his and he squeezed hard enough to crack one of her knuckles. She glared and tried to pull her hand away. He held fast.

"Miss Byrne, it is a pleasure to be in your company. I look forward to the day when we shall share all of our moments." He kissed her hand with his teeth out and she pulled away. Remembering a small curtsey before staggering out of the room, she made her way up the stairs two at a time.

She knew then. She knew that if the original Lillian Byrne had drowned in the river, it was not an accident. If she had been promised to Mr. Sutton, and he found her displeasing, he had every indication of being the kind of man who would dispose of her. Had Lillian only ensured the deadly outcome with her brashness?

She wished she had someone she could talk to. Someone who would be on her side, to really listen to her fears and misgivings. But she was alone. While she wanted to believe her father was certainly someone who cared for her and hoped for her happiness, he was no longer here. She didn't know when or if she'd ever see him again. Her cousin could be relied upon, to be certain, but he had little power to change the outcome.

She remembered Matthew's words on that rainy hill. He knew what poverty would do to young women. He begged her not to choose that course. But what could be worse than marrying such an abrasive and horrible man, whose only intent was to parade her as some child-bearing trophy and beat her if she did not comply?

She wished she could talk to Matthew right then, to tell him about the afternoon while it was fresh in her mind, but it wasn't as though they had instant messaging or texts. She closed the door to her room and stared at the small writing desk beneath the window, its inkwell, quill, and paper at the ready.

"I wish I had taken greater care in Mrs. Babel's cursive classes," she whispered. She hadn't written a letter in over three years, and certainly nothing so formal as he would expect.

But then again, he knew her to be strange and not entirely proper, so perhaps he wouldn't expect her language and penmanship to be as poetic and perfectly formed as from other ladies of the era. He would, hopefully, remember their vow of honesty and respond with some other solution to the horrible matter at hand. Despite his affirmation that she was the bane of his existence, at the very least, as his patient, and a lady, her well-being must mean something to him.

Dr. Blackwell,

I hope that you will pardon my horrid scribbling. Please know that I would not dare to write, but it is with great fear and concern that I take pen and ink to you now. I have just had a visit from Mr. Sutton. His temper is quite pronounced and he demanded that I obey him, but not in the lovely caring way you have. In a frightening, horrible way that makes me think he means to do me harm should I not do exactly as I am told. He says I can no longer walk as I am accustomed to, by myself in the fields of this blessed land, even though it brings my heart such joy and calm. He says I have forgotten myself and am a threat to his reputation. He threatened to beat me with his hands and even a riding crop should I not comply!

My dearest friend. You once swore a pact to me and I to you, that we would in all things be honest. I know that I've upset you the day of the picnic and it was my own fumbling mouth that over spoke and caused your good and noble heart to be filled with guilt. I cannot apologize enough, but I would spend every day trying to if you could help me devise a solution to this situation. At the very least, I beg of you come visit. I miss you terribly.

I have put so great a pressure on you in asking, and I hope truly that you know, I do not do so lightly. You've become the one confidant, with whom I feel my heart can express itself most fully. Please, Matthew. Understand that I cannot marry your cousin, or I shall surely live a life of regret, pain, and solitude.

Your Lily

Lillian sealed the letter carefully with the wax and metal stamp on her desk and pulled the bell cord next to her bed. She had never used it, always finding the maids more attentive than she cared for, but tonight, she needed an ally, and Miriam had proved her worth as a true and faithful friend. When she arrived, red cheeks and asking if the missus was alright, Lillian handed her the letter.

"First, I must thank you for sending Mr. Byrne to interject, you are a true friend and I owe you a large debt," Lillian paused and took Miriam's hand in hers and pressed a kiss to her cheek. The older woman blushed but looked pleased, as if she'd never received such affection from her charge nor children. Lillian pressed the letter into her palm.

"I'm afraid I must ask of you one more favor. Please see that Doctor Blackwell, the young Doctor Blackwell I mean, gets this as soon as possible, Miriam. I will owe you a great debt for your help in keeping it secret. I assure you it is not improper, it is simply something I can only speak to with my physician about," she lied. Miriam looked as if she really didn't need so much explanation to deliver a note to the handsome doctor.

"Aye, Miss Lillian, I will see to it that the *young* doctor gets your love note," she winked.

"It is not a—"

"Sure'n it's not, child," Miriam nodded. "And no woman would blame you, even if it was." She turned and left the room. Lillian sighed and paced in the room, watching from her window as, minutes later, the stable boy took one of the fastest stallions down the road, lamp in hand at the encroaching dark. She watched the small yellow light disappear over the hillside and wondered if all her hope of survival was going to disappear with it.

～

Matthew was never a man to take to drink. He knew the effects of the poison could be quite disastrous, and the altered states men took whilst under its influence could have harrowing consequences. It could become addictive. It could cause great trauma to the liver and a man's ability to reason. That being said, he was drinking. And doing so with a concentrated effort.

The dinner he'd just excused himself from with his father and uncle had been strained with the unspoken disappointment in his suggested future. When Frederick had joined them over brandy and cigars, after meeting with his 'beloved' fiancée, and proceeded to burst into a tirade about Miss Byrne's deplorable and pretentious obstinance, Matthew had swallowed his snifter whole in an effort to keep quiet.

"I've never met a woman so petulant. She should count herself lucky that I did not take a hand to her right then and there. When we are married, by God—" and he went on, disgustingly callous and barbaric about his intentions to tame her spirit until the older gentlemen had insisted that he calm himself with a drink and a warm fire. Matthew sat in the corner, arms and hands gripping at the chair in an effort to not exact the kind of violence on Frederick that he'd so horribly described about Lillian. Instead he excused himself, feigning an early morning call to the town's apothecary the next day.

Except, instead of peace when he'd arrived in his quarters, he found her letter laid on his bed, no doubt placed there by some valiant servant. The shaky lines, apologizing for her poor penmanship, the plea for him to help her find a way to make the situation not so. The threats that she'd received from his cousin. A riding crop? His hands against her? The horror of it was enough for even a well-intentioned stranger to want to take action against such a union.

But what beat against his heart and brain even more so was the admission that he was her confidant and friend. The person that she could be honest with and who she missed terribly. Then to read her neat signature,

Your Lily

As if she were his. As if that could ever be. What she asked of him was impossible and social suicide for him, much worse for her should even the simple slip of paper be discovered. He knew the reach of his cousin was growing, that he was making powerful friends in high-level places and was using such engagements to render himself immune from the shadier dealings of his business overseas.

Matthew had no power to help her find release from her situation. He was teetering on the edge of respectability as it was with his unconventional ideas of dealing with the poor. He could not respond to her letter. Instead, he had a bottle brought to his room and was obsessing over all the ways the day had gone badly. Foremost in his mind was the thought of what would happen once she was married to his cousin.

He couldn't very well take her away. And he couldn't allow her to leave; an orphan in the world, facing poverty and unsavory ends in the harsh and bitter slums of some industrial city. She had not the constitution, as a properly raised young woman of some means, to survive the working world. The best he may be able to offer was to continue to offer his friendship even after the event of their marriage and try to talk to his cousin about being more open and forgiving to the quirks of her personality.

But he knew his cousin. And he knew that his cousin did not

approve of the opposite and fairer sex having opinions of their own, nor did he approve of them being much else but meek mice, scurrying through the house on quiet feet and warming his bed on demand. He supposed that Frederick would also demand that she bring boys, not girls, into the world. He would demand a lot of her. And she would fight.

Matthew's gut fell and he took another healthy swig of brandy, feeling it warm the churning mess of his intestines as he thought further of her sprawled beneath his large and imposing cousin, fulfilling the demands of his nature without him having the slightest care for her comfort or enjoyment. What if she fought him not just in words as she was prone to do, but also against any physical advances she did not want? What if Frederick held her down, against her will, feeling justified in his marital rights?

Matthew's face turned red and his head pounded as he took the expensive bottle and threw it against the fireplace, shattering the glass and causing the fire to erupt with a roar. His eyes welled with tears. He could never live in this county again. When they married, he would have to leave. He could not see her in such a state and not murder his cousin outright. Just knowing what lay ahead of her filled his chest with such a sense of hopeless despair that he hung his head, dropped to the floor, and sobbed.

Your Lily

What a fine mess they were in indeed. He hadn't been wrong when he'd told her that his greatest regret was meeting her. Meeting her had meant falling so instantaneously and irrevocably in love with her, that the remainder of his days would be nothing but a tortuous hell. He didn't know if he should leave his father's home tomorrow, or rush to her side. So he locked himself in his room with another bottle and her letter, and there he stayed.

She'd received no word and had therefore stayed in the confines of her room the next day, refusing food, tea, even light. She sat in the same dressing gown, her hair in tangles and matted to her cheeks from the tracks of tears. She was giving up hope. Lillian Byrne, stubborn, self-made woman was about to marry a man that would no doubt drown her in the river and she would become nothing more than a journal entry that would be read by some stubborn young fool two-hundred-and-twenty years from now who may very well take a trip down a magical staircase and start the blasted cycle all over again.

Lillian hugged her knees to her chest and thought through it again and again. Could she have lived this before? She closed her eyes and rocked back and forth, trying to unlock some secret subconscious, some past life knowledge that could help her get out of this mess.

She sat in front of the dead fireplace, the chill in her room reaching a frosty degree in the evening. Still, she would not allow anyone to enter, not even her beloved Miriam. She had even refused to see her cousin who had so sweetly saved her from the parlor meeting with Mr. Sutton. Lillian couldn't rely on Fitzwilliam to save her. She couldn't rely on the useless sympathy from Kitty, and she was becoming more certain that she could not rely on her father to come back.

It became clear, after the third morning that Matthew, her guardian angel, had turned a deaf ear to her plea for help. She'd even heard the maids talking in the hallway outside her door that the good doctor might not be coming to visit Westbury Manor again, as he had decided to make the long journey back to the south of Wales within the week and was much too preoccupied with the details of such an event to do anything else. They said this all with clucking tongues and shaking heads. Lillian should have known that she and Matthew had not been as duplicitous as they had thought and that whomever had seen their interludes, or knew about her secret letter, would have ascertained their growing affection.

She thought through it, from the perspective of the era and realized that he must have been going away to save his reputation. Maybe to save hers as well, since she was too daft, and irrational, and senseless to halt such destructive behavior. Perhaps it was the norm for husbands to beat their wives, keep them under lock and key, own them as property or livestock. It was probably the norm for women to not mind.

What would she do? Submit and hope that it would ensure her survival for a longer period of time, until she could find a means to escape? What kind of survival would that be?

If the choice were to be strangled to death by her husband or sustain months, if not years of abuse first, Lillian would prefer to be the instantaneous victim of a crime of passion. Lillian shivered in front of the cold and dark grill of her fireplace. She wished her mother were here. Her heel-wearing, ladder climbing, glass-ceiling exploding, tough-nut mom. The woman, who even though allowed herself to be whisked away in flights of romantic fantasy occasionally, never put much dependence on her flyaway husband.

She'd tell her to run.

She'd tell her that she wasn't like the women of this age and if she ran she could find a way to make a living, to support herself. Or she could find a way back. She would tell her to stop moping around and start looking for ways out. There had to be some sort of fairy ring or magical standing stone site, or something that could send her back. Her mother wouldn't let her give up. Her mother would want her to do everything in her power to get back to her.

Hell, even her stupid brother would tell her to stop all the dramatic self-pity and be the stubborn Lillian he knew. Her resolve began to glow, somewhere deep inside of her heart. She had a family to get back to in the future. She did not know where her father had disappeared to. She did not know if he would return. It would be up to her to save herself. She had it in her to be cunning, she could act the innocent bride-to-be with some skill, just long enough to dissuade suspicion and find a way to get back to her time.

After all, there wasn't anything left worth staying for in this time now that Matthew Blackwell had abandoned her.

AN EXCITING AFTERNOON

Lillian stared out into the gardens, her eyes dreamily relaxed so the view muted into vibrant greens and dark blues, splashes of reds and pinks along the rose-lined paths and greys of statuesque fountains. She was taking reprieve in the parlor, after a busy morning helping Miriam and the staff in the kitchens and gardens. The fresh air and labor helped her to feel stronger. She listened to the housemaids and cooks, heard town gossip, and hoped for any word of strange happenings, like where one might find an underground group of time travelers in Westbury. Most of it just normal superstition of the time or juicy improprieties between the sexes.

As hands were always needed to help out with the requests of the missus and Lillian didn't feel as uncomfortable in the lower worlds of the kitchen and garden, she found solace and peace in the dirt. Digging up vegetables and pruning fruits, snipping herbs and feeding chickens, she'd spent the last two days trying to sort through her thoughts in the pens and rows of peas, and the soft, firelit kitchen alongside the quiet but watchful Miriam who sometimes cocked her head, as if trying to discern where exactly Lillian fit in.

If all went to plan, Lillian would be gone within the week. Far away from the gripping strength of Mr. Sutton. She relished her alone time in the parlor for only a few minutes.

"Pardon the interruption, Miss—"

"My dear Miss Byrne!" the two voices coalesced at once as Miriam tried to slow down the young woman who followed her. Lillian refocused and looked from the exasperated expression of Miriam to the desperate and saddened face of Kitty, her bright blonde curls bouncing from their opulent updo as she crossed the room to take Lillian's hands in hers.

"Oh my dearest Kitty, what a surprise!" Lillian struggled to speak. "I thought you would not be returning so soon from your trip to the coast."

"Your cousin tells me that you had a relapse whilst I was gone and I am simply dismayed that my absence would bring you such darkness. Oh, how frightened you must have felt after your quarrel with Mr. Sutton. Are you recovering? How do you feel? I did try to see you straight away but this dreadful Mrs. Shaw would not let you be disturbed. She had the gall to suggest that my conversation would not be welcome and you needed quiet to regain your strength. As if seeing your new best and dearest friend might be a trial!"

"My dear, Kitty!" Lillian burst out, disrupting the deluge from rattling through her head. "I am quite recovered. But please do not place any blame of my condition on yourself."

"You should not be standing, you should sit. Mrs. Shaw can you please bring us some tea?"

Miriam looked at Lillian as if to see if she really wanted tea before she listened to Kitty. Lillian made a small shrug and Miriam nodded.

"Yes, mum," she muttered as she left the parlor.

"My darling Lillian, you are quite flushed, please, come away from the sunlight and sit. I will have Mrs. Shaw bring you your embroidery work from the conservatory. It looks as though you could use a relaxing endeavor."

Embroidery, relaxing? Lillian's stomach turned knots before her fingers could even attempt them.

"Uh, thank you, Miss Darlingwood, you are always so thoughtful and kind."

"I would not wish for you to fall behind and face your aunt's wrath," she giggled conspiratorially and led Lillian to the couch.

It seemed that wrath was all Lady Mayfield had for Lillian. She recalled a stiff and scowling reprimand at dinner following her 'tea' with Mr. Sutton.

Lillian sighed. "I fear this is not the art I excel at," she said with a pout and sat heavily down beside the light cream of Kitty's delicate perch.

"Oh darling!" Kitty twittered. "I know it is not. Why you are simply horrible at the task, but I am here to offer your fingernails reprieve from the dirt and flour of your other pursuits. Lady Mayfield is simply horrorstruck at all the time you have spent not pursuing the tasks and skills of your station."

"Those menial tasks she is so concerned with keep her fed and taken care of," Lillian said suddenly. Kitty's light countenance faltered and she emitted a tiny scowl, complete with puckered pink lips. Even in her indignation she was as cute as a goddamn button, Lillian thought.

"That indeed may be true, but you are not a common young lady, living in a London hovel. You are part of the Byrne family name." The tone was a reminder to Lillian that this was not a game. It was a very delicate balance of keeping history intact so that when she did find a way home, it was the same one she left.

"You are quite right, my dearest. I apologize for my brashness. I am not myself in these moments. I do appreciate the skill and time you have offered to help me become a better woman, one suited to be a—wife," the last word stuck in her throat.

"Oh, my dearest, I know you have been through such an awful

ordeal." She forgave as easily as a breeze blew through a summer garden and she placed a delicate hand on Lillian's knee briefly. "I simply cannot express how concerned Mr. Byrne was after your quarrel with Mr. Sutton. I have never seen him in such a state of worry," she said.

The sunlight lit dust motes between them that seemed to dance down to the thick imported rug beneath their feet. Lillian watched them and heard the fading notes of something in Kitty's voice that could only be attributed to longing. Lillian looked over at her downcast eyes and the small quiver of her lips.

Kitty was in love with Fitzwilliam.

Lillian thought back to her cousin's reaction to the mention of Miss Darlingwood's name and smiled to herself. Even if it was her brain concocting a Jane Austen book, she might as well play along. She'd read *Emma* enough times to know what had to be done. Besides, she'd promised, when he'd come so bravely to her aid, that she would do everything in her power to see to it that Kitty gave him a chance.

"Fitzwilliam is already so dear to me. He has been such a constant and caring person, but I would be remiss if I did not tell you, while in the confidence of our solitary task, that I think my impending doom—er betrothal—has left him feeling anxious," Lillian tripped over her words.

"Why, whatever do you mean, Miss Byrne?" Kitty said and shot an eyebrow up to the ceiling.

"I fear that he sees in my matrimony the lack of a womanly presence in his own life. I feel there must be a great hole in his heart. I fear he quite often finds himself awash in loneliness," she said, nonchalantly, pulling the thread through the stitch a bit too tight and puckering the material in the process.

"Awash in loneliness?" Kitty said, just as undisturbed in tone but her eyes darting back to Lillian in quick interest. "I'm afraid I don't understand."

"I mean, I am saddened that he lacks the affection of a good woman to fill his heart," she said softly, stilling her hands and looking at Kitty. "And his home."

Kitty's face washed with pink like a rose garden had bloomed in each cheek and she suddenly stood, gasping for a breath and walking to the window. The blush only deepened when she saw the lonely, soon-to-be-left bachelor walking through the garden, cane in hand and deep in thought. Lillian joined her at the window and felt as though fate were stepping in to solidify the romantic seeds she was planting.

"He is such a dear hearted man. So patient, kind, doting." Lillian looked at Kitty and then down to Fitzwilliam's wandering path. She went on. "During my time of need, he has been by my side. He is a true and gentle man," she said again, and they watched as he reached down to pluck a rose from a bush, immediately turning to look up at the parlor windows. Their eyes met; Kitty emitted a small exclamation of surprise and ducked away from the window.

"I dare say, you are not immune to his charm?" Lillian asked hesitantly looking down at where Kitty had crouched to hide, her lip coyly bitten.

"I—I cannot say. I have not allowed myself to think on the matter for too long." She sat down with a huff and returned to her work, steady fingers now trembling.

"Well, we are here, alone for a time. Perhaps you should allow your mind to wander." Lillian sat beside her, taking up the puckered fabric and trying to right it before continuing. "I do believe he thinks of nothing but you. He compared your lips to a ripe strawberry over breakfast the other morning."

"Lillian!" Kitty gasped in shock. The sound of the tea tray rattling into the room distracted their discussion and allowed Kitty a much-needed reprieve from the subject. They worked through the afternoon, sipping tea and shifting on the stiff settees and uncomfortably humid air that had settled into the stuffy room. Lillian looked towards the door at every creak somewhere further down the halls.

She was postulating how she could access the Colonel's personal office to see if there were any records or journals her father might have left behind. She wondered if the stairs weren't the only tear in time. There must have been others, or her father would not have left. If that did not pan out, she thought, delicately dabbing at the sweat on her brow, she wondered if she could find any money in the office to afford a ticket to America, and what the soonest day was that she could leave. She wondered if Matthew would ever think of her. She wondered if she'd ever be able to forget him.

Lillian felt faint. Heartbroken and weak. Miriam had opened one of the garden windows, but the afternoon air did not improve the quality of the room. It only filled the space with the heady scent of roses and lavender.

Much to Lillian's dismay and Kitty's expectation, her embroidery did not improve with the hours of diligence and Lillian's frustration with it grew. You would think, as a person possessed of brains and relatively nimble fingers, she could manage to draw on cloth with thread, but it simply was not happening. In the crux of another failed knot which had damaged her cloth beyond repair, and the undercurrent of worrying she may never get home, that she may not be able to escape Mr. Sutton's wrath and that Matthew was probably gone from her life forever, Lillian allowed the curse to cross her lips.

"Shit," she whispered. Kitty, in sheer horror of the word, gasped, rose, and upended the tea tray, causing it to spill across the rug and splatter over Lillian's decidedly-ruined cloth.

"Shit!" Lillian said again, this time more surprise than anger. A scuffle behind them added to the cacophony of chaos in the quiet parlor and Mr. Byrne and Matthew Blackwell rushed in. Kitty rose, looking pale and on the point of fainting.

"What in the hell—" Lillian stopped to see Fitzwilliam not rush to her side, but to Kitty's.

"My dear Miss Darlingwood, are you ill?" He turned, from his bended knee before Kitty, to the doctor who was staring at Lillian, himself looking gaunt and drawn. "Doctor Blackwell, have you any smelling salts?" Mr. Byrne asked.

Doctor Blackwell turned briefly to the case he'd set down and handed it to Fitzwilliam. "Third pocket on the right-hand side. Miss Darlingwood, are you quite alright?"

"I'm just," Kitty breathed but her gaze settled on Fitzwilliam. Color returned to her pale cheeks. "I was startled by Lillian's very unladylike outburst."

"Well, I'm sorry! But it's damn hot in here and this damn stitch is—"

"Miss Byrne!" Doctor Blackwell reprimanded sharply.

"What are *you* even doing here?" she argued back, and the heat of their mutual unrest filled the room. "I thought you were supposed to be leaving Westbury. Abandoning m—" she stopped "your father's clinic, for good."

Kitty gasped, "Miss Byrne!"

Matthew looked back at Lillian with a sharp scowl.

"Mr. Byrne was giving me a tour of the herbal garden and offering me to refill some of my personal apothecary before my journey. I had no intention of disturbing you further." The tone of his voice made her throat close up. "We came to investigate when we'd heard the upsetting of a tea tray. Naturally, I'd assumed *you* had fallen." He scowled down at Lillian. She rose up to her feet, unknowing that the long sitting spell, her skipped meals, days of worry and missing him, the heat, the frustration, and the lack of fresh air in the room would cause her to swoon.

"I do not randomly fall—" her words trailed off as the world went dark.

. . .

Kitty made a shocked yelp as Lillian's knees buckled. Matthew leapt over the end of the couch and caught her before she could hit the floor. She heard his soft voice, calm in the face of pressure.

"Mr. Byrne if you please, the third pocket," he said over his shoulder as he settled her exhausted body into the couch.

"Of course," Fitzwilliam said distractedly Matthew uncorked the small bottle and ran it beneath Lillian's nose. She sat up abruptly, coughing and flailing. Her first fist caught him squarely in the jaw. The second he caught in his hand with a firm grip. She focused her vision on him.

"I believe you were saying something about not being the fainting damsel?"

"I dislike you," she returned with a scowl. Matthew smiled and Lillian wanted nothing more than to slap the smug expression off his face.

"Perhaps it would do you great benefit to get some fresh air," he said.

"I simply do not think I'm recovered enough to accompany her," Kitty said, back of her hand to her forehead. Fitzwilliam stared, doe-eyed, at her.

"Of course not, my darling—" he stumbled on the word, "Miss Darlingwood."

"Not to worry, as I am the doctor who prescribes it, I shall be the one to complete the arduous task," Matthew said and rose offering Lillian his hand with a quirk of his perfect brow. She scowled at him and struck his hand away.

"I do not need your assistance."

"Nonetheless, you have it."

Lillian wanted to tell him where he could shove his assistance as she rose and stormed past him. He took a feather-light scone from Miriam's tea tray and pocketed it before following her down the hall with a calm and knowing pace, talking as if they had not just had a very public argument.

"I would very much like to know more about your herb garden. Mr. Byrne has been telling me that you have personally been attending to it recently," he said, nonchalantly to her back as she bounded down the stairs.

"What is that? An insult against me working in the garden, growing flowers instead of perfecting my useless skill of stitching them?" She turned on him. Matthew kept his hands firmly clasped behind his back but leaned into her scowl. His smile and curiosity at her returning fire caused her to feel open when she'd worked so hard to close that door.

"My God but it is good to be in your presence again. I've missed you, so terribly, every scathing, proud, and vulnerable inch of you."

"What?" Lillian's breath caught.

"In response to your skill, I feel a woman who understands nature and plants is of much better use. The world has plenty of pillowcases and tapestries. More interesting is the woman who does not fear a little dirt in the spirit of growth," he said. Lillian stared up at him, and his smile. Her eyes softened.

"I thought," she swallowed hard and tears filled her eyes. Matthew's smile faded. "I thought you disliked me. After the letter, I thought—"

"On the contrary," he said softly.

"But you said," she hiccupped back a sob "you said meeting me was the paramount regret of your—"

He pulled her into his arms and silenced her with a kiss. Hot and demanding, his lips pressed to hers and his fingers tangled into her hair. He pulled away just as quickly and she stood speechless with fire in her cheeks and breathy gasps.

"If I had known that was the key to silencing you, I would have done so much sooner," he said but his breath came heavy and fast.

"You—you kissed me."

Miriam came from the back door and appeared in the hallway, startling Lillian silent.

She adjusted her laundry basket and looked the both of them over suspiciously. "Alright you two?" she asked as though they were children, up to no good.

"Yes, Miriam."

"Yes, my lady," they both rushed at once.

"Saints, child," Miriam glowered. "You best treat her right, I'll not attend to another one of her moping spells on your account," she admonished and bustled away. Matthew put his hands behind his back and rocked on his heels.

"You moped on my account?"

"Do not assume that every bad day I have, has anything to do with you," she grouched and turned to walk out, with or without him.

"That my lack of response hurt you so…Lily, I could not be more aggrieved," he said, using her name in the quiet and dark hallway, away from prying ears. She turned. He took one of her hands discreetly in his.

"I do not wish to be a bane to you," she said.

"You are not."

"I do not wish to sully your good name or your soul."

"You do not," he whispered. She swayed closer to him unbidden.

"I hold you so dear. You mean a great deal to me, Matthew." Her hand grazed over his brocaded vest, the hard muscles of his stomach and hip, her forehead touched his chin.

"Lily, you are not to blame for my vexation." he whispered. "I am sorry I was not here, when my cousin came to call."

"If you had been, what could you have possibly done?"

Matthew hung his head. "Thrown the bastard out," he growled.

"My skirts prohibited me from doing just that, myself," Lillian responded. Matthew smiled and nuzzled her cheek.

"I fear I am of no help to you," he whispered, lowly as they heard people conversing in the kitchen off of the hallway.

"You have every right to leave me to my own devices," she said softly. He sighed as if the words ripped his heart in two. He held her fingers tighter against his hip bone. His eyes closed.

"I may be within my rights to leave you, but I am not within my heart's reason to do so." Matthew turned his head, his lips pressed to her temple.

"Will you still walk with me? I do not mind going alone."

"Please," he said, shook his head and took her wandering hand in his own warmly. "Allow me to accompany you."

Matthew cleared his throat and stepped away, gesturing to the back door and the open garden waiting beyond.

Lillian had to shake the strange and heady thoughts from her head. She needed to get home. She wasn't here to stay forever, but his lips on hers, the sweet and beautiful words he spoke, made her heart less troubled. She could not expect him to spirit her away from the madness she'd fallen into. But for now, on this fine day, she would enjoy the time with him. She took a shawl from a hook beside the back door and her bonnet. They stayed a respectable distance apart from one another through the garden.

When they'd reached a shabby gardener's gate, at the northern boundary of the property, Lillian raised her eyebrows at him.

"What disastrous plans are you hatching in that pretty head of yours?"

"Would you like to run away with me?" she asked. Matthew's brow drew in and he sighed.

"Surely, you jest."

"I never joke about rebellion," she said and pushed the creaky gate open, bending back the overgrown bushes around it. Matthew sighed heavily behind her.

"Lily, please! If they find you missing, with me—"

"If they find me with you, I will not be missing. They will

think I led you astray and you merely stayed with me to keep me safe from my own poor decisions. Someone must." She shrugged and continued on. It took him approximately thirty seconds of standing obstinately on the other side of the gate before he followed her.

She didn't say much and he didn't lead her in conversation. He stayed a half step behind, and to her left, hands clasped behind his back. Lillian wondered if it was to keep them to himself. Given the heated exchange in the hallway, she wished he wasn't such a gentleman. While she tried to look anywhere but at him, her eyes fell to a stone with a strange marking along the fence, separating their lands from the road. Before Matthew could catch up to her, where she knelt to touch the moss-etched trinity, from just over the next hill there came a loud crashing of branches followed by a cry. Matthew took off at a hard run before she could even stand and see what had happened. She followed him down the road, slowed by her skirts.

When she crested the hill, she saw him kneeling at the side of a young boy, crying and writhing in pain, pawing at his tiny and contorted arm. Matthew looked up at Lillian, worried and flushed.

"You really ought not be here." His voice was worried and stilted as his hands grasped onto the arm of the boy who was in horrible amounts of pain.

"You really ought not tell me what to do," she returned, breathless, as she rushed to his side.

"What in God's name," he stopped, blushed, and lowered his eyes as the concerned mother came from the house to the scene. With a deep breath he controlled his tone. "What are you doing, Miss Byrne?"

Lillian settled, her thigh brushing against Matthew's knee, next to the boy as his mother sat next to him, crying with worry. Lillian searched beneath her skirts and found two small and straight branches, broken in the fall. She maneuvered closer, put the boy's head in her lap. Her long fingers were quick and steady as she placed the small stick in between the boy's teeth. She took his head between her cool palms and stared into his eyes.

"You are so brave and strong. We are going to help but it will hurt," she said to the boy and then looked to the worried mother, tears running down her cherry, round cheeks. "We will hold on to him and to each other." Lillian nodded to her.

"You don't have to do this," Matthew began.

"He is hurt, you are helping. I will not stand idly by when I could be of assistance."

"But you have no experience, you cannot—"

"I have seen a bone set before, Doctor Blackwell. I will not faint if that is your fear."

The child's crying grew louder and Matthew sighed, blowing out a nervous breath with flared nostrils. "On three," he said, more calmly, but with a tight jaw. Lillian nodded, held the boy's shoulders against her knees while his mother held his other hand and stilled his writhing legs.

"One, two—" the sickening crack of the tiny bone popping first out and then back into place was the herald of an excruciating wail from the boy. With gentle shushing and steady pressure, Lillian and his mother held tight while Matthew immobilized the bone with the other branch. Lillian peeled off her own shawl to fashion a sling for the boy's arm and to further keep it stable. Matthew checked the circulation of the boy's fingers and adjusted the wrappings until he could see a healthy pink filling each tiny finger. The pain must have eased as the boy's cries calmed. His mother took him gingerly in her arms and rocked him reassuringly while the doctor and Lillian sat back on their heels and calmed their own breathing.

"Miss Byrne," he began.

"I already know the reprimand on your lips, 'that was most unbecoming behavior from a young woman of my station,'" she said, breathless from crouching in her tight-waisted dress and wiping the perspiration from her brow.

"You were most outstanding and brave, far calmer and in control of your emotion than I have ever seen in any young woman or young man for that matter. You amazing, fearless, girl." He sat back, against the tree, swiping at the sweat on his forehead before rising to help the boy and his mother back to their small quarters, where Lillian assumed some of Westbury's staff lived. Lillian stared after him. Her cheeks felt warm, her heart still not settled after the event. She could hear his voice filter out from the open door, giving care and instructions to the mother and answering questions.

"I beg your pardon, good sir, but simply cannot afford to pay you for your time."

"It is not necessary that you do."

"But sir!"

"Madam, I insist. I am only happy to have come along when I did. Just see that he rests and stays out of trees for a few months."

How could anyone think him crude? How could anyone balk at the generous and kind heart of this man? Lillian feared her own heart would show through her eyes when he came out. And she didn't know how she would keep from pouncing on him, kissing him, and convincing him to run away with her. She rose to leave and looked for the shawl that had been draped around her shoulders. She spun in place, lifting her skirts in confusion.

"I believe it was commandeered in the essence of necessity, I'm afraid it must stay where it is until he's farther healed," came Matthew's voice from the doorway. He was drying his hands and rolling his cuffs down. Of course, she had forgotten in the stress of the moment pulling it off to offer it.

"It is of no consequence. I am glad to see it in better service."

"Are you not cold?"

"I am quite fine; it is a sunny day."

"It is," he said, and she watched the way the light dappled in from the branches filtered down between them. "A lovely day for a walk."

"It is indeed." She looked at him and saw him turn his gaze to the dirt walkway. "Made better with the continued company of a dear friend?" she asked. Matthew looked up at her and smiled.

"Friends do not yell at one another even as they are coming to one's aid. I'm afraid I behaved very badly."

"I interrupted you in the throes of your work. I would expect nothing less than your best effort to direct me to mind my manners."

He chuckled at this, "Something of which you never take heed."

"I'm quite intolerable," she said with a sly smile.

"I am in your debt. You are quite quick-witted. Where did you learn to mend a bone?"

"I—" she couldn't very well tell him how she'd been a nurse in a different time. "I've learned a few things in my time in the orchards and gardens. I see all manner of spills and cuts in the kitchen."

"Of your own making, to be certain, but other people's maladies?" he said, and the corners of his mouth turned up in a light-hearted laugh. She couldn't help but follow suit as the musical sound set her heart on fire and joy bubbled up in her chest.

"Oh you!" she picked up an acorn from the ground and threw it at him. He chuckled joyously and returned the volley. She squealed in delight and ran around the oak tree to collect more. As she rounded the large trunk, hand full of acorns, he surprised her from the other side and pinched the underside of her arm lightly. Lillian let out a squeal and a laugh and dropped her ammunition. Her laughter was truncated when his arms went suddenly around her waist and his breathless laughter met her neck, his lips turning to steal a kiss, sweet and warm in the shade of the tree, before breaking away quickly to collect his jacket and his decorum.

"Miss Byrne," he said, looking down remorsefully.

"Do not worry, Matthew," she said his name softly.

"I shall escort you home," he said and looked up at her.

"Only if you promise to not let the heavy weight of guilt walk alongside us," she said and took his elbows in her hands giving him a gentle shake. "The stress of what we've just endured, gives cause for hearts to seek comfort. I feel no ill will towards you. So, you mustn't feel it towards yourself," her quiet words brought his eyes to level on hers and she could sense a relief settle back into his countenance.

"Perhaps you are right."

"You'll find, good doctor, that I am nearly always right."

To this he smiled, kissed the back of her hand demurely, and settled into a comfortable walk, not behind her, but beside her. Their shoulders touched in the warm and relaxed walk back to Westbury Manor, where he surprised her with the stolen scone, tucked in his pocket, to share.

11

THE COLONEL'S SECRET AND INVITATIONS, BOTH DISASTROUS AND SWEET

Colonel Mayfield, a man once known in the year 2023 as John Hawthorn-Byrne, watched the entire exchange between his daughter and Matthew Blackwell from his third-floor study. He had only returned that afternoon to talk to his daughter. Now, as he watched her with Matthew Blackwell, his heart paused at the way they walked, bumping shoulders and smiling coyly. The light in Lillian's cheeks and the softness in the way Doctor Blackwell watched her, he recognized new love and hope budding in each of their hearts, the way two people who care truly for one another would behave. Even with the protectiveness of a father, he could not help the joy at seeing her so happy.

He had wasted so much of her childhood jumping through time, working with an elite agency to try and right past wrongs, that he'd created his own wrongs in abandoning her. When a rogue Timekeeper had called him out of the field to tell him that his daughter, possessed of the same genetics as he, had inadvertently crossed back into time through an unsanctioned portal, he jumped backwards, two years prior to her fall, and inserted himself into the timeline, in expectation of her arrival. He'd assumed a new identity, acquired lands and titles. He placed himself in the best possible position, so that when she fell through the torn fabric of time, he could prevent the historical murder of his own daughter.

He knew that the timeline ran in a loop. In the original timeline, Lillian had fallen into the past and created her own loop by blindly marrying Frederick Sutton, only to die at his hands, and be reborn two-hundred years later.

John had spent most of his lifetime jumping, assimilating to the era in need, and setting history right by seemingly insignificant actions. But this jump was a selfish prayer to the gods of time to save his only daughter. He wanted to refuse her engagement to Sutton, but that meant putting Fitzwilliam and Kitty's chances at marriage in jeopardy. And if they never married, Lillian and her brother Will would never be born.

John bit his nail and watched the couple. Even with all of his preparation, the 'Colonel' had not foreseen this unintended match. He saw the way Lillian looked at Matthew. The way Matthew looked back. Could he be the interruption in her loop that would save her life?

He watched as Miss Darlingwood pulled Lillian through the front gates, rather gruffly for a woman so small. Doctor Blackwell's eyes never left his daughter, until she was once again inside the manor and the door had closed behind her. John sighed.

When he had returned and gotten Fitzwilliam to open up about the episode in the parlor between Lillian and Mr. Sutton, he knew the timeline was on track. But in his research of the original timeline, Lillian hadn't stood up to Mr. Sutton. She had been more dazed and compliant. Until she wasn't, and ended up with marks on her throat and drowned on the banks of the Avon. But this time, Lillian seemed different than what the records had described and her father felt, since the first time since he'd jumped through the portal in search of a way to save his only daughter, that they may be closer to changing the past than ever before. He had gone to the Timekeepers field office in Westbury to ask for their help. They had sent him on a side mission and, in exchange, had promised to send him the coordinates of a portal, and a time she could safely return back home. It had wasted weeks, and he knew that his leaving only reinforced Lillian's distrust in his intentions.

John sighed, rubbed his tired eyes and put pressure on his temples. He had been told to wait, and had to have faith that the Timekeepers would give them the information to send her back where she belonged. He'd pledge the rest of life to the agency, if they could just save his daughter. At least he had some time back with her now. He would try to explain everything and apologize for the childhood he missed. He hoped that she understood that his leaving was all for a greater good. Genetics aside, and having had her own accidental jump, he would not wish this life on his daughter for anything. He'd been jumping through time for years and it was starting to affect his mind and his body in ways no human could have predicted.

He was deep in these thoughts when Lady Mayfield bustled in, full of venom and righteousness. Lord, but his only regret was having to marry the woman.

"Colonel Mayfield!" She never used his first name.

"Yes, my darling," he sighed.

"Dispatch with the romanticism. I've heard that your niece has gravely insulted her fiancé and they had a very public argument in our very parlor not three days ago."

"Is that so?" he said, knowing very well the truth, and glad of it. "I hear tell it was but the two of them and Miriam. Nary a public to be found."

"Do not mock me!" When he wiggled his mustache at her and did not try to guess what direction this conversation was going she huffed. "Well?"

"Yes, my dove?" He smiled at the rise it got from her.

"Well, we must hold a dinner party. Immediately! So she may

publicly apologize and make things right. Lest she live here as a spinster, sucking off the teat of her unearned position."

The Colonel raised his eyebrows. The woman's stately form, and tiny mouth was the epitome of puckered, and he thought of how tight her ass must be to not even spare a small living for a niece that, by all accounts, earned her keep in the kitchens and gardens.

"A dinner party sounds a fine idea. I've heard rumors and it might be the perfect place to encourage young love," he said, his mind not on Lillian and Mr. Sutton, but on Kitty and Fitzwilliam, whose match was imperative to history.

"I do not care if it encourages love. Just see that it puts her back in his favor." And with that she bustled back out just as stormily as she'd entered. The Colonel sighed and folded his hands behind his back.

Perhaps a dinner might be a good way to distract Lady Mayfield enough so that he could spend more time with his daughter while they waited for the Timekeepers' coordinates. Lillian would, of course, hate the prospect of having to sit across the table from Mr. Sutton, and surely to be forced to give an apology he did not deserve would enrage her. By perhaps by inviting the Drs. Blackwell, it may help to keep the evening more civil. Though, he thought sitting back in his chair and remembering the way Lillian and Matthew had arrived, it might make for even more tension.

"Engagement dinner? But must we?" Lillian's reaction to Lady Mayfield's decree was not demure.

"It is high time you two solidified yourself as a united couple in the presence of our friends and neighbors, and that is the last of it." Lady Mayfield insisted before dismissing Lillian. Lillian stormed out of the conservatory and made her way outside and through the gardens. The harpy was quickening the process and now the time Lillian thought she had, was starting to disappear.

She paced among the rows of beans and peas, the soft folds of warm earth holding her feet while the bees buzzed along beside her. There were so many more now than in her time. She stopped to watch them. She had the brief thought of just continuing to walk, out of the back gates, away from this mess. She could find a way to make it on her own, even if she couldn't make it back to her own time.

"There you are."

The voice stopped Lillian in her tracks and she quickly swung around, where her father was walking toward her. She was not prepared for the way her heart rose and fell. Part hope that she would soon get to go home, and part agony at the thought of leaving Matthew.

"Where the hell have you been?" Lillian said. "Did you find a way back?"

John looked around the garden and shook his head. "Things have been … complicated. I spoke with my contact in Westbury and they told me they could get the coordinates to me as soon as they could calculate them."

"When will that be?" Lillian said, wondering how many days she had left with Matthew. Her eyes stung.

"I wish I knew."

"How did this happen, Dad? I feel like you owe me an explanation."

Her father came near and tried to put his arms on her shoulders but she shied away. He nodded in soft acknowledgment and sighed.

"There exists a secret society called the Timekeepers, whose job it is to keep the timeline of humanity relatively intact and always progressing towards a better world."

"Go on."

"They have discovered that certain people have an easier time traveling between timelines, and have employed them to help set wrong things right. I am one of those people. They offered me the job just as I met your mother. I thought I could have both, the adventure I craved, and the family I loved. Only—well, I guess we both know I failed at balancing that ledger."

"So how did I fall through?"

"Portals are like shifting doors in the time-space veil. They are exceptionally hard to find, and they only open at certain moments in time. My best guess, is that you are like me. You have the ability to open them."

"How in the hell could I have opened the portal? I was falling!"

John shushed her and looked around. "I think there was a weak spot in the veil, a normal person would have walked past it. But you fell, and the portal opened to accommodate you."

"So why can't I just open it now and leave?"

John shook his head. "Unfortunately, you entered in a moment in time that must play out to some extent if we are to ensure your birth happens."

Lillian was quiet for a moment before meeting her father's eyes. "Kitty and Fitzwilliam."

"Yes."

"So that means I have to go through with this dreadful engagement party?"

"I'm afraid so. But I will be with you, every moment until it's time to send you home."

Lillian rolled her eyes skyward and blew out a frustrated breath. At least she might get to see Matthew again. Little did she know that Doctor Blackwell was, at that very moment, opening the formal invitation to her engagement dinner and wishing he could leave himself.

∾

"Must we go?" Matthew growled to his father and threw the invitation down on the table by his untouched breakfast.

"Frederick is your cousin! And the Colonel and Lady Mayfield are our closest neighbors and friends. Of course we will be there. I thought you were fond of Miss Byrne."

"Precisely the problem," Matthew grumbled under his breath as his father was now lost in a different discussion about the newest methods of surgery out of London. She must not be happy about this at all. Would his presence help her or only make things worse? After their afternoon walk, it was different now.

After their kiss...

Would he bring her comfort or only more emotional conflict? Matthew was not sure, but he thought the honest thing to do would be to ask her himself if she would want him to attend. He rose, finished his tea and slung his coat over his shoulders.

"Where are you off to at this hour?"

"I think I shall take a walk," Matthew said and took his gloves from the sideboard.

"A walk?"

"I'm in need of air." He left with the departing admonishment from his father that he was indeed still a *strange boy*. Matthew had no argument. He was strange. Strange in the head and heart over Lillian. Strangely in need of her presence. Strangely falling ... he sucked in a deep breath as he crested the hill between their properties and slowed his gait. He must not barrel into the house like some lovesick animal. It must seem merely by coincidence that he found himself at their manor.

He was admitted, by the younger maid, Sarah Jane, and told that the Lady and Colonel had gone into town to shop for clothing for the approaching dinner with Kitty and Fitzwilliam. No one but the young Miss Byrne was home. Matthew sighed in relief and excused himself to the back gardens. He went back into the house through the servant's door to look for her after failing to find her in the dirt and sunshine.

He must have been through five rooms and yet had not seen any sign of her or even that she had occupied the room. He used his nose, knowing in a strange way the particular notes of her delicate scent. He had spent a whole afternoon after their walk, trying to determine what it was exactly that she smelled of. Something like flowers, or fresh linens, or sunshine on warm bread. Her skin, her neck, the hair thick and black on her head. He longed to run his fingers through the silky length of it. Matthew sighed, stopped in the deserted hallway and calmed his thoughts. He was only here to ask her one question. Then back to his own life.

If he were Lillian, and had just been sentenced to a public dinner with a most hated man, where else would she go to avoid it all, besides the garden? Matthew ducked around the entrance to the dining room and found himself in the kitchen. The sweet smell of bread and the delicate spice cake now being prepared, washed over him and he realized that part of what made up Lillian's scent may have been due to the time she spent in the kitchen.

And speaking of the angel he sought, there behind the skirts of Miriam who was kneading dough for the next morning's rolls, sitting beside the fire, head tucked away from him while small droplets of tears dripped off her nose, was Lillian.

"Beggin' your pardon, Sir, but you can't be here!" Miriam said and bustled around the large rectangular work table where fresh vegetables and eggs were lined up in different stages of a process he couldn't even begin to decipher.

"It is I that should beg your pardon, my good lady." He bowed to Miriam eliciting a scoff of disbelief from the old maid. He lowered his voice and looked back to the undisturbed door, as if assuring her he was there in secret as well. "I merely am concerned for Miss Byrne's state." He tried to peer around Miriam's girth but she swayed to block her young charge from him.

"Her state is none of your concern," Miriam said brashly and Matthew smiled, bowed his head. Miriam watched him with her eagle eyes as he blushed and worried over his gloves.

"I assure you, good Miriam, I have only her best interests in my heart," he whispered. "I've just received a most distressing correspondence, and I feel she may not be pleased about it. Is she quite well?"

"I'm fine," Lillian said suddenly with a sniff behind Miriam's aproned guard. "It's fine, Miriam, he can—" she paused to wipe her nose on a tattered piece of cheese cloth she'd been worrying over in her hands. "He can inquire after my health. Before returning home where I'm sure his father and cousin must be missing his presence," she sighed. Miriam rolled her eyes, before stepping aside and moving to the far corner of the room to start another concoction meant for the impending guests.

Matthew sat on the other end of the hearth. The stone was warm beneath him and the crackle of fire was comforting. He looked over to where the soft orange and yellow light bathed Lillian's milk-soft skin in a golden glow. Today her dress was a creamy yellow, soft and simple, her dark hair tied with a yellow ribbon and up off of her neck. Her eyes were red, and her fingers shook.

"I know," she began before hiccupping and recuperating her resolve. "I know I should not be angry about my engagement to Mr. Sutton. I know it was not my place to reject his offer or to be mad about Lady Mayfield's ridiculous show of social propriety with this dinner. But the way he behaved last time we met, the things he said, I—"

"I am not here to berate you, Lily." The use of her name made her eyes rise to meet his. He couldn't stand the swell of tears that made them even more liquid and soft. "Except that I am angry that you have to spend even one more hour in the man's company, and I can offer you no viable solution to avoid it as of yet. I am here to ask if my presence at the ridiculous show would be beneficial to you, or only make things worse." They were quiet for a moment.

"I fear your presence will not change my fate," she said and stared into the fire. Matthew's face fell and he stared into the flames with her.

"Lily—"

"Will you—" she stopped herself.

"Yes," he said, mesmerized by her beautiful brokenness and everything that made her the Lillian he knew and loved, emboldened by their relative privacy.

"I know it is not prudent to ask, but will you hold me?"

"But Miriam is here, surely she could—" he began to say something a proper gentleman would.

"*She* is much too busy." Miriam interrupted, crossed back closer to them, and eyed Matthew. "My hands are stuck to my tasks. I think yours would best do the same."

"My tasks?" he asked from his seated crouch by the fireplace.

"You are a physician, are you not?"

"Well, yes."

"So, see to the patient's pain then," she said it exasperated as if he was the thickest-skulled idiot she'd ever known.

"The patient's pain." He looked to Lillian in her upset state, trembling and hurt.

"You don't have to." She shook her head.

"Miss Byrne," he whispered with a smile and stood. "I would not be a credit to my profession to leave a human who is suffering in need of care. It would be much against the oath I have sworn, for me to keep my distance in this time of your acute distress." He quickly removed his coat and hung it from a hook beside the hearth. He then removed his cravat and unbuttoned the top two buttons of his shirt for comfort.

"What are you doing?" Lillian said, almost in shock and looking at Miriam who watched with the fascination that does not pass from a woman of any age, when seeing a man shed their clothes. Doctor Blackwell walked to Lillian and sat in the corner, behind her, and slung one long leg around, closest to the flames, encircling her body with it.

"Come now, sit back."

Lillian's eyes went wide as she looked up at Miriam.

Miriam raised her eyebrows. "I think I've some things to do in the pantry," she said and bustled off to door leading down to the cold cellar. Lillian looked over her shoulder where he stared expectantly back.

"Is this not the treatment you had in mind?"

"It is."

"But now you are afraid to take your medicine?" he said and held out his arms. She stared at his chest and then back up to his face.

"I am not," she scowled but did not move. "If anything, I'm afraid I will take too much," she said coyly over her shoulder. Matthew took in a deep breath before pulling her back into his arms, against his chest. Her fingers wrapped around his hands and her head tilted back to rest on his shoulder as they stared into the flames together. He could feel her heart thrumming.

"I wish we—" she began but swallowed back the thought. He stared into the flames and wondered if her thoughts ran parallel to his. To wish it was his right and privilege to hold her, every evening beside the warmth of the fire, her body against his, her long neck beneath his kisses, her cheek pressed to his chin. Would that they were destined to share such wedded bliss. Would that she were his.

"Lillian, I—"

"Please do not," she whispered, and her nails trailed up his forearms. "Please do not tell me I shall find happiness in some way with him. Please, Matthew. Remember your oath to me and pray do not lie. Especially not while your heart beats as though it is my own."

Matthew kissed her forehead then and fell silent. If he dared speak the truth of his heart, that he loved her, would always love her for all of the days of his life that remained, she might be moved to do something brash and foolish. Like run away with him, and keep running for the rest of their lives, perhaps never to have peace and solace.

Matthew buried his nose in the crook of her neck and inhaled.

"You smell of sweet cream and sugar," he said.

"I helped Miriam with the cake this afternoon. Which would be much to Mr. Sutton's consternation, I'm sure." An unexpected chuckle rose in her throat and he felt it bubble up against his neck. She continued in a deep and serious voice. "A woman of your standing, and one that is soon to share my name and hearth should do *no* such low-born work."

"And how would you respond to such an opinion?" Matthew pressed, trying not to let his smile shine through the words and truly wondering how she felt about harder work, as he delighted in it himself.

"I would probably say that if my hands were left idle, they may find much worse mischief to partake in."

"Is that so?" Matthew's nose traveled up the delicate skin of her neck and his warm lips paused just behind her ear. "What sorts of mischief could these beautiful and delicate fingers find?" his hands caressed hers and wove between them.

"Pray tell, what would *you* do with them? If you had full license to use them as you wish?" her whisper was quiet in the kitchen and Matthew's heart raced. His imagination ran wild with thoughts of those fingers curled into his hair, scratching across his back, wrapped around his hard—Lillian took in a deep breath as his body swelled and pressed into the small of her back. Miriam was giving them a few minutes, not an entire night. He cleared his throat but would not let her move away. "Would you keep me from 'lowly' work, even if it brought me happiness and peace?"

Matthew took in a deep breath, trying to compose his thoughts but her neck smelled so sweet and the warmth of the fire with her pliant body between his legs was more temptation than he'd ever suffered.

"I believe a woman should do whatever work her heart leads her to, especially if it leaves the delectable taste of sweet cake to linger on her skin," he kissed her neck slowly at first but as Lillian gasped and arched into him, he continued down the length as if trying to taste every inch with deliberate and slow heated warmth.

"Matthew," his name was a breathy plea, and his hands began a slow and deliberate trail across her collarbones and cupped her shoulders, holding her steady against the heated caress of his mouth and tongue down her neck and shoulder. Lillian responded with heat and longing. She pressed closer to him, her fingers running up the length of his thighs.

A purposeful banging in the stairwell followed by Miriam singing, sudden and loud, roused the two from their impassioned state. Matthew took his hands from her body and sat up. His breath was ragged and pained.

"Are you quite all right, Doctor Blackwell?" Lillian asked, breasts heaving as she turned a fraction towards him. His jaw tightened and he took a slow breath through his flared nose, smelling not just her buttery cream scent but also the delicate layer of desire that radiated from her skirts. Miriam came through the pantry door and looked over a basket of carrots and parsnips to the blushing and bothered couple.

"I do not believe I will be set right again," he answered tightly, then leaned in, farthest from the table where Miriam had begun washing and peeling the vegetables and whispered. "Until I have you in my bed, or I am, by some lucky happenstance, killed from the sheer force of wanting you."

Lillian gasped and nudged her forehead into his lips. Matthew rose quickly, righted his clothing as well as he could for the obvious discomfort he was suffering, and slung his coat back onto his heaving shoulders.

"I hope you are much recovered, Miss Byrne," he said stoically.

"I scarcely can remember why I was even upset before," she said and smiled up at him in a way that made him wish he could clear the table of all vegetables and spread her out like a feast, to savor every inch of her.

"Nor I," he said, though it was not entirely true. In less than a month's time he would have to relinquish every thought and desire he held for her when she married his cousin.

"I shall be there, at the dinner, with my father, in the event you need any assistance, or simply," he sighed with a sad smile, "need a friend who is on the side of your best interests." He arched his eyebrow seriously and Lillian looked relieved.

"I look forward to seeing you then." He adjusted his cravat and nodded gratefully to Miriam.

"Thank you, Madam, for the moment of respite."

"T'was my pleasure, good sir," she said with a mischievous smile as he stumbled away from the hearth, stealing yet another two of her angel-like scones before he left. "Or was it yours?" She winked at Lillian who toppled over in a fit of giggles before composing herself.

12

NEW LOVE, OLD PROPRIETIES, AND AN ESCAPE

Lillian suspected that the dinner was Lady Mayfield's attempt to force some propriety on her wayward ways. As a result, the guest list grew and more food was ordered and soon a small quartet was hired to play, and the largest room of Westbury Manor was cleared to allow for dancing. With such an opulent use of their resources, Lillian knew the expectations were greater on her to give up her reluctance to the impending nuptials to Frederick Sutton.

Every day, at least twice, Lillian would stop her father in his role as Colonel and ask what news he had. Every day, the answer was the same. Not yet. She watched him grow more agitated and kept her distance the closer the engagement party got.

Meanwhile, Kitty was also growing more and more distressed. More than once, Lillian would see her worrying over a handkerchief that she kept close to her heart.

Lillian had seen enough movies to know what might be at the center of the girl's troubles and found an excuse the morning of the dinner-turned-ball, to steal her cousin Fitzwilliam away to the orchards, under the ruse of picking apples for a tart.

"So?" she asked, from beneath her bonnet while he glowered at each apple as if he didn't know if any were perfect enough to pick.

"So?" he answered back.

"Don't be dreadful, Will. Are you going to ask Miss Darlingwood to marry you or not." Fitzwilliam dropped an apple at his feet and turned to face her quickly.

"Kindly lower your voice!" he hissed, as though Kitty would be hiding behind a tree, listening in.

Lillian laughed, "There is no cause for worry, she's presently in town having her gown fitted for tonight. She will be a vision in soft pink, and her eyes will be on you alone."

"I wish you would not tease me so," he said and stared down at his feet, the sad apple nestled in the grass between them.

"I am not teasing."

"A fine young lady such as our Miss Darlingwood, could have her choice of men in the county. It would be a miracle indeed, if she should ever agree to accept my affections. I have even given her my favor but for all I know she has thrown it out." He bent to pick up the apple.

Lillian thought back to the handkerchief that had rarely left Kitty's hand during their last meeting. "Will, are you an idiot?"

"I beg your pardon?" He straightened up and looked like he might lob the apple at her. She smiled at him.

"She's desperately in love with you! If you cannot see it, it is simply because she is a far better woman than I am and is much more refined at hiding her true feelings."

"But how can I be sure?" He looked down at his hands, worried, and nearly in tears. "I love her so, dear cousin. She is the light in my world, and I could not bear it if she refused."

Lillian walked over to him, hindered by skirts and grass. She looped the apple basket through one elbow to free her hand and took his.

"Will, my darling. I have kept her company these last weeks and the only truth I know is the love I see between you. She plays coy and shy, to keep her own heart safe. But I have seen her watch through the windows while you are in the garden. I have seen her lean into the sound of your voice through walls and crowds. When she nearly fainted at my unladylike behavior in the parlor, you were so kind and attentive. I feel certain she will never love another the way she loves you."

"Truly?" he asked, with happy tears in his eyes. "How this does my heart much good to hear." Lillian smiled, tears of her own forming. Whoever thought the era of stoic masculinity was toxic, forgot the genteel and true romanticism that also coexisted.

"Do not waste this night, cousin. The crowd will be merry, the food and music fine, and all hearts," she paused, not thinking of her own, "will be light. It is indeed a night to make promises." Lillian leaned over and kissed Fitzwilliam on the cheek. Tears sprung up in her eyes. How she missed her family, and how blessed she was to still have one here. She actually wished Fitzwilliam was her brother. He pulled a handkerchief from his pocket to dry her eyes.

"There, there now, funny girl. You've your own happiness to attend to."

"Oh no," she sniffed then and shook her head. "Tonight will be absolutely dreadful for me. But you mustn't concern yourself."

"Surely it will not all be dreadful." Fitzwilliam looked around the orchard and lowered his voice. "There will indeed be merry company, even our dear neighbor Doctor Blackwell will be in attendance."

"It is to have my heart cleaved in two," she whispered. Will lifted her delicate chin with his fingers and met her eyes with his, a strange look passed between them, as if he were just seeing her for the first time.

"Do not fear, sweet cousin. I feel this is not the end of your story. I feel you have a few surprises both to give and receive." Will kissed her forehead and they walked back to the kitchen both hearts in states of worry for very different reasons.

When Lillian returned to her room, the odd thought came that this would be the perfect night to disappear. With the merriment of the occasion and hopefully an additional betrothal from her cousin, everyone would be distracted to be sure. If history was right, she didn't have much time. And the longer they waited, the more certain her marriage to Sutton would take place. Given that she'd already angered him, he might not wait that long to murder her. Her father hadn't been forthcoming, but he had mentioned a headquarters in Westbury. Perhaps if she pleaded her own case, they would see the severity of the situation and help her find a way out sooner. In any case, she would surely get more information from them than her father.

Lillian's heartbeat clamored inside her chest at the possibility of running away, and also the fact that in a few short hours she would have to see Mr. Sutton. Last time she had made him terribly angry. She must not be left alone with him again, and she would feign an illness if need be, to escape the party.

Even as Lillian contemplated these thoughts she smiled and nodded when Fitzwilliam rushed into her room and relayed his plans to take Miss Darlingwood for a secluded walk in the gardens that very evening to confess his undying love for her. Lillian tried to shut out the thought that Matthew would never ask her to marry him. He wasn't hers to have. He probably was meant to marry some kind and simple milkmaid in the far off 'wilds' of Wales. She would be robbing history of a whole family, children, grandchildren, someone who could be a doctor or a scientist someday.

The thought that she might actually be stealing Matthew

away from his destiny only made her feel more certain that she needed to go.

~

The dinner had turned into the event of the season, much anticipated and prepared for in fits and waves of decadence and lavishness. The handsome Mr. Byrne, tall and slight with dark hair and lavender eyes like his cousin's, was dashingly dressed a fine blue and gray tailored suit and his dark curls neatly coiffed as he waited, with bated breath, at the bottom of the stairs for the ladies. Miss Lillian Byrne, the soon-to-be Mrs. Frederick Sutton, descended with her best friend, Miss Caterina Darlingwood from the magical process that produced exceedingly beautiful specimens of soon-to-be-married and hoping-to-be-asked young women. Their dresses were of dusky lavender silk and creamy pink, and their hair was piled in curls upon their heads, pinned with pearl clips and silver fasteners.

Lillian's head felt like it must weigh six hundred pounds and she worried she'd topple over on the stairs at the slightest misstep. She would forever be known in the county as the girl who couldn't stay upright. She had loved the gown that Kitty had picked for her in her absence, but hated the occasion to wear it. The capped sleeves were nearly translucent and the low-cut bodice coupled with the boniest, and hardest undergarments she'd worn to date, left the dove white flesh of her breasts precariously on display. She tried to throw a shawl over herself before leaving her room; but Kitty would have none of it and pulled her down to meet her guests.

"You cannot hide your light under a bushel. Besides, I think they are most distracting features to the young doctor."

"What?" Lilly had looked at her in shock and nearly tumbled down the last few steps to the waiting escort of Colonel Mayfield and Fitzwilliam. Mr. Sutton was nowhere to be seen but Lillian swore she heard his preposterously pompous voice echoing from the study. "What did you say?" Lillian looked back at Kitty whose eyes were only for Fitzwilliam.

"Hm? Oh nothing, dearest." Kitty smiled and continued on. Lillian adjusted her hair, so that one curl touched her cheek demurely.

The manor was impeccably decorated, with white lilies, foxglove, ivy wreaths and crisp white cotton sashes tied at the end of every banister and baluster. The gentlemen wore their finest brocaded vests and suits, the ladies a sea of fine cotton, lace and silk. Voices teemed from low to jovial and Lillian was assaulted with the sounds of at least three dozen people chattering, dancing, eating and drinking in the halls and rooms of the manor.

Lady Mayfield caught her eye and gave her a stern pout along with a nod towards the study where she presumed Mr. Sutton was drinking and having manly discussions about hunting or kicking puppies. She gripped her father's arm. She simply could not face the man without an ally.

"Are you well?" he whispered in her ear. Lillian's eyes scanned the crowd.

"Do you know Colonel, if the Drs. Blackwell have made their appearance yet?" she asked.

Her father stared knowingly down at her. "I suspect they will be along shortly." Lillian only nodded with the sad despondency that made him smile. "I daresay he would be daft to miss the opportunity of your aunt's greatest social success to date."

Lillian cringed. "I don't think he's much impressed by societal showmanship."

"No, but he is much impressed by you," her father responded. "I suppose we should go at least pay our respect to Frederick Sutton." Lillian loved the way he did not call him her betrothed, or her fiancé, or even by a respected title.

"Ugh, must we?" she rolled her eyes, at ease on her father's arm.

"It would keep that old hag's glare from our backs and I shall be with you for the entirety of it." he reassured. Lillian grasped his elbow tighter and felt dizzy, the heat of the parlor, the noise, the ache in her head, the tight corset... *she was nine and her father was walking her in to the dentist for her first round of braces. I'll be with you the whole time ...* he'd said. And he'd never left her. Her father, her dad. The Colonel.

Lillian stumbled and he held fast.

"Are you well, my dear?" he asked and looked down at her. Lillian's moist eyes stared back up at him, confusion, elation, anger; whatever her thoughts of her father's past behavior, she was beginning to understand how precarious his job had been.

"I've missed you, Dad," she said softly. Her father's eyes became misty and he put his hand over hers.

"I've missed you too, Lil'. I'm sorry this has happened." He gave her hand a squeeze.

"Well, I'm happy I get to have an adventure with you." She smiled up at him.

"There you are." The stern voice broke their gazes from one another and a coldness descended in the study as they stepped in. The other men in the room, turned and bowed at the young lady and the respected Colonel. Lillian closed her eyes, shook off the truth of their situation and bowed in turn to all of the men. When Sutton came to stand before her, she did not bow but offered him a cold glare.

"Mr. Sutton."

"The future Mrs. Sutton," he returned just as coldly. He reached out to take her hand, but she pulled away. He grabbed her wrist harshly and moved to pull her to him but the Colonel stepped in, removed his hand and took it with his own in a hearty handshake.

"Frederick my boy, nice to see you again. Are you enjoying

yourself? Have you had the brandy? Please, let us toast to your happiness." He stood between Lillian and Frederick. Lillian breathed a sigh of relief.

"I had hoped I could have a word with my darling betrothed. So much to discuss. I've just come into possession of a new whip for the horses and wanted her approval before I broke it in," he said menacingly over the Colonel's shoulder. He flashed a sharp-toothed grin at her and Lillian felt the blood drain from her face. Her gut turned; her world spun.

"Please, excuse me, Colonel Mayfield. I am faint and must take some air."

The Colonel could barely protest before Lillian bolted from the room and ran, skirts held high, down the least crowded hallway and up the back kitchen stairs to her room.

Matthew did not want to go.

He was, by all accounts, late and currently trying to build up his nerve to face an evening devoted to the engagement of the woman he loved, to his most-hated cousin. The man was simply terrible towards women. He believed them to be only slightly higher in value than livestock. Barely more important than cattle. Meant for a specific purpose.

That is what he feared for Lillian if she were to marry his cousin. The only hope that she might someday find contentment in was that Frederick often traveled for months at a time and they would rarely be together. He adjusted his coat and stared into the mirror, the hollow eyes of a man in forbidden love. If he had only spent the last years making money instead of administering to the poor, he might be able to ask for her hand from Lady Mayfield first. But as it was, he was too poor to do anything about it, even if she did love him enough to marry him. Blast it.

"Are you coming? We shall be late!" His father yelled from the foyer. Matthew sighed. Was any man in a hurry to watch his dreams die?

Matthew entered Westbury Manor, begrudgingly behind his father, and was greeted coldly by Lady Mayfield, given a warm handshake by the Colonel, and then followed his father into the boisterous crowd. He scanned the crowd but saw only Miss Darlingwood, Mr. Byrne, and several of his father's colleagues and friends milling about. No raven crown of hair. No lavender eyes to find his. He felt the tight anticipation more acutely in his chest.

Where was she?

He found his cousin, lounging against the fireplace in the study with a glass of brandy. His large presence and booming voice bragging of his latest kill to the other men surrounding him.

"A stag, nearly six feet tall, I dare say a larger beast has never been brought down!" When Mr. Sutton's eyes fell to Matthew, they narrowed. "I always get what I want, isn't that right, dear cousin?"

Matthew was never one to believe in violence, but he would have given anything to launch his fists into the smug face.

"And where *is* Miss Byrne on this happy occasion?" he asked.

"She is taken quite ill with a headache. You should have seen the beautiful gown! The purest purple silk, exceptionally well fit to view her best attributes." He leaned in closer for Matthew's ears only, "the purest white flesh for a man to sink his teeth into."

Matthew nearly pushed him into the fire. He cleared his throat and loosened his tie around the throbbing in his neck.

"I'm sure she was very fetching, tis a shame your company has caused her a headache," Matthew said blandly.

"I beg your pardon?" Mr. Sutton stepped towards him. Mr.

Byrne, who had chuckled beneath his hand at the comment, came between the two men. Though he was slighter and much younger, his sweet and jovial countenance seemed to defuse the tension just enough to avoid a most socially disastrous occurrence.

"I am quite certain that the good doctor meant that the general merriment has affected the sensitivity her injuries have left her. Sometimes I barely whisper whilst reading out loud and she must leave for the noise." Mr. Byrne cleared his throat and Miss Darlingwood came to stand next to him.

"Please, Mr. Sutton, tell us what happened then, with the stag?" she said, wide-eyed. Her interest pried Mr. Sutton's eyes from his cousin. If it was one thing Frederick was more inclined to than anything else, it was pontificating on his own greatness. Matthew bowed.

"Excuse me, I have forgotten to offer my respects to the Colonel," he lied.

Matthew left the room in haste and wondered if he could climb the staircase, but other couples and merrymakers were blocking the passage and it would not do for him to go alone to her quarters.

So, he went outside. In some ways, he was most grateful that he had not seen her in her dress as it would make her eyes even more alluring. He was also grateful that he did not have to see her stand beside his cousin, the perfect flesh of her on display while she tried to smile, though she did not mean it, or worse, look as though she was on the verge of becoming ill from the thought of what she'd been thrown into. The picture of Frederick's teeth marring any part of her body hit him in the gut.

"What ever would I do? Shy of killing the bastard?" he whispered as he rubbed at the incessant pounding in his chest. Never had he held such ferocity of emotion for a woman. She was so wonderous a creature. Demanding, smart, and strong, and yet still so unrefined in moments.

He stopped in the midst of his pacing beneath the half-moon's light and closed his eyes. No one would have believed how she turned to fire and heat in his arms as she had beside the fireplace. He shook with thoughts of her perfect breasts heaving against his forearm, begging for the tender and not so tender ministrations of his mouth and tongue. The trembling of her thighs against his, through the thin fabric of her skirts.

He was enchanted with the adamant way she denied affection for his cousin. As if love had anything at all to do with marriage. To be married to a woman one loved? One desired above all others? Not just for the proper and chaste reasons of familial obligation?

Matthew's thoughts went to the next logical place. Could he allow himself, even for a moment, to picture Lillian as his wife? In his bed. Long legs wound around him, naked in sweat and flesh, touching as he pleased, allowing her every opportunity to use him in any delicious way she desired? Teaching her all he knew about the beauty and desires of her body and what they could accomplish together. And all of this wild and painfully enjoyable wonderment under the blessing of society? Matthew sighed in frustration.

His thoughts were such a distraction that he nearly missed the small, very real gasp of surprise that came from above him as Lillian dropped from the drainpipe and into his arms. They both collapsed in a heap of skirts and surprised grunts on the ground.

Lillian sat up suddenly, straddling his waist, pink cheeked and breathless, confused as she looked into his face. It was as if heaven had dropped her straight from his fantasy into his reality. Matthew held his breath and his hands went instinctively up the length of her thighs, and around the gracious curve of her backside.

"Matthew?" she gasped. Matthew's air had been stolen in the fall. Now the warm weight of her pressing in just the right and magnificent ways he'd only moments before been fantasizing about stilled every worry and thought in his head except for that which ached to lift her skirts and pleasure her beneath the moonlight.

The brazen thoughts made his head swim and as the adrenaline subsided and his body began to ache from the actual fall and of her hitting him on her way down, he closed his eyes.

"Miss Byrne," he groaned. "You would address me so improperly?"

13

AN ESCAPE FOILED, A MEETING TO SAVE FACE

Lillian was still reeling from the good luck at making him a soft landing. Well, not *so* soft, she thought, and her eyes melted into his with desire. She leaned down closer with an uncontained smile. His hands still gripped tight, unabashedly, on her derrière.

"I'm not the one being improper," she whispered and shifted her hips back along his swollen desire. Matthew grunted and sat up, his hands moved to her shoulders and he seethed in frustration before gently pulling away with the utmost self-control in the deserted courtyard.

"But by what luck has the angel fallen into my arms?" he whispered. "When I was assured, the fair mistress was upstairs, in bed, with a headache."

Lillian didn't answer but searched the dark pathway for her satchel. Matthew rose slowly, watched her with a furrowed brow and a frown.

"It seems you are feeling rather adventurous for a woman who should be resting. Perhaps you should rejoin the party and take your part in the celebration," he said with his eyes narrowing, trying to ferret out her reason for escape.

"I have very little to celebrate," she glanced at him. "I just wanted some air."

"Air?" he said, and studied her traveling cloak and bag. "Truly, Miss Byrne, do you think me a fool?"

"I think nothing of the sort," she said and brushed the pebble dust off of her skirt. "I am sorry that I landed on your—you." She cleared her throat. "You may be on your way, back to the superficiality of the merriment inside. I am quite fine."

"I will do no such thing, and you shall not dismiss me so lightly. Not after all we have been through. What kind of man do you take me for?"

"I assure you, sir—"

"You are making plans to run away, in a most shameful act of cowardice."

"Cowardice! You think it cowardly to climb out of a window?"

"Miss Byrne, have you hit your head again in the fall?"

"No! Did you?" she argued hotly.

"A young, unwed woman cannot simply take a stroll on her own at night or," he paused and looked at the satchel "run away into the dark unknown. It would be folly indeed to believe your safety is secured. It simply is not done." He straightened his collar angrily and brushed the dirt from his trousers.

"Well, we both know that unconventionality is kind of my jam," Lillian said, looking for a way around him. The prospects of her plan dimmed the longer they stood there.

"Preserves aside, I cannot believe I am reminding you again of the precarious position you are in."

"I can't believe it either, when you know I haven't taken such advice before and why you'd knock your head against a brick wall in an effort to make me take it now," she said strongly and secured the satchel beneath her cloak. "I will not marry that man, I do not love him," she said finally.

"But it's already arranged," he said desperately.

"I'm in love with someone else!" she burst out. Matthew stopped and stared at her.

"But—" his brow drew down. "You hardly know anyone here."

Lillian looked at him and scowled. "Are you really so dense?" Before he could process her confession or her question, a call came from the lit doorway.

"Miss Byrne!" They both turned, surprised and breathless. The Colonel came down the stairs, glass of wine in hand and a pipe at the ready for lighting.

"It was my belief that you were in your quarters, held hostage by a monstrous headache. What ever are you doing in the gardens and how did you get through that crowd unnoticed?" He looked around at the deserted grounds and back up to Matthew, who now blushed profusely at being caught in such a compromising position.

Lillian swallowed, if she was not careful, her father would know she had tried to take matters into her own hands. He might also think Matthew was somehow involved. Plans to escape that night were ruined, there would be no leaving. The only thing she could do now was try to control the damage by any means necessary.

"Colonel, thank goodness you're here," she breathed out quickly. Matthew tensed beside her.

"Yes, dear girl, I am here. What is it? What has happened?"

Lillian took a brief moment to look into Matthew's concerned eyes.

"The good doctor has been giving me much needed advice on the very delicate matter of my health and that of my future prospects. You see it's—" she blushed and fidgeted with her cloak. She pushed the small satchel she'd been carrying beneath her cloak further, discreetly, and cleared her throat.

"Yes? Go on, girl, you know you are more than safe to tell me anything that is on your mind." Her father's eyes narrowed on Doctor Blackwell as he crossed the garden towards them.

"Are you mad? You cannot hold counsel with him," Matthew whispered.

"Kindly do shut up," she seethed under her breath. "Do you think me an idiot?" Her eyes found his and he clamped his lips tightly closed, trying to keep the answer firmly behind them.

"Good sir, I was feeling quite ill, especially—" she leaned back and gently touched the injured ribs. "Here, sir. I could not seem to take a full breath in my room and so I snuck out to get some fresh air. I know it was not proper, but I did not want to take anyone away from the lovely night to accompany me on such a foolish and boring interlude. It is, after all, a lovely night with the moon and stars hanging so—"

"I quite understand your reasoning, Miss Byrne. However, it is lucky I found you and not your Aunt in your current unchaperoned state. For the sake of your reputation and your *family's*." Her father's gentle reminder that the reputation of Fitzwilliam was paramount. Lillian's cheeks lit up almost instantaneously and her breath quickened. Matthew groaned and shook his head.

"This is not at all what it seems. I came around the corner from the kitchen, where I had snuck out unseen by the party guests, and Doctor Blackwell was merely strolling there. It was all very coincidental. And happily so. You see, he was just the very person I needed to talk to. And the privacy with which we could discuss such a delicate topic was most important."

"Oh?"

Matthew shifted beside her and she saw from the corner of her eye that he was clenching his jaw in anger.

"Having run into the doctor I inquired to him about my ribs. He and I both wondered if they would be an impediment to my upcoming nuptials." She blushed and looked down at her hands demurely. Matthew watched her and his brow furrowed in confusion until understanding dawned. He shook his head at Lillian before sighing.

"Colonel, after discussing her condition privately, I am concerned with the extent of her internal injuries, which are still healing, that the anticipated consummation of her upcoming nuptials might be, detrimental to her health and safety." He looked the Colonel in the eye as if he were the professional doctor not a love-sick boy. Lying about a condition to save them both the embarrassment and social ruin.

Lying to buy her time.

Lillian looked up to the Colonel with cheeks beet red. "I'm quite embarrassed to have brought it up to you, sir."

Her father looked between the two of them, and she swore she saw the glint of pride in her ruse to delay the engagement before he sighed. Without a blush or worry he cleared his throat.

"Well, if that is the way it is, it is. I shall talk to Lady Mayfield this very evening about delaying your wedding until a later date. Do you think, Doctor, a few more weeks to be a sufficient amount of healing? Would you be willing to stay your leave for the South until such time? I realize this is a tremendous request and you are under no obligation to comply. But, perhaps, for the good of our Miss Byrne?" Her father's knowing voice tapered off.

Our Miss Byrne.

Matthew looked at her.

"Yes, Colonel, I think she will be quite right in body and mind by then," Matthew said.

"It is settled then! Now, Miss Byrne, please return to the party. Doctor Blackwell, I would be much obliged if you would accompany her back to the dinner and stay as close to her as possible for the evening, in the event she should need you," he said, and Lillian's heart sang.

"As you like it, Colonel. I shall be happy to offer my expertise in any manner I can." Matthew gave the Colonel a bow. She curtseyed to the Colonel.

"Thank you, from the bottom of my heart, Colonel, for being

such a calm and understanding guardian," she said. Her father looked at her briefly.

"It is the least I could do," he said it with an air of sadness. Lillian tried to meet his gaze. "Now please, go on and enjoy some part of the evening if you can," he said and returned to his pipe.

Lillian nodded. She bowed again and followed the very quiet and stoic doctor back towards the house. Matthew walked with such a hurried pace that she wasn't sure she could catch up to him in her skirts, even in her best walking shoes. Hiking her dress and determined not to show frailty, she charged up after him.

"Is there a fire we are rushing to? Why must you," she paused to breath as he stormed up the short set of stairs to the back entrance, watching her feet instead of seeing him stop until she'd run into his chest and they nearly toppled over. Matthew steadied her with his hands and quickly let her go.

"I used to think a woman's greatest enemy was poverty, but for you, Miss Byrne, I believe it may be stairs."

"Are you very angry with me?" she asked and looked up at him.

"I am," he said, nostrils flaring as he gazed down at her before turning and continuing up the stairs.

"But there was no harm done. You got what you wanted. I am confined to my fate once again and you and I were not guilty of any impropriety. I daresay I was very clever in coming up with—"

"I am not getting what I want," he said and stopped, refusing to face her. "And despite the fabrication you gave to a respected friend of mine, you have set my mind and heart against themselves."

"But how? I merely prolonged the inevitable."

"You have taken away my future prospects in Wales, you have put me into your orbit for at least another month's time. You have also put into my mind the picture of—" Matthew stopped and took a deep breath.

"Of what?" she said and came to face him. She looked up into his eyes, searching for the honesty they were supposed to keep counsel with in one another. Voices from the party inside floated through the doors towards them.

Matthew looked skyward. "It matters not." He paused at the door. "Please let us get this tumultuous evening over with."

"It does matter. It has greatly upset you, and if you are upset then that matters to me," she said.

"Kindly keep your voice down," he said back.

"You first!" she retorted. With stealth and grace, he pulled her away from the doors and behind a decorative column beside the entrance. He kissed her, deeply, with warm lips and tongue, angry as they searched her mouth for reason, for truth, for the words of love he could not seem to speak himself.

"You've put the image into my mind of you and my barbarian of a cousin together."

Lillian looked into his downturned face with understanding. "Consummating our marriage vows?"

"Please do not—"

"If it causes such a reaction for you, imagine what it does to me." Her satchel fell to her feet and her shoulders slumped. He looked at it on the ground.

"My anger is misplaced," he cried softly, caressing her chin before kissing her gently. "It is myself I'm most angry with. I have foiled your attempts at saving yourself. I am angry that I am not a better man, deserving of you. Able to financially support you." he confessed.

Lillian untied her cloak and satchel, folding them neatly into her arms. Matthew was silent as he stared at her in the lavender gown. His eyes fell to her breasts, before darting away. Perhaps Kitty was right, Lillian mused, maybe they were the doctor's favorite feature.

"But now I have time. We have time, to think of something better," she whispered, while the voices beckoned them join the party before suspicions could be aroused. Lillian sighed and came nearer to bury her head in his chest. Her arms went around his trim middle and his shoulders gave way their tension to hold her close while they still could. His hands caressed up her back and delicately touched her hair.

"It was brilliant of you," he whispered as he gently wove her hair between his fingers. "You're quite brilliant, Lily."

She looked up at him and he down at her. She wanted to kiss him again, to crawl fully into his arms and throw her middle finger at the constraints and rules that kept them so far apart. She nestled herself into his chest before stepping away again.

"Only because I surround myself with brilliant people," she said softly.

"Thank you," he whispered and kissed her temple. "Thank you, thank you, thank you." More kisses to her cheeks, her neck, beneath her ears.

"For what?" she whispered back and lavished in his warm mouth until it found her lips and gave her an aching slow kiss. His hands framed her face. He broke away to look at her.

"For giving me more time with you."

Lillian's heart leapt and fell and ached. Time. Time was all at once her friend and the worst enemy she could have. Weeks until her murder. In an era she didn't even belong in. Time with a man who she was falling so horribly in love with, that surely couldn't be meant for her. She felt tears form, and took her hand in his, kissed his palm and stepped away.

She took in a deep breath and walked slowly towards the doors. Matthew followed, at a good distance away and hands behind his back. When they came inside, she set down her cloak and bag on an unoccupied bench before continuing on into the great hall. The party was a loud and bright affair. Lillian looked back once over her shoulder, winked at him, and he blushed before finding someone else to talk to.

When dinner was served, they sat next to one other, with Mr. Sutton across from Lillian. He leered crudely at her and Matthew's fist tightened on the white tablecloth between their fine dishes.

Next to Mr. Sutton were two of his business associates that he'd invited, without asking, to the party, allowing the family of his fiancé to pay for his guests, taking disgraceful advantage of the generosity of the happy event to further his business.

He barely spared a warm glance at Lillian. In fact, Matthew found it quite indecent how Frederick's heated looks were always directed at her breasts and never at her face whenever he spoke to her. Lillian, to her credit, gave measured and bland responses, as though she'd put a mask over her beautiful brain. Matthew wondered if all women possessed this skill when trying to deter the unwanted advances of a man. He rarely interjected and tried to remain neutral.

Mr. Sutton, put out by Lillian's refusal to be drawn into his conversations, began compounding on the business of the day and loudly using language that belonged in a dockside pub and not at a respectable party. Matthew's head swung to Lillian, who was watching him too.

Even despite her own brash and uncommon use of grammar, she was deeply upset by his cruel and foul language. Kitty gasped. Lady Mayfield even turned bright red. Doctor Blackwell could see it was also affecting the rest of the guests as a hushed horror made its way up the table to them. Matthew opened his mouth to change the topic, when Lillian's strong voice rang out over the table.

"Mr. Sutton! I simply will not stand with such vulgar and inappropriate language at the table of my beloved family. If you must talk like an uneducated dock worker, you may do so in a barroom with your compatriots, but not over dinner in the presence of such merry and genteel company."

The silence of the table was quite complete, and Mr. Sutton choked on his wine abruptly before falling into a fit of coughing. When he finally contained himself, he stared in horror at his future wife, then to the expectant faces around him whom, he suddenly realized, shared her feelings but would not have dared to speak so boldly to him. His face grew red.

"Forgive me, my dear, Miss Byrne," he seethed. "I have gotten carried away in the spirit of the day. Still, it is hardly your place to speak that way to me, and you needn't accost me with such *hysterical* reprimands." His eyes bored into her with such intensity that she swore they'd send a spike of lightning right through her heart. She lowered her gaze, cheeks pink, and excused herself with such a quiet request that no one seemed to hear it.

"My dear Lady Mayfield," Matthew said quickly, covering her escape "Forgive me for I have not heard, where did you find the time to plan such a magnificent gathering?" The distraction, one that put the attention on a host, most willing, seemed to ease the table with smiles and a return to the merriment. The Colonel looked gratefully to Matthew and smiled, starting off with his version of the events, which were quickly taken over by the Lady herself, who had no shortage to say on the painstaking details of planning the party.

But it wasn't with the weight of cotton, hiring of musicians, or food preparation that Matthew's thoughts lay. Lillian had excused herself and Mr. Sutton had not gone after her. He was quietly hunched over his conversation with his friends, shooting angry glances down the table every few minutes.

Matthew leaned over to Mr. Byrne and Miss Darlingwood.

"Excuse me, my dear friends. I'm afraid I have forgotten to send a patient a message about a very important meeting tomorrow. May I ask the favor of the use of your study for a moment, and your porter?"

"Oh yes, of course," Kitty said, as though they were her things to offer. Then she leaned in towards him. "Thank you, so very much for the diversion. I thought it would be a very unpleasant memory in the making."

"The pleasure was mine, Miss Darlingwood," he said with affection and rose to leave, but she placed a hand on his arm.

"Oh, if you happen to cross Miss Byrne's path," she said, barely above a whisper. "Please ensure that she is quite well." Kitty winked at him in a very Lily-like way and he blushed.

"Should I encounter her in the vast wanderings of your halls, I will do my best to comfort any concern she may be suffering."

Mr. Byrne smiled at him as well and contributed to the conversation with such lively excitement that no one noticed the good doctor taking his leave of the dinner table.

14

HYSTERIA IN THE GARDEN

He found her in the garden. Not trying to escape this time, but head bowed to the gathering clouds in the east, soft sobs escaping her. Matthew came up slowly, and did not touch her.

"Miss Byrne," he whispered. "Are you quite well?"

"I am not," she sniffed. "I am not enjoying this party at all."

Silence sat between them. Matthew stepped up next to her and watched the growing storm in the distance. Its rumbling warning seemed to send shivers up both their spines simultaneously.

"Do you think I'm hysterical?" she asked.

"I do not."

"Did you know, my dear Doctor Blackwell," Lillian began but stopped as the strange fact lodged in her throat.

"Yes, *my dear* Miss Byrne?" he said, half light-hearted, half listening for anyone else approaching. What did it matter if she said something? She'd be gone soon and hadn't they sworn an oath of honesty towards one another?

"It has been postulated that women diagnosed with severe cases of hysteria can be cured with the simple method of sexual release," Lillian said, rationally, as though they were in a scientific lecture hall. Matthew swung his head to either side of the empty balcony, and the dark garden beyond.

"I beg your pardon? I do not know where you acquired such information."

"I would think that you, being a man of science, would appreciate the effective properties of such a method."

He lowered his voice and tried to cover the disruption with the charm of his smile. "Please, let's discuss the weather."

"Oh, I've embarrassed you. I am sorry," she said and but when he looked away from the storm to her, her smile was anything but apologetic.

"I very much doubt you are." He shook his head.

"Does it upset you so? To think of such a method as a medical practice?"

"It upsets me to think of," he paused considering his words carefully. "Of you and I discussing such a treatment. Or that you would even suggest it. My cousin's barbaric accusation was incorrect. You were right to stand up to him. You are not hysterical nor in need of," he stopped at the thought. Lillian stopped too, thinking of being under his knowledgeable hands, bare and weeping with pleasure while he administered to her condition. He shook his head and closed his eyes. "Where on earth did you hear such information?"

Lillian smiled at him and the flush of his cheeks. She'd watched a PBS special on it.

"I read a lot."

"I very much doubt that you would be privy to those types of books."

"You'll find I'm nearly always learning. Even things I should not be privy to. Did you know, for instance, that an orgasm a day can be incredibly beneficial to one's well-being." Matthew turned to put his finger over her mouth to silence her, before realizing such public touch was inappropriate. He drew away but the heat of his touch still lingered. He stared at her lips, his eyelids falling softly. She read the darkening of his gaze as he leaned closer.

"Are you thinking of kissing me?" she whispered. When he said nothing but clenched his jaw and opened his eyes to glare, she continued. "I was thinking about your hands. Your fingers. They're exquisite, you know? I often wonder what they'd feel like —" He took her elbow and steered her farther out into the garden.

"Does it trouble you so?" she asked, breathless in his rush.

"It does."

"Pray tell, why?"

He looked behind them, assured that no one was outside and that they were alone. He looked down at her, studying every detail before he closed his eyes and took a deep breath.

"Lillian, please."

"Does it disgust you? The thought of helping me in such a manner?" She took her elbow back with force. "I only thought you'd find it interesting, as a doctor."

"Did you, Lily?" he turned on her, anger and something else causing his voice to lower, his eyes to stare at her hungrily. He gripped her arms. "Or did you bring it up to tempt me further into the sinful thoughts I can't seem to pull away from on a daily basis concerning you?"

The touch of his hand on her sent shivers through her. She looked down at where his fingers trembled.

"It would not be a sin if it were for the sake of my well-being," her eyes were tied to his lips now, and his to hers. Heat blossomed between them and the world blended away. They stumbled towards one another.

Matthew pulled Lillian around the thick cover of bushes and into a secluded alcove. He pressed her against the strong height of a tree with his body and his head fell to her neck. Lillian arched to make contact between her skin and his lips.

"You are indeed feverish," he gasped against her skin. "Quite possibly not within your reasonable senses," he breathed, hot on her neck, and dipped to taste her skin. He gently bit her neck, nudged beneath her ear, and allowed his hands to caress down the length of her torso.

"One might say I'm practically hysterical," she gasped and curved her body into his capable hands. Matthew growled low in his throat, nipped his teeth along the tender line of her collarbone and she responded by threading her hands into his hair.

"I'm afraid, I am only in possession of my hands to attend to you," he said, drunken and dreamy on the smell of her skin and the sound of her sighs.

"Yes, please, employ them," she begged and turned her head to capture his lips finally in a kiss that sent heat and shivers rolling through her body. Matthew groaned at her words and swallowed her gasps with his kiss. He took his time, tasting and teasing the delicate warmth of her full bottom lip between his teeth. She whispered his name and all felt lost, his hand trailed up over the confined pulse of her heaving breasts.

The quiet darkness of the garden was punctuated by the frivolous conversations of party-goers through the open windows and the distant sound of soft thunder. The low rumble was just enough to cover the delicate moan that escaped Lillian's lips as Matthew's nimble fingers gently pinched the hardened tip of her breast beneath her dress. She pulled at the confining skirts and wrapped her leg around his thigh, putting the pressure of his muscular leg against her sensitive core.

"Lily, I am lost," he gasped as he felt the warmth through her skirts and the cool wind rushing up around them.

"Find yourself in me, I beg of you," she whispered. Her thigh clenched and slid against his and she trembled. Her hand held his head to hers, while the other caressed down to his straining cock, painfully hard with want. His body responded in waves of pressure against her hand. He continued to kiss her while his hand reached down and tugged at the length of silken fabric. She inhaled sharply when his fingertips trailed up the soft skin of her inner thigh.

"Is this too much?" He wasn't sure if he was asking God or her. The two were one and the same in the moment.

"Not nearly enough," she whispered and bit his lip. Matthew traced kisses along her jaw, bit her neck as his deft and long fingers found their way through the layers of fabric.

"Matthew, please," she gasped as he parted the cloth and slid one long finger inside of her. Lillian threw back her head and he groaned at how wet and tight she was. His thumb caressed the swollen peak of her, while his fingers moved in swift and precise strokes, curling delicately against the most sensitive spot. Again and again, her back pressed tightly to the tree, her body bound by his arm and chest. Her gasps became cries, lost to the wind, and he silenced her with kisses. Her whole body tensed as the rush of pleasure rolled through her like the deep thunder around them. Lightning struck in the field far off and illuminated her face to him. He watched her face as she crested and clung to him.

His fingers continued to pulse, until she was writhing and she dug her nails into his shoulders, traced hands up into his hair to hold his forehead against hers while her breath spiked and rolled. She wanted to bite him and take him, and pull them away from the world waiting inside.

"My sweet Lily," he breathed her name like a prayer.

"Stay with me," she shivered, hands shaking as she freed his thick cock from the confines of his clothes and wrapped her strong fingers around him. As the rain began to fall, peppering their clothes and hair, running in droplets down her neck, she continued her silken, tight strokes. He drank from her collarbone, dipped his tongue between her breasts only to rise again and kiss her swollen lips, his body tensed and pressed against her, straining for release. She gasped and tightened her hand. Matthew felt the wave build inside and he surged in an explosion that drove him to bite her neck and push her harder against the tree, grunting in a pained and beautiful way. His body softened down in waves, even as their mutual breathing began to still. The tension and worry had drained away.

It was indeed a viable method.

"Lily," he gasped.

"My love," she sighed. He looked into her eyes and righted their clothing. His hand traced up her waist, her shoulder, and around the back of her neck and he brought her forehead to his own with a sigh. He kissed her tenderly and the world felt right and beautiful.

"I do not wish to go back."

"Nor do I," he agreed throatily into her neck. "I can't imagine a time when I will no longer want you," he whispered the incoherent promise. "I wish I could have you, all of you, to be—" he stopped and Lillian looked into his tortured eyes. She swore there were words behind his lips he would not speak and it broke her heart. The world was all at once too cold and unfair, and this was maybe the only moment they could have for their own. The rain had slowed as if driven by their mutual passion, and calmed in their satisfaction.

"So you do not think less of me? Not behaving as a refined young lady should?" she said and a small smile played on her lips.

"You are all the more a woman. A strong, passionate woman, not faint of heart or body."

"I do feel wonderfully faint, currently," she said softly and her lips brushed his. Noises from the opposite end of the garden caught their attention and snapped them apart from each other, damp, flushed, and wanting.

"My darling Kitty, please," Fitzwilliam's voice implored. Kitty rushed ahead of him, a flush in her cheeks, hair undone from the rain. Lillian moved to follow but Matthew held her hand firmly.

"We cannot interfere without ourselves being found out," he whispered, and they watched, from the shadows as Fitzwilliam followed.

"It was not my intent to behave so ungentlemanly. I should not have let the thoughts of my heart cloud my judgement, please!" Kitty turned, in the middle of the deserted garden, tiny fists balled up at her sides as she thrust her pert nose up at him.

"I am not angry at your supposed transgression."

"Then tell me, please my dearest, what is it I have I done, so that I may make retributions to you?"

Kitty stamped her foot and Lillian had to smother the snort of laughter that bubbled up. Matthew covered her body with his, the dark jacket sealing them into the shadows, and shushed her. Kitty continued.

"I have given you perfect and ample opportunity to kiss me and yet you have not. If you do not wish to kiss me it is not fair nor gentlemanly to leave me aching, incorrect in my assumptions about your affection. I do not wish you to play games with my—" she did not finish her tirade as Fitzwilliam moved swiftly in, taking her by waist and claiming her mouth with his own. She gasped in her throat, arched her body up against his and sighed with release. He continued tenderly kissing her lips, her jaw, dipping scandalously low to her neck before returning to her lips.

"Will," she whispered, the rain reduced to a soft caressing patter. "Oh, my sweet Will, how you undo me," she threw her arms around his neck and kissed him back ferociously, causing Fitzwilliam to stumble backwards before catching her fully and laughing into her lips.

"Seems there is a family propensity for unchecked passion when boundaries are crossed," Matthew whispered in Lillian's ear. His lips found her neck, they watched from the shadows, somewhat guiltily, somewhat in pleasure, as the young couple nipped and kissed at each other until the quickening of breath and building of heated caresses caused them to stop.

"My dear Kitty," Fitzwilliam gasped. "If I do not stop now, I fear I would quite—"

"Sully my honor?" Kitty gasped, equally wanting.

"With fumbling joy, yes," he smiled, placed a kiss on her nose contritely. She cleared her throat and stepped away. "I hope you are no longer angry with me?" he asked as they walked back to the house, a respectable distance between one another.

"Only at fate, for making us stop. I shall hold you to a joyful sullying, once we are wed, be assured." The tone and guarantee with which she spoke caused Lillian and Matthew both to laugh into one another's bodies in the effort to keep quiet. Matthew's warm breath on her shoulder made the world feel right and beautiful. When he looked down at her and smiled, her heart gave up any hope of leaving Westbury Manor.

"Are you well?" she asked, knowing they, too, should be returning.

"I am quite calm, more so to know I have done my sworn duty to help my favorite patient in her time of," he stopped to smile, "great need."

"I am quite certain the need will arise again," she smiled back.

"You are indeed troublesome, Lily."

"And unfortunately, I am all yours," she whispered, not knowing why or how the words formed, only that it was the truth, deep into her soul, and undeniable. He stopped and turned back from moving to escort her inside. He stared into her eyes. "No matter what future greets us when we leave this garden, I will always be yours. I cannot be anything else."

"Lily," he gasped, his eyes filling. Before he could speak, the sharp call of her name cut through the darkness and desperation.

"Miss Byrne! Miss Lillian Byrne, where are you?" The shrill tone of Lady Mayfield set them apart and Lillian sniffled. Matthew closed his eyes, sighed, withdrew a handkerchief to give her and stepped away, hands clasped behind his back just in time to see a sizable party of people round the corner.

"What is all this? What has happened? What dishonorable actions have taken place here?" Lady Mayfield screeched. Lillian's head snapped up; Matthew cleared his throat. They stepped farther away from one another. Mr. Byrne stepped out from behind Lady Mayfield and studied their position just behind the tree of the garden he had, not minutes before, been snogging Kitty in. He looked to the angst in Lillian's eyes and pushed his way to the front of the crowd.

"I'm sure there is a perfectly rational and innocent explanation," he said.

Kitty was suddenly at her side. Lillian didn't know where she'd come from but she touched her back lightly before she spoke.

"She was with me! She was walking with me in the garden, quite upset about—well, about Mr. Sutton's behavior at dinner. She needed air, you see. I stopped to fix my slipper. It is only just now that we've met with the doctor."

The readily offered defense squelched Lady Mayfield's plans to dishonor her wayward niece. She huffed and barged back through the crowd. The recent upset left guests to make the swift decision to leave for the evening to avoid further discomfort.

Fitzwilliam came down the steps to be closer to his cousin and Doctor Blackwell. "Are you quite alright?" he asked, looking between her and Matthew.

"Quite," she answered and looked at Kitty and took her hand.

"Gardens can be," Kitty stopped to clear her throat "easy places to get lost in."

"Especially beneath the moonlight," Matthew finished, looking hungrily at Lily. Fitzwilliam mirrored his own desire to Kitty.

"I think it is sufficient to say that what happens in the garden at night, shall remain in the garden. Would you not agree?" Lillian said and looked coyly into each face.

"Quite," they all answered in unison with small smiles, cleared their throats, and firmly folded their hands in front or back of their own bodies.

~

From their love-soaked glances, none of them witnessed the angry and scorned man, watching them from the parlor window. The same room in which he'd once promised his fiancée just retribution for her actions. Where he resolved not only to break Lillian Byrne but to remove any obstacles in his way that may protect her.

Frederick was no idiot. He knew she was close to quitting their arrangement and making him look like an absolute fool. That his own cousin was in on the plot and now, having witnessed them walking from the garden together, flushed and obviously enamored, he was determined to ruin the budding romance before it began. Perhaps it was Matthew's fault that the girl was acting so petulant.

He would break his cousin. And then he would break Lillian. Sutton stared down at her flushed cheeks as she smiled at her coconspirators. She was nothing more than a common harlot and he would have his way with her, violently, so she might never hold the idea that it was a pleasurable event, but a price to be paid for making him look ridiculous. A price she owed him.

He would punish her in delicious, painful ways. His body responded with a quick reaction and he blew smoke slowly out from his fleshy lips. When the couples dispersed, he turned away too. Plans formed in his mind to drive a wedge between the two fawning lovers for good. It only made matters worse, when Colonel Mayfield entered the parlor and gave Mr. Sutton the very untimely news, that his engagement would be postponed.

15
HEARTS ARE BROKEN AND
STITCHES HEAL

Matthew could think of nothing more than seeing her again. While he'd accompanied his father home in their carriage, glancing over his shoulder at her waving all of the guests goodbye, his mind and heart were filled with longing and confusion. What they'd shared in the garden was certainly, by all standards, scandalous. And yet, he felt no remorse. If anything, he felt closer to her, emboldened by his love and sureness that everything he did with and for Lily was the right course of action, and damn the governing laws of the times. Humans were hearts before they were subjects and what the heart wanted, the heart should have.

So, when he arose the next morning having slept deliciously well, he reminisced over the dreams of her in all manner of undress. Laughing in bedsheets and dining on picnic blankets beneath warm sunshine, sitting on his lap, kissing her neck as she read to him. He donned his clothes quickly, washed his face and made haste to visit his favorite patient.

He did not make it out the front doors.

There, in his father's parlor, was Frederick, dressed to hunt, with his rifles lined up against the settee in a barbaric manner.

"Cousin," Matthew said warily and looked at the guns once more before he met Frederick's cold stare.

"Ah, good you're up. As you should be for a *virile* young man."

His tone was tense, his eyes fire above a calm smile. Matthew's father came in, his own hunting clothes on and blowing his nose into a kerchief.

"Wonderful, Matthew, go change. We'll leave presently." His father said and adjusted his tie in the old mirror above the fireplace.

"Leave?"

"Of course. Don't be dull, cousin. I'm taking you hunting!" Frederick slapped Matthew hard against the back. A little too hard for good nature. A cold rush of sweat coated Matthew's body. He stared at Frederick. He must have gotten the news about postponing the engagement.

"I was unaware you would want me to accompany you as I have previously expressed my distaste for the sport."

"Well, today, is a new day, and I feel it's important that you witness my skill at bringing down even the largest prey."

Ice ran in Matthew's veins when Frederick's eyes never left his. His voice shook. "Did Lady Mayfield speak with you last night regarding Miss Byrne's condition?"

"I understand enough," Frederick responded a tight whisper. "It matters not a week or a year longer. She will be mine." He kept the tone of his conversation low enough that Matthew's father was unaware of any other interaction going on and started to tell them a story about the best hunting he'd ever had in the south of France as a young man. He was too preoccupied with the memory to hear his son or Mr. Sutton continue.

"She is no one's to own," Matthew argued lowly.

"She is mine."

"That is her decision."

"We cannot trust the frail mindedness of their sex to make

their own decisions. And I know that you will do what's best for her and her family."

"I'm not sure what you're insinuating, Frederick. Her best interest is always in my heart."

"It surely is somewhere, but I very much doubt it's your heart," Frederick glared down at Matthew's groin. "If she will not marry me, then I will see to it that the reputation of the entire Byrne family suffers. If she will not marry me, I will ruin her and those she loves without mercy. If she will not marry me, she may not even live to see the love of another."

"You cannot—"

"You know that I can. Pray cousin," Frederick leaned in, large hand on the wooden stock of his rifle as he pressed the cold metal up into Matthew's thigh, "help her to make the right decision. If you care anything for her at all. If you want her to continue to walk among the living." With that Frederick cocked his weapon with a vicious snap and Matthew's father came out of his monologue at the sound.

"For heaven's sake, Frederick, not in the house!" Frederick backed away from Matthew but their eyes never parted. Matthew's heart skipped and ran in his chest. Frederick would, and probably with great relish, be the financial downfall of her family. He would have no qualms about making sure that Lillian would suffer in every way possible. Matthew believed now that he might even kill her. He backed away three steps.

"I will not be hunting today," he announced, voice raw.

"Why ever not? Surely it is a fine day for it, and it would continue the bright spirit of the last night."

"I—I have to pack. I'm leaving for Wales as soon as it is prudent to do so." Matthew said softly. He left, climbed the stairs, reached his room, and threw up into his wash basin. They were at a deadly and painful impasse, and he had failed the only woman he'd ever loved.

∽

Days passed and the light and full heart Lillian carried since the night of the dinner began to fade into emptiness. No word had come. Her letters, unanswered. When she'd gone for a walk, over the hill to see if he were at home, his father, a serious gentleman with the same beautiful blue eyes assured her he was not. Matthew was very much occupied in London that week, gathering equipment, and paperwork for his anticipated move to the South. When her face fell and her eyes filled with tears, the old man's stern expression softened. For a moment, Lillian saw the quiet and compassionate bedside manner that Matthew had. The doctor shook his head.

"I'm sure he will be sorry to have missed you, Miss Byrne."

She nodded, bowed and turned to walk back home. It didn't feel like Matthew was sorry. It felt like he was avoiding her. Had the garden scared him? Had she, once more, gone too far and now might never again reach his good graces? Lillian pushed her food around on her plate that night and could not bring herself to enter into the conversation. The Colonel asked quietly if she were alright.

"He has not spoken to me in days," she whispered. "He's left for London and his father mentioned him leaving for the South." Her voice broke and she took a swallow of wine, to keep from sobbing.

Lady Mayfield interrupted them, demanding to know what all of the secrecy was about and proceeded into a tirade about how unfortunate and inconvenient the delay of the wedding was. Mr. Byrne looked as though he wanted to break in with happier news of his own but the Lady would not be dissuaded from her reprimands to her wayward niece. Lillian merely nodded, voiced a meek and teary apology, and excused herself to her room.

She had ruined it. By her desire and her lack of self-control, she had ruined everything. She had bought them time together and now he was determined to make her spend it alone. She wept herself into a dark and haunted sleep and refused to leave bed the next day. She wished he'd never interrupted her escape. Though the garden and the time they'd spent in its safety was a dream world, if she had known it would lead to his leaving, she never would have seduced him into getting lost there.

She lay in bed and her fingers ran through her disheveled hair. Her stitches itched.

She wanted to pull them out but she didn't know how, with such archaic tools as the iron tipped tweezers she had on hand. She hadn't had a tetanus shot since the tenth grade and didn't want to risk what strange kinds of bacteria she might infect herself with. Still, she sighed as Miriam bustled into the room and set out a clean gown, layers, and dress for her, there were worse ways to die.

When Kitty had caught her trying to remove the stitches herself that afternoon, in the dusky old mirror with her embroidery scissors, she'd issued such a horrid and unnecessary squawk that the scissors had slipped and gave her a puncture wound that then began to bleed.

"Damn it, Kitty!" she'd yelled without thinking as the blood dripped down her cheek and down the front of her dress.

"What on earth are you doing? I cannot leave your presence for a moment without you launching yourself into danger." Kitty rushed over and confiscated the scissors, pressed her own clean handkerchief to the new wound and promptly had to sit down for the faintness she felt at the sight of Lillian's blood.

Worst of it, Kitty took the scissors and instructed the staff to keep all sharp objects away from their young and troubled charge. Then, she skittered away, promising that someone was coming remove them within the hour.

"Someone?" Lillian fumed by the side of the piano and plunked a few keys madly. "She had better not come back here with Matthew Blackwell," she grumbled to herself in the dialect of her time. What was the use in pretending after all? Perhaps, if no way to her own time could be found, she would secure passage on a boat to 'the Americas' and start over in a country that might be more accepting of her brutish and forward manner.

Matthew woke with a horrible hangover, just like the day before. And the day before that. Today he was packing, so he resolved that he was done with his binge. After all, spies from Westbury Manor had assured him that she was now out of her room, which meant, in true and tried Lillian fashion, she was moving forward having lifted herself from her slump of despair by the strength of her own stubborn will.

She would be fine. She would somehow manage to either change his brutish cousin, or survive whatever was thrown at her. He had to believe this to be true. He had to believe that she didn't need him and that it would all work out in favor of her happiness.

Unfortunately, he believed, in equal parts, that he was wrong, and that the more stubborn and strong-willed she was, the worse it would be for her once the vows were exchanged. He was leaving in a week. He would never again look into those lavender eyes, never kiss her pink pout, never hold her lithe body against his.

Matthew couldn't bear the thought of facing her, since abandoning her after their night in the garden. She most likely thought he'd gotten what he'd wanted. That he'd simply used her. He left her letters unopened, ached with every one that arrived until they stopped arriving. He hadn't gotten what he'd wanted. Only Frederick was getting what he wanted. And Matthew was a damn coward, for not having come to her rescue.

He passed back and forth trying to dissuade himself from the idea of going to see her one last time before leaving for Cardiff. Perhaps try to explain that it wasn't only her reputation now at stake. But the whole happiness and safety of her family as well.

He was stirring his tea slowly, poring over the medical journals in his room, deciding which should accompany him on the journey and which he could send ahead by freight, when the door resounded with a knock.

"Yes," he said simply, not wanting to speak too loudly for the sake of his head. He did not expect Miss Darlingwood to follow his butler into the room and stood quickly, dropping the book in his haste.

"Miss Darlingwood." He bowed and she curtseyed. "This is an unexpected surprise. I hope not warranted by tragedy. Are you quite well? Your father? The Colonel?"

She smiled from beneath her bonnet. "I am quite well, in perfect health both in heart and body," she smiled in a way that lit her cheeks with a rosy glow and Doctor Blackwell saw in her the look of a woman in love. He had seen the same glow beneath the stars that night in the garden. In Lily's face. He dropped his eyes and felt tears sting them, before composing himself.

"Then to what do I owe the honor of this visit?" He motioned for her to sit and motioned to his butler to fetch a fresh pot of tea.

"I do come on behalf of a patient in need of care," she began and looked at him pointedly. He stared back, his head still filled with cotton and the remnants of brandy.

"A patient?"

"One you have treated in the past."

"Oh?'"

"One who is in desperate need of your particular expertise." Her blush grew as she looked down at her hands. Matthew's heart leapt and his nerve endings shocked. She was now so bold as to send people to fetch him when letters could not do it.

"Miss Darlingwood, please inform Miss Byrne that she is no longer in need of my—"

"She did not send me. I came of my own accord, to see to it that you do what is just and right for her heart." Kitty paused, taking in a deep breath to gather her courage.

"Please, Miss Darlingwood—"

"I have come tell you that the stitches are healing into her skin and she needs help removing them. I have been able, thus far, to dissuade her from taking the embroidery scissors after them herself, as we both know how inept she can be with such sharp instruments. But I fear she is impatient."

"God in Heaven," he cursed and his sullen mood turned to annoyance.

"So, please, good sir," she shook her head as if talking to a stubborn child. "Yours are the nimblest fingers, and I know that you will save her much harm and possibly more loss of blood if you would see to the stitches yourself."

"I cannot. It is no longer in her best interest."

"Her best interest?" Kitty's mouth pursed.

Matthew looked at her, feeling his face pale at the memory. "My cousin," he paused, sighed, and covered his eyes. "Threats have been made. Grave ones."

Kitty stared at him and her eyes narrowed. "What do you mean, grave threats?"

"It is not of any importance—"

"That is a lie!" Kitty burst out. "If it has kept you from her side when she loves you so unfailingly and you her—"

"Miss Darlingwood!"

"Then they must be grave threats indeed and something must be done about it."

Matthew stared at Kitty, her cheeks pink. "I wish that I could. But he has tied my hands, in fear of retribution for both herself and her family." Matthew stared at her hand pointedly. Kitty twirled the engagement ring against her finger with her thumb.

"Please, it is best if someone else attend to her," he said and went back to perusing a manual on disease that he had no will to read while his mind was preoccupied with Lillian on the brink of poking her own damn eye out with sharp little blades.

Kitty scoffed. "Do you not wish to see her? Not at all? Not even once more before you abandon her?" The rise in her small voice reiterated the same words that had whispered in his brain for the last few days. The rain clouds outside descended rapidly as if gauging his mood and contributing to the solemn darkness in his heart. He sighed and hung his head. The tea arrived and he barely nodded, so deep in thought and turmoil.

"There can be no other for the task. I believe you have taken an oath and I shall hold you to it." She rose and he stood quickly in response. Kitty nodded to the butler without taking tea and bowed to Doctor Blackwell. "I shall expect you at five o'clock this evening."

"This evening? But that's—"

"Plenty of time and fair warning to gather what you need to meet me at the gates of Westbury Manor to assist our dear friend," she finished the thought for him and strode, more confidently and maturely than he'd ever seen Kitty do, out the door.

16

MIRIAM'S STORY, SHREDS OF HOPE, AND A DEAR FRIEND DEVISES A SECRET MEETING

Lillian was pissed and wished she could leave now. She was still angry when Miriam brought tea and a wary look.

"Saints, child, you're lucky you didn't put your eye out there," she grumbled in true motherly fashion. Lillian rolled her eyes and sat down with a huff. As Miriam poured the tea she looked over at the new wound and placed the pot heavily on the tray with a clatter. "I don't know why ye couldn't have just waited."

"Well, I'm not very patient, and while I once was very good at putting in stitches, I am not very skilled at removing them on myself. I'm not very skilled at anything," she said lamely and took the teapot back up and poured Miriam a cup of tea as well. The old maid studied her curiously before sitting next to Lillian with a sigh.

"Now, that's not true. Though I've heard you used to play the piano well, but the fall caused you to lose your skill, and Miss Darlingwood says your embroidery is something terrible —" Miriam stopped, realizing that she wasn't being of assistance in making Lillian feel better. "But, now, the gardener James, tells me you spin a fantastic tale and I do love a good story," she said and sat back, bringing the tea to her lips and blowing gently. Lillian had told the gardener the wild tale of a young space knight with a twin sister who saved the galaxy. She watched Miriam for a moment while the stupidest idea came to her.

"Would you like to hear a story?" Lillian said.

"Why, yes, if it pleases you. I would very much like that." Miriam said. Lillian blew out a breath.

"Once upon a time," Lillian began and took her own warm cup in hand. "There was a gangly, young girl. She lived in a magnificent world, over two-hundred years in the future. Where trains sped across the countryside at hundreds of miles an hour, great flying machines took people across oceans, and the whole world was connected by a vast network of magical boxes that allowed for thoughts to pass freely from person to person."

"Oh, this is fantastical, it is. I can't even imagine!" Miriam whooped and helped herself to a biscuit. "Well, do go on. Tell me about this girl."

Lillian had thought for sure that just the beginning would have scared the old maid into sending for a head doctor, or at the very least a priest. Apparently, Miriam had a greater sense of adventure than the upper-class people she'd been sharing company with. Lillian looked at her and continued.

"The girl lived in the Americas but was in England, tracing the history of her family. She was visiting this very same manor, enjoying the beautiful and stately grounds. The girl's mother, her brother, and she were researching their ancestors from here."

"Where was the girl's father?"

Lillian paused and thought about all those years she'd assumed he'd just been a vagrant, hopping from job to job. In a way, he had been. "The girl's father abandoned the family, years before. Disappeared without a trace and left the girl's mother to raise them herself. She became a very successful stock trader and could afford to travel."

"How odd the future must be, that women can trade cows on

their own and travel without a man to keep them safe along their journey." Lillian paused and blinked at Miriam.

"No, stocks are—you know what? It's—yes. It was a *fantastical* time indeed. And even though they were without a patriarch in the family, they were happy. Well, as happy as anyone could be."

"Tell me more. Go on about the adventure!" Miriam, whose legs were short compared to the couch where they sat, swung them like a little girl up past her bedtime. Lillian smiled.

"The girl was daydreamy and brash. She was stubborn and had just gotten into a quarrel with her brother."

"Oh, she reminds me of you!" Miriam chuckled and brushed the crumbs from her apron.

Lillian paused, wondering if she should continue. She looked at Miriam. Miriam stared back at her and nodded in encouragement.

"Go on, then."

"After the quarrel, the girl was running down the stairs of the manor, intent on leaving the stuffy old house and getting some fresh air, only," Lillian's voice shook and her eyes clouded up. "Only she was quite clumsy," Lillian paused and sobbed inadvertently. Miriam put her cup and biscuit down and took Lillian's trembling hands in hers. "While she was running down the stairs, she tripped and fell."

When she didn't continue, Miriam searched Lillian's face.

"What happened then, child?" Miriam asked softly.

"She, she woke up to find herself very far from home. In a completely different time. Two-hundred years before she'd even been born." Lillian sniffed and her teary eyes met Miriam's, whose brow fell in deep thought. "To a place where everyone knew her, though she did not know herself."

"Miss Lillian," she said softly. "What did this young woman do, upon finding herself in such a situation?"

"She just wanted to go home," Lillian said. "But she didn't know how to get back to her own time. And she feared being trapped in a time, with a," Lillian hiccupped, "with a man who would surely be the death of her. So, she did the only thing she could do. She tried to fit in. Tried to behave in the ways that were expected of her. Tried to be the woman that everyone thought her to be. To do the things they asked of her."

Miriam took her hands from Lillian and wound them together in a prayerful pose. "Saints, child," she whispered. Lillian sat still and silent beside her, folding her hands as well. It felt good to tell someone even if she was sure that Miriam must think her mad, or ridiculous, or both.

"How would you end this story, Miriam? What should a girl do?" Lillian sniffed and wiped her nose unattractively on her shawl. Miriam watched her.

"I can't say," she said softly. "But I know a story myself. Akin to yours," she said and sat up. Miriam looked over both shoulders and listened for footsteps in the hall. Lillian perked up and looked back as well.

"You do?" Lillian asked.

"Not far from here, south along the river Avon, where it bends to the east, there lies a great stone." Her brogue seemed to deepen and the effect of it was ancient and magical. Lillian leaned in. "Some say it was the fae folk that brought it, laid it down as a gateway to their world."

"Have you been to this stone?"

"Oh, aye. Once, when I was a young girl, hired on by the first master of Westbury Manor. I had brought my friend Charlotte to see if we could catch a fairy. We was silly and unrefined you see," Miriam's eyes sparkled. Lillian began to lose hope. Fairies were one thing. Time travel was a completely different set of physics.

"Did you catch a fairy?" Lillian asked in an effort to show Miriam the same kindness of an open ear. Meanwhile, her mind conceded that if her father did not provide her with an alternate plan, the only road out was to head for the coast and see if she could catch a boat to at least her own country.

"Oh no, Miss! Blessed be," Miriam laughed. "But the stone was engraved with strange and ancient letters. Ones I couldn't read for sure. Charlotte said they was from before us; before Rome, sometime when those druid folk ruled the land," Miriam stopped to shiver.

Lillian's mind flashed back to the day she'd walked with Matthew, the beautiful day when they'd kissed, saved a boy, and escaped their societal confines. The strange marking on the stone outside of Westbury Manor. She closed her eyes and saw it clear as day. A triskelion, carved and filled in with moss from years of standing still.

"What do you know about the druids? The fae?" Lillian asked.

"Oh, I always heard tales when I was a wee girl. About how they could walk from world to world and from time to time. Like they didn't have to obey the same rules as us. That they could skip through space if it pleased them."

Lillian sat up and the gears in her brain cranked to life. It sounded an awful lot like what her father could do. What she had done, inadvertently.

"Did you ever go back to the stone?" Lillian asked. Miriam looked around again to check for any ears that might overhear.

"Oh, aye, I did. Without Charlotte of course, she was scared of the fairies. She was a sniveling twit she was, no sense of adventure." Lillian couldn't help but smile. "I was on my way to town, about two years past, and thought I'd just look in on the stone. To see if it was still standing. That morning I scrambled through the underbrush and I watched the sun hit the stone and the ruins. The symbols lit up like wee blue flames."

"And then what?" Lillian was perched on the edge of the settee. Miriam looked far off across the room. Her brow fell in and she seemed to be picturing the exact moment, her breath came in short gasps and Lillian watched a bead of sweat form on her forehead.

"A great whorl of wind swept about me, tossing up the leaves and debris, and the doorway—" her shaking hand reached out as if stuck in the memory and trying to grasp the exact vision.

"Yes? The doorway?"

"It was like a clear window to the other side of the field, but different somehow. And a man—a man—"

"What man? There was a man?"

"A man stepped through—"

A great ruckus erupted from outside as the dogs barked, heralding the arrival of someone. No doubt it was Kitty. Lillian looked to the door quickly.

"Did you see this man? Who was he?" Lillian took Miriam's hand in her own, desperate to know more before they were interrupted. Miriam came out of her haze when the downstairs doors were opened and Sarah Jane's voice floated up from the stairs welcoming in a guest with a familiar and warm tone.

"Who was who?" Miriam asked and looked to the hall, suddenly snapped back into reality. "I must get back to work." She heaved herself from the couch and looked down at Lillian. "The story you spin is a sad tale indeed. One that I would very much like to see you write a happier ending to. An ending where the young woman finds her way home." Miriam's eyes darted to the hall, behind Lillian. She smiled knowingly. "Or perhaps, she could find a happier future right here, where she's at. And of a good heart, make a home." Miriam bustled out of the room.

"Here she is!"

Lillian looked up to the sound of Kitty's voice and the very upsetting arrival of Doctor Blackwell close on her heels. Lillian's brain froze its plotting.

He looked pale, and dark circles ringed his eyes. As though he had not been well himself. How her heart hurt to see it and she stood up quickly, torn between tears and elation, at not just seeing him in such a state, but in the new information that held her thoughts hostage. The world seemed to spin and she felt the blood empty from her head to her feet.

"Kitty what have you done?" she breathed softly and felt dizzy. Doctor Blackwell came in swiftly, forgoing the formal bow or even the pleasantries of introduction. Seeing her in such distress caused his whole demeanor to change.

"You are so pale. And too thin," he gasped as his eyes traced over her shoulders and collarbones where her blue cotton dress hung from her. He studied the small trail of blood down the front of her dress and it caused him to clench his fists to his sides. "And a more appropriate question might be, what have you done?" he said.

Without reserve for present company, his hands came up to frame her face. The warm fingertips were gentle but firm, holding her still so he could assess the damage. The smell of tobacco wafted up from his coat pocket. Parchment, ink, lavender, tea, and rain-tinged grass, all hovered over the surface of his earthy, male scent.

Now she was going to faint, thought Lillian. She stared into his eyes, wanting to memorize every fleck of light within the blue. He stared only at the new wound and the stitches that had become far too comfortable in her skin.

"I was trying to—"

"Gouge your damn eye out?"

"Doctor Blackwell, please!" reprimanded Kitty. A sudden flush lit Lillian's cheeks.

"I am perfectly capable of cutting out a few stitches. You needn't worry about me. I could have removed them myself if Kitty hadn't taken my damn scissors." Lillian threw his curse back in his face and his eyes dropped to hers. Then to her lips.

"You both should be ashamed for such language," Kitty scolded. "I'm simply *so* upset that I *must* take my leave." She winked and left the room. Lillian turned away, tears in her sore eyes, as she covered her mouth to keep from sobbing. She did not make it far, before Matthew took her by her wrist and pulled her back to him.

"Please," he whispered. "We are given this moment. I do not wish to waste it."

"Waste it?" Lillian yanked her arm away and stared at him through the burgeoning tears. "You have wasted days! Days when I ached to be with you. Days of time by my side and days' worth of kisses. Days that are running out. It is not I who has wasted time." She turned to leave and Matthew took her by the waist and pulled her back to him. He held her tightly in his strong hands and pressed her body close to his.

"Forgive me," he gasped. "I had no choice."

Lillian pressed her fists against his chest and pushed, but he held fast. She growled in frustration and he returned by kissing her deep and full, biting and hungry. He pressed the length of his muscular body against her and his hands gripped into her back tightly as he continued to kiss and bite at her eager lips. Lillian's body melted as a small and needy sound pressed through their lips.

"You lie," she cried even as he continued to kiss his way to her chin and jawbone. "*You* always have a choice."

"My cousin," he gasped, pressing his hard and needful body into her soft curves. "My cousin threatened to dishonor your whole family, the entire Byrne name. I think he intends to break apart our dear Mr. Byrne and Miss Darlingwood's happy future, and even to—" he gasped and pulled away. She stared up at his face, the tracks of his own tears, his own desperation, his own bottled-up sadness coming to the surface.

"What else?" she whispered.

"To kill you," Matthew choked. "He threatened to kill you."

Lillian's world spun and her body sank into his. Matthew led her to the couch. Had she been creating her own problem this whole time? Her behavior with Matthew had threatened Fitzwilliam's engagement. It had angered Sutton into quite possibly playing out the history of her death. Lillian Byrne would die. She cried and clung to Matthew and he sat next to her and held her close.

"I am a coward and an idiot, and I should have fought him then and there. You have no cause to forgive me," Matthew whispered. Lillian nuzzled her face into his chest and inhaled deeply. His beating heart calmed her. Whatever would she do? What was to say Mr. Sutton wouldn't murder his own cousin, especially if Matthew stood between him and claiming Lillian as his bride?

"You are not either of those things. Mr. Sutton is a frightening and horrible man, who will stop at nothing to get what he wants."

"I mourn the time I've spent so far from you, for both our sakes. But also in giving him the satisfaction of winning, through our ruin."

"Especially when it's my job to ruin you," she whispered and looked up at him. Matthew looked down at her, the softness of his smile made the world feel suddenly right again.

"Such a deceptively sweet smile, hiding such a quick and sharp tongue. Ruin me indeed, I should like to know how you intend to do that," he teased. He was close enough to feel her breath on his chin, soft as a whisper and his hands caressed her cheek.

"I assure you, good sir, my tongue can be quite soft."

Doctor Blackwell inhaled a small gasp as his brain ran away with the idea. "Yes, I think that would quite do it." He tilted her chin up to kiss her lips softly. "Whatever shall we do, my brilliant girl?"

Kitty cleared her throat from outside the room. "Doctor Blackwell, your satchel, sir?" she said and peeked around the corner. They both sat up and a respectable distance apart, though both now knew Kitty had no mind to make judgements. She placed the small bag that he'd dropped upon seeing Lillian, at his feet. "For the stitches."

"Miss Byrne, please do sit still. So that I may attend to you properly," Matthew whispered in a manner so seductive that Lillian's knees trembled and wanted to part. She complied and he stood to closer inspect the stitching and the small wound she'd given herself. So close that his thigh pressed her knees open slightly. Kitty cleared her throat but remained across the room, suddenly involved in a new embroidery project for her upcoming wedding and casting small, conspiring smiles their way, while keeping a watchful eye on the door.

He was not as quick as Lillian had expected him to be with the work, taking his delicate time, not just with the stitches but pausing to stare at her face, as if he were memorizing it, every line, eyelash, laugh line and freckle. He did not speak and she tried not to look at him as he deftly cut and removed each stitch. The thread pulled at her skin and caused a small discomfort which he apologized for quietly. He took a clean white cloth to the droplets of blood released and blew out a tense breath at the agony of hurting her even in this small way.

His breath smelled of peppermint and tea, and pipe smoke and she wanted to taste him again. As he snipped the last knot and pulled it out, she felt the familiar painful tugging and her hand went around his thigh to squeeze instinctively. He paused, hands steady over the stitch, and his eyes fell to her face, locked in concentration, mouth and lips inches from his still swollen desire, long fingers pressed to the tense muscles of his thighs. She wanted to nuzzle into him, please him, make him as weak in the knees as he made her.

"Are you quite alright? Do you need a respite?" he whispered. She loosened her fingers and the nails grazed the skin behind his thigh. He inhaled and closed his eyes, his hands shook.

"Do you need one?" she whispered back. He opened his eyes, shook his head and swallowed thickly. He removed the final stitch and nodded.

"There you are." He gathered up his tools in a towel.

"I fear I am again indebted to you." Matthew looked like he

had ideas on how she could repay him, and his moral code was battling with them. He looked at Kitty and once more at her.

"Please," he said and stepped away, handing her his handkerchief to catch any errant drops. "Keep both the new and old wounds clean. The new is not so wide or deep for stitches but do not attempt any further surgery on yourself. That will be payment enough for me."

"That I will," she said and stood before curtseying to him with a demure bow. "I believe this is yours." She held out his handkerchief but he shook his head.

"For you to keep. For when you find yourself in need." He bowed to her, his cheeks a slight tinge of red, and took a deep breath. He turned to bow to Miss Darlingwood.

"Thank you, Miss Darlingwood, for your help in assisting the patient. I know it must not be easy to keep her from danger."

"I feel it is a time-consuming occupation. She could most benefit by having the both of us assigned the task," she teased and gave a small wink to Lillian that was not at all subtle.

"If you have no further need of my services, I am afraid I must take my leave," he began.

"But won't you stay for tea?" Lillian asked quickly and motioned to the full service that she'd started with Miriam. Matthew looked longingly at the divine scones in particular. Lillian wondered how many he'd stolen in his time at Westbury. Not that anyone could blame him.

"I am afraid I cannot. Not today. But soon." He bowed again and took his leave. Lillian hung her head. Kitty murmured her goodbyes to his retreating back and bowed again.

"Oh, Kitty," Lillian reprimanded.

"He was available to remove your stitches."

Lillian felt tears well up, poetry behind them. "You have torn the stitches of my heart wide open with your bringing him here." She looked down to her closed fist, the handkerchief crumpled within.

"But don't you see, dear Lillian?" Kitty took Lillian's hands in hers. She gently opened the tightened fingers and they both looked at the bloodstained cloth with his initials. "He has given you his token. He said, for when you find yourself in need."

"I don't, I don't understand what that even means."

"It means, my dearest, that he will always be at hand, for you."

"But he—"

"It is his way of telling you, that you are in his favor, and he has not abandoned you. He is working on a plan." Lillian stared at the linen cloth and felt sick to her stomach.

She sniffed. "I fear I need to go lay down. Please excuse me." She took the handkerchief and left the room for the safe and dark quarters of her room once more.

She curled up around the sweat-moistened and blood dabbled piece of cloth, putting it to her nose to catch the notes of tobacco, medicinal herbs, something that was intrinsically his own. She wished that he had not given it to her. It only confused her more. She must leave, mustn't she? If she stayed, she would be dead within a month.

Her feelings for the good doctor did not matter. No matter if they had connected on some deep, ethereal level, she was not meant to be in this time, was she?

LILLIAN VISITS THE FAIRY DOOR
AND THE LADY MAYFIELD INSISTS

Lillian's father warned her that Frederick Sutton intended to call on her the next morning. He'd advised her to remain neutral, to not be her usual self. Lillian had rolled her eyes, and asked him when they could leave. John shook his head and told her soon. The lack of action and the idea she should behave complacently for the horrible Mr. Sutton set a determination in Lillian's mind. If her father would not do more, then she would investigate the lead Miriam had given her. Scouting out the so-called 'fairy door' stone presented a perfect opportunity for her to feel as though she were doing something to get home, and also to simply not be there for whatever violent nonsense Mr. Sutton intended to spew. She prepared the best she could for the trip. Rising early, she took her tea and a biscuit in the kitchen away from the family, then quietly gathering her things to slip out even before Miriam was aware she was leaving. If the housekeeper's suspicions and story could be believed, if she had indeed seen someone coming from the gateway, the fairy door may be her way home. She tried to push thoughts of Matthew to the back of her mind. This was only an experiment.

She could have had faith in love, and believed that Matthew

might find a way to keep her from marrying Sutton. But she was never raised to allow a man to save her. Besides, if Sutton was not above murdering her, he certainly would enjoy taking Matthew's life as well. She could not risk that. She had to go home.

She had an easel, paint and canvas. It was to be her excuse should she be discovered. She knew that Kitty found painting dreadfully boring, and thought it was one of the lowliest skills a well-bred woman could possess as it left one with discolored fingers and exposed the skin to too much sunlight. Lillian knew she would not begrudge her going alone. Perhaps she might even think Lillian was meeting Doctor Blackwell. Lillian stopped in her path, thought of his long fingers on her cheek, eyes searching hers. She could almost hear him whispering,

What are you doing, stubborn girl? You should not be here alone. Why would you leave me?

The loneliness and ache of missing him that followed nearly made her turn back around. But, when she looked up from her daydreaming, she saw the same strange, three-vined, triangular marking on the short wall beside the road, that separated it from the river. She looked around the deserted, early morning path and hiked her skirts up to gingerly climb through the brush. She continued on for a few hundred yards, and the wall climbed slightly higher, still covered in moss and undergrowth, until it was a full-sized gate. Nearly hidden in the overgrowth, the stone archway sat undisturbed in the forest. Beside it, and through more pristine forest, she could hear the rushing waters of the Avon close by.

When Lillian approached the doorway, she found nothing spectacular about it. The stone wall on either side of it seemed to lead off in an endless line through the forest, separating the road and the river, but the growth of the forest did not give a clear view of anything except more trees and flora on the other side. The undergrowth was thick around the door and creeping up and over the wall itself. It was a wonder she, or Miriam for that matter, had found it at all.

The doorway was unassuming and plain. Not more than a progression of height in the dilapidated old wall. A large slab of stone sat in the archway, effectively blocking it as a useful pass through. The arch around it was carefully constructed of small cut stones. She put aside her painting things and walked slowly towards it. Holding her breath, she reached out her hand, pads of her fingers grazing the cold and wet stone.

When her fingers met it, tentatively, an electric shock shivered through her arm and tingled down to her toes. She jumped away and stared as faint markings etched across the top of the slab glowed briefly. It felt as if the gate could sense that she was not made of particles from this time. The recognition of the old magic frightened and assured her at once that if there were a way out of this place, away from the certain fate of death, this would be it. She sat against the cold stones of the wall and watched as the markings faded. Her heart raced and she hugged her arms close.

This discovery brought about all kinds of new questions. If she survived, and made it out of this time to the present, what year would it be? If she survived, did that mean history would change? Would her disappearance simply be interpreted the same? How would that affect the timeline? The history of the land? What would become of Frederick Sutton? What of Kitty and Fitzwilliam?

What of Matthew?

She closed her mind off from the worry and stood to pace around the stone. She knew too much worry might cause her to falter and she could not falter in her goal of getting back home. But what kind of home would she return to? And who's to say this gate would even bring her back to the future? What if it sent her to the past, or another dimension? Lillian nibbled at her fingernails and paced.

She knew very little about the specific magic, dates and moon phases and newt eye potions. Her heart ached in her chest. She crumpled back down into the dirt and leaves and saw the sun twinkle through the forest cover above. She should return to Westbury Manor before someone sent a search party for her. She didn't know if this was the route to saving herself, but she knew that it was something.

She stopped briefly along the way, set up the easel by the bank of the river. She had no idea how long it took to paint something. If a finished product was expected she could hardly hope to complete something in the short time left her of the morning light. She had just started the background colors, the rolling green hills of the English countryside, when hoofbeats sounded from the path behind her.

Clutching her bonnet to her head she turned quickly to see a horse approaching. Fear tripped up her heart and she gripped her paintbrush as the backlit figure approached.

"There you are," Fitzwilliam said, relieved. Lillian squinted up at him until he came around and dismounted. Her cousin sighed. "I was sent by the illustrious Lady Mayfield to fetch you back to the manor."

Lillian rolled her eyes and her shoulders slumped "Ugh, must you? And must I?"

Fitzwilliam chuckled and came over to the mess of a painting. He studied it carefully and shook his head.

"Well, perhaps we will find you some other genteel talent." Lillian struck him on the shoulder and they both laughed. He helped her gather her things and walked beside her, leading his horse. For a few paces they were silent and then Lillian turned to him.

"What is your impression of Doctor Blackwell?" she asked, hoping to judge his willingness to run away to America with her should the gate not work out. Fitzwilliam looked mischievously at her from under a quirked dark brow.

"He is a stiff and doddery old man, but I believe generally good of heart."

"Oh you!" Lillian pinched him behind his arm and he yelped, before smiling down at her, handsome and dark curls across his forehead. Lillian would miss this family she had found. At her sudden downturn of mouth, Fitzwilliam continued kindly.

"Matthew has been my friend for a great many years, since I moved to Westbury. A kind, if serious, gentleman. Though he is less serious with you. I have never seen the man smile so much, except in your presence. I have not seen him get so flustered either."

"But you do not find his temper too hot?"

"No." Fitzwilliam paused in thought. "Certainly not to the extreme and distasteful level of our other 'acquaintance'," his voice was dark. "Doctor Blackwell's anger comes from worry borne of frustration."

"I do not wish to worry or frustrate him."

"Not even a little?" Fitzwilliam nudged her.

"Well, maybe a bit." Lillian blushed and looked down.

"He is very much enamored with you, Lily. I daresay his heart is completely in your hands and he wishes only good things for you."

Lillian felt like crying. "Whatever will I do?"

"What choices are before you?" Fitzwilliam asked, serious but open. On one hand she could escape the whole mess and leave Matthew, possibly grieving the loss of her. Or on the other, stay and risk dying. Fitzwilliam was not asking for these options and would be shocked to hear them.

"Dishonor my family or spend the rest of my days with a cruel and horrible man?"

Fitzwilliam continued to walk, the horse snuffled beside him. "I am sorry," he said quietly. "It is a great injustice to you, so sound of mind and body, to have to be reduced to only those options. You are brilliant, and worth so much more a choice in your own life."

Lillian took his hand with hers and they walked closer to Westbury Manor.

"Ah so you've found her!" the Colonel's voice came from the gate.

"Yes, she was butchering a canvas in the woods. It would be best if we could burn it and bury the ashes." Fitzwilliam said with an air of formality. Lillian released his hand and stuck out her tongue at him.

"You are such a terrible cousin." The smile they shared was near sibling love.

"Come my dear, let's put the thing to rest." The Colonel offered to carry her painting supplies so that Fitzwilliam could take his horse to the stables. As they walked to the house together, the Colonel lowered his voice.

"Where the devil were you?"

"Trying to find a way to get me out of this mess, like you should be doing," she whispered harshly back. Her father stopped and scowled.

"If you anger Sutton there is a good chance he will ruin the reputation of your cousin, then no marriage, and no Lillian."

"If I don't leave soon, he's going to murder me! So, also, no Lillian," she said rather loudly, and they both stopped to look around. Her father took a deep breath into his nostrils, a trait she remembered from childhood, when he was trying to find the patience.

"I won't let harm come to you. I've given up a great deal—" he paused and looked down, "to assure your safe passage back to your own time. I need you to trust me."

"Well, you'll forgive me if I'm a little short on trust. I seem to remember you leaving me to my own devices quite often." Lillian stormed away towards the front door, where she was met with the loud squawk of Lady Mayfield's voice.

"There you are! You petulant girl!" She bustled down the stone steps of the manor and grabbed Lillian's arm rather forcefully.

"Now my dear—" began the upended Colonel.

"You are insufferable, and I shall be glad to be rid of you! What would have transpired if someone had heard of you missing your future husband's calling? The whole county would shun us. And the engagement of your cousin would also be ruined!" She led Lillian away without so much as a backwards glance.

Lillian tried to turn around back to gauge her father's expression, but Lady Mayfield closed the door between them and led her to the sitting room where she pushed Lillian into the chair.

"My Lady," Lillian began.

"You will silence your sharp tongue for once and listen." The command was abrupt and menacing. "You will change from these filthy rags and pay a visit to your much maligned fiancé. While there you will make amends as a proper young lady should."

Lillian lifted her chin proudly. "And why would I do such a thing?"

Lady Mayfield's face turned red with fury and she leaned in, her hot clove-laced breath blowing on her cheek.

"Because if you don't, I will tell all the loudest mouths in the county that Matthew Blackwell has sullied your honor and is nothing more than a perverse cad, who ruins young women. I would be more than pleased to turn you out into the street, with or without the Colonel's agreement, and you would be left to the sharp teeth of the world."

Lillian wanted to pull Lady Mayfield's wig off and slap her in the face. She felt heat rise in her cheeks. She did not speak, but folded her hands in her lap and dropped her eyes.

"He did no such thing. He is a man of honor."

"It matters not. What I tell society to believe, they will," came her growling reply. Lillian looked up into her blazing eyes and took a measured breath.

"If you'll excuse me, Lady Mayfield. I will go to my room and prepare."

All the way up the staircase, Lillian's heart played an erratic rhythm that seemed to climb to near hysteria. Walking into the snake den of Frederick Sutton's home to apologize and beg for mercy for her justified behavior was the worst possible thing that could happen.

Aside from Matthew's reputation being completely ruined.

She washed her face, changed her gown, and tried to put her hair into a simple updo. She pushed away the thought that this meeting with Sutton could lead to her death, if she was not careful. With a steady hand, she left a short note to Fitzwilliam and the Colonel. Where she was going, what she was meant to do, and to please check in on the progress of the negotiations should she not return promptly.

"At least then they might find my body sooner," she grumbled and put a final pin in her hair, sweeping back the front pieces so that her pink and garish scar was clearly visible.

18

THE TRUTH OF MR. SUTTON AND A
TERRIBLE VIOLENCE

Lillian did not want to go. But she thought if she didn't at least try, then she had no doubt that Lady Mayfield would see to the ruination of Matthew's reputation and possibly even have his medical practice dissolved. And if she didn't apologize to Mr. Sutton he might decide to try to ruin their entire family and cause Kitty to rethink her engagement to Fitzwilliam. And if they never wed, she would never be born. Even her pestilent brother would be snuffed out.

Lillian was not a fainting damsel and if this must be done to keep up appearances, she would play the part. The insistence of her marriage to Sutton must have been some cosmic glitch in the timeline that had to occur, otherwise, the Lady would have allowed her to end it after the disgraceful conversation over their engagement dinner table.

These thoughts and more filled her head, distracting her as she rode in the carriage, past the safety of Matthew's residence and onward to his cousin's imposing manor. It was cold and monolithic. No gardens, but precisely-cut shrubbery surrounded the main entrance. The windows were dark and foreboding like the man's eyes himself. Lillian shivered as she looked up at them and the carriage came to a halt. In her best gown, gloves and bonnet she allowed the porter to help her down and her steps were small and faltering as she was led inside to Sutton's sitting room. His porter, a sharp faced man with hard eyes, studied her.

"The Master will be with you shortly. Please do not touch anything," he scowled. Lillian sneered at his retreating back and vowed to touch as many things as possible as soon as he left. She thought it odd that it was not questionable for her to meet with Sutton alone. Perhaps because he was her betrothed. Perhaps because in his manor he was allowed to entertain young women alone. Perhaps because her horrible aunt knew this would seal the necessity of their marriage.

She did not sit, but walked around the room and studied the various taxidermied animals hanging in poses along the walls and mounted in corners. The room smelled of musty death and her stomach turned even as the gears in her head continued to work. Maybe if she married him, ran away the night of their wedding, and faked her own death she would stand the best chance. Though Fitzwilliam and Kitty would be greatly saddened, there would be no dishonor and they would have each other and their love for solace. Matthew would be heartbroken, but he would be alive and have his work. Life would go on as it was supposed to. She just had to avoid that little detail about actually being drowned.

As she perused the bookshelves, she thought about Matthew. She wondered if he would find solace in someone else. If she could return, she would look up every detail she could find about Doctor Matthew Edward Blackwell. Who would he marry? How many children would they have? Would his descendants survive all the way to her time? Would they look anything like him? It wouldn't matter, she thought sadly and picked up an old leather-bound journal, absentmindedly flipping the pages. They could look exactly like him but they would never be him.

No one would ever compare, and she was destined to lose

him. She turned through the first pages of handwritten notes. Thoughts of Matthew faded quickly when her eyes lit on a picture scratched in black ink inside the page. The blood drained from her face as her mind made horrific sense of the images.

The sketches, in great and disturbing detail, showed the capture of African people and accounts of one such 'restocking' mission. The disgusting pictures showed men pulled limb from limb as they were forced into chains and ropes. It showed sailors raping the women, setting fire to villages, throwing children into the pyre or having them suffering the same fate as the women. The detailed written notes in the margins made Lillian's breakfast come up into her throat. She gave out a strangled cry and covered her mouth.

They were all signed, Frederick Sutton.

"What are you doing?" The sudden reprimand caused Lillian to physically jump, drop the book, and gather her shawl tightly around her shaking shoulders. Mr. Sutton stared at her and then down to the journal at the base of her skirts.

"What right do you have to snoop in my private study?"

"I was not snooping, I was merely—"

"You are so petulant, Miss Byrne. I shall see to it that when we are married, you are held to proper restrictions both in space, and in behavior." He came closer with a stealth she was not ready for. He grabbed her by the shoulders harshly, large hands digging into her skin and making her cry out. "By any means necessary." His voice was dark and his breath hot on her cheek as she turned her face away.

"I was overjoyed when I heard you had come," he licked his lips. "Lady Mayfield tells me you have had an appropriate time to formulate a groveling apology."

"I will not grovel—"

Sutton cut her words short when his hands tightened, nearly reaching the bones of her arms, and bruising her skin. He shook her. She cried out and his breath quickened.

"You are pale, my dear," he whispered in her ear and his tongue, thick and wet traced up her jaw. "Did you like what I drew? My own personal experience will be something you will get to enjoy." He bit her chin harshly, and Lillian cried out. His hand quickly went over her mouth and nose, stifling her voice and blocking her airway as he pressed her up against the bookshelf. She turned her head away and her eyes met a coiled cobra, tongue out and glass eyes staring into hers. She tried to scream but his hand was too tight.

"Your flesh shall know the same rightful punishment." With that he uncovered her mouth and swallowed her lips with his large and suffocating kiss. Lillian was shocked but she remembered the classes her mother had insisted she'd take in high school. Her survival response took over and she steeled her nerve.

She bit his lip hard, nearly clear through, and caused Sutton to howl with pain before pulling away to cover his bleeding mouth.

"Unhand me!" she yelled and while there was a small distance, she hiked up her skirt and kneed him squarely in the groin before running towards the door. She had almost reached it when his large meaty hand closed around her shoulder. She turned back to fight and met his other hand as it struck her across the cheek. The room spun and pain erupted in her eye and forehead, the bruised bone of her skull protested. Lillian tried to stay on her feet but he was pulling her back into his hard body.

"No! Let me go!"

"I will tear you apart," he growled in her face and pressed his hard and throbbing body to hers. Lillian struggled and stomped at his feet.

"Leave me alone!" she cried just as the door swung open and her father burst into the room.

"Mr. Sutton, unhand Miss Byrne this instant," he bellowed and the hands around her body slackened. Fitzwilliam followed close behind, hat and cane in hand, with a look of murderous rage on his face. She fell into his arms and sobbed.

"Mr. Byrne, please escort your cousin to the carriage." The Colonel stood with his full height and breadth in challenge. Sutton was still bleeding profusely from his bottom lip. He stared at Lillian.

"Colonel Mayfield, you have no right to take her away. You have adopted a petulant and dangerously feral hellcat and I will see to it that she is properly refined. You are lucky my offer still stands, and I can remove the dark blemish from your house." His words were slurred through his injury and his eyes were raving mad. For all the pain she had caused him, he only seemed to want her more.

"You will do no such thing," the Colonel's voice seethed. "The engagement is off. I see you now for the villainous character you are." The Colonel looked down at the open journal and the drawings within. "I dare say the entire county shall be made known of your dealings both here and abroad."

"You know the world of men is something much above the understanding of a stupid, sniveling, spoiled girl!" His spit was bloody as he spewed the words at the unshaken Colonel.

"The world of a true man, of the man we should all aspire to be, is not the world you are building. Either with your relations in the deplorable trade of human life or the mistreatment of the fairer sex." The Colonel gave him a harsh look that seemed to halt Mr. Sutton's impassioned raving, and caused a calm deadliness to come over his features. He stayed silent as the Colonel departed, though is mind and thoughts were racing ahead to the solution that must happen.

19

THE PAST BEGINS TO CHANGE, AND SO MUST PLANS

Fitzwilliam held Lillian gently from the side as they traveled home in the carriage. The bruises on her arms were already starting to darken. The teeth marks on her chin and neck stung, and she could feel the angry red mark across her cheek throbbing. Fitzwilliam looked at her, and the blood on her face, and paled.

"It is not my blood. It's his. I tried to fight him, I tried," she sobbed.

"I know dearest, I know. You did well. You did brilliantly. I do say you gave him back in turn." Fitzwilliam lost decorum and whispered. "You are such a brave girl. A heroine in your own right and had I been there, I would have likely murdered the sodden bastard." The bouncing of the carriage jostled her pained body and yet the horses could not be driven fast enough away.

"But I shall be ruined. He will ruin our family and your chances with Kitty. Oh, my dearest Will, I'm so sorry!" She began to sob again.

"Darling, do not trouble yourself so." He kissed her forehead. "Do you think Miss Darlingwood's affections are solely for my estate or name? Do you think me so horrible a catch?" he chuckled into her forehead, trying desperately to be the levity she needed "There is no way in heaven or hell that I would allow that horrible monster of a man to step anywhere near you again, let alone have you be forced to make good on that betrothal. I dare say our angelic Miss Darlingwood will no doubt agree." He kissed her forehead again as the carriage carried them down the road. The Colonel followed them closely on horseback, watching behind them for signs of Mr. Sutton if he was fool enough to follow.

Fitzwilliam had given her his handkerchief and she wiped away what she could of the blood from her mouth and her tears, feeling dirty and shaken and horrified that any woman should have to suffer such violence and worse. What if they had not come in at that moment? What if she had not left the note for them? She shivered and the tears started fresh. They welled so much so that when she saw the lone rider ahead, she sunk into Fitzwilliam in fear that it was Mr. Sutton, cutting across their path to fetch her and finish what he'd started. But as they drew nearer, Fitzwilliam squeezed her gently.

"It is all right, dear cousin, it is our much-beloved friend."

When she looked up, the road dust settled at the chestnut legs of Matthew Blackwell's steed. When his eyes found her, his jaw tightened at the sight of her broken despair and bruised body. His horse jumped and neighed, and shied with his rage. He circled the carriage and addressed not Lillian but the Colonel.

"What has happened? Who did this?" He looked back to Lillian who could only meet his eyes but not speak.

"Doctor Blackwell, we've just come from your cousin's. I am ashamed to say he has been caught in the act of most deplorable behavior—"

"You needn't say more," Doctor Blackwell growled and set his sights on the road leading back to Sutton Manor. His heels twitched to dig into the sides of his steed but Lillian's voice broke out of its cage to yell at him.

"Pray, sir, do not!"

Matthew stopped, circled back around and came close to look at her, teary eyed, bloody and shaking. Lillian's head began to swim and her vision clouded, but rather than faint, she saw the pages of her mother's journal, and watched as the words blurred and changed before her eyes.

A duel, death...a woman drown herself from grief.

This history was in danger of an ending more tragic than the first and she was the one changing it. She must stop him.

"Please, Doctor Blackwell," she said composing herself. "Please do not confront him in his angry state."

"And you think me *not* angry, Miss Byrne?" he growled.

"I think you too angry to let your good sense win out. I fear for your safety. And the oath you have sworn."

Matthew paused, the Colonel and Fitzwilliam were quiet in their observation.

"You needn't worry about my safety, Miss Byrne. I only mean to have a discussion with my cousin."

"I beg that you do not," she whispered and shook her head at him while her tears fell. Matthew's horse pranced back and forth along the road, torn between the mixed signals in his master's body and the pull of indecision in Matthew's heart. Fitzwilliam spoke.

"Doctor Blackwell, please. My cousin has sustained injuries in the altercation. She could use your expertise and I feel there could be no better physician for her current state," he looked down to Lillian whose eyes had dropped.

Matthew looked frustrated with the situation, he glared at the road behind them and then down at her. Lillian could tell he was torn between wanting to take her into his arms and the very acute desire to murder his cousin.

Promptly. Painfully. Without remorse.

"Please, Matthew," she said again, using his name despite the company of others and shook her head to the angry and vengeful thoughts she could read on his face. Matthew grunted and veered his horse in the direction of Westbury Manor.

"I shall accompany you to safety and see to Miss Byrne's injuries," he said to Fitzwilliam, avoiding looking at her. His horse huffed under the tension he was pouring over with. "But make no mistake, I will be paying a call to my cousin."

"Perhaps we should consult the authorities?" Fitzwilliam offered. "I do not know much of legal proceedings but I would wager a constable from London might be called?"

"No," Matthew said simply. "I know my cousin. The length of his reach in the county and in London are powerful. I fear that if justice is to truly be served, it must be done outside the laws of this land."

"Matthew," Lillian said, as her vision was pulled back to the haze of the journal once more changing with his words. Her eyes glazed over and all she could do was try to keep up with the changes that seemed to shift in the journal's pages, unsettled and all things possible.

It was a murder of a most heinous nature, Doctor Blackwell was taken away to prison, and shortly thereafter, the gallows. Our cousin became a woman so deep entrenched in grief of her fiancé murdered and her lover hanged, she was driven towards the Avon with nothing left to lose.

Lillian passed out promptly and Matthew had very little choice but to help assist Mr. Byrne in seeing her safely home.

When they arrived at the gates of the manor, the Colonel rushed ahead to prepare Lillian's room and to send for Mrs. Shaw who knew what the doctor might require. Fitzwilliam, being strong of heart but somewhat slender of body required that Doctor Blackwell help him take Lillian from the carriage and the good doctor carried her up the grand staircase to her room.

"From where does this blood come?" he barked at Fitzwilliam as he laid her in the bed and looked at her mouth. "Where is the wound?" his hands moved frantically over her face, her neck. The

Colonel helped to adjust the pillows and move a table closer to the bed.

"'Tis not hers," Fitzwilliam responded intensely to match the Doctor's lack of decorum. "It is Mr. Sutton's. It would seem that she, well, she bit him I think, his lip. Quite hard."

Matthew's frantic pace to inspect every delicate inch of her neck slowed and he looked at her peaceful face as she remained unconscious but still lightly breathing.

"Bit him?" he said. Such lack of decorum indeed. "Good for you, Lily," he said softly and smoothed an errant strand of hair from her forehead.

Miriam came with the hot water and bandages and gasped to see the horrifying state of her young charge.

"Saints, child! What's happened? Did she fall?"

"She was attacked," Doctor Blackwell said and wet a clean towel to wipe away the dried blood. He must remove as much of it as he could and as quickly as possible. He would have her rinse her mouth thoroughly with brandy as soon as she was able. Who knew what darkness resided in that man's blood?

"Attacked? But she was just going to call upon Mr. Sutton per the Lady Mayfield's orders." Miriam covered her mouth and gasped. "You mean to tell me that *he* done this to her?"

"I'm afraid I am not privy to all of the facts madam, but it would appear that is the case," Doctor Blackwell said.

"That bloody bastard, I'll string him up from the old oak, I will, bare handed," Miriam seethed as her round cheeks turned red.

"Madam!" Fitzwilliam said, but Matthew smiled back at her.

"Together you and I, Lady Miriam, we will sort that bastard out," he said as Lillian's eyes fluttered open and she flinched in response to the memory of being struck, backing up into the pillows with frantic effort. Tears renewed, gasping breaths heaved in her chest, still speckled with blood.

"Find ease, dear cousin, you are safe," Fitzwilliam came to her bedside and soothed her with soft words of comfort. The Colonel stood at the foot of the bed and watched, a mixture of pain and remorse on his face. The same look Lillian had seen when she had broken her collarbone at six. When she'd suffered the flu in fifth grade. When he'd walked away from them two years ago.

"I have failed you," the Colonel said softly. The other men and Miriam stared, between the two people. "Doctor Blackwell, Mr. Byrne, dear Miriam, if we could have a moment?"

"I will not leave her side," Matthew replied plainly. The Colonel smiled and chuckled. He nodded his head.

"Of course you won't. You love her. I had so hoped it wouldn't come to this."

Matthew looked down at her, but Lillian's eyes stayed on her father.

"Whatever affection I have, it was not her fault," Matthew said.

"Of course it was not. She is merely Lily. One cannot help but love her," the Colonel said. "Even when she infuriates you."

"Once I address her wounds, Colonel Mayfield, I beg you accompany me to Sutton Manor to set things—"

"You can't go! You'll murder him and be hanged for it," Lillian said suddenly, and only the Colonel lacked a surprised expression.

"My darling, you do not know that," Matthew said. But Lillian's eyes went far away as though she was reading letters on a wall above his head. The Colonel stepped forward and cleared his throat.

"If you please, Doctor Blackwell, our Lillian knows a great deal about possible future events," he said.

Miriam looked to Lillian, and the memory of their conversation about Lillian's fall swept over her features. "Because she fell from the future," Miriam said then covered her mouth with her hands. Both the Colonel and Matthew looked at her in surprise.

"What in the devil are you talking about?" Matthew breathed. The Colonel sighed.

"I think we all need to take a moment. Calm our nerves, until we are prepared to discuss all that has happened."

"Why not discuss it now?" Lillian started.

"This is not the time!" her father returned.

"If you please, there's no need to shout," Fitzwilliam broke in.

"Now please everyone, stay calm," Matthew held out his hands.

"Tell everyone who you really are!"

"Lillian, you don't grasp the implications—"

"What does she mean?"

Everyone's voices rose in a cacophony of noise and emotion until the room was nothing but a den of accusations and confusion.

"Enough!" shouted Matthew with such a commanding voice that it sliced through all of the rest and immediately cut them all short. "That is enough! I have no knowledge of the lies or traumas that have befallen this household. But I do know that Miss Byrne has suffered great injury and you will all leave this room until her safety and physical well-being are taken care of! It wouldn't harm any of you to retire to separate rooms whilst we calm our nerves. I myself will stay here so as to not," he looked at Lillian, "upset our patient further by confronting her attacker. Though he justly deserves it."

The room was quiet and they all looked at one another in more shock than agreement. There was some uncomfortable dawdling but one by one they walked, sullen and haltingly out the door.

"You will let us know if you should need anything?" Fitzwilliam said over his shoulder.

"I will," Matthew said dismissing him with a nod. "Miriam," Matthew said, avoiding eye and body contact with Lillian while he readied a bowl and towels. "If you please, more warm water, boiling if you have it, my medical kit from Sarah, and some brandy if you can dig up."

"Yes sir, right away. Er, will you be using the brandy for the instruments, or—"

"Yes and for myself. And the patient should she need it. Hell, bring yourself a glass while you're at it," he said smugly and rolled up his sleeves. Lillian watched his sinewy arms lit by the late afternoon sun. The rays caught on the golden hair and taut muscles. His hands, deft and nimble, meant to heal not to hurt.

When Miriam left the room, Lillian swung her head suddenly to him. "You must believe me. I swear I did not ask for the attention he so brutally bestowed. I did not go there for the purpose, he—"

Matthew held up his hand. "There's no point in explaining."

"But I must! I could not bear it if you thought me the sort of woman who would do such a thing."

"I know," he said calmly again and closed the curtains. He lit the lamps beside her bed and went about setting a table closer to her bedside. "I was told you were required to go by Lady Mayfield."

"She threatened to tell the entire county that you sullied my honor." Lillian rolled her eyes and waited while he came to her with a clean and wet cloth. She leaned into his deft and firm touch as he took the blood from her skin.

"Did I not?" he whispered. Something akin to shame and sweet memory played on his downturned face and she wanted to pull him into bed with her, lock the doors and truly commence with a good sullying.

"You did not. You are," her voice broke, "so good and true a man."

"Lillian."

"I must leave," the words left her mouth before she had time to consider them. Silence sat between them as Matthew carefully removed the blood.

20

LILLIAN'S RESPITE

"What do you mean?" Matthew said softly.

"I fear he is still intent on ruining us all, especially now, after what has transpired," Lillian said as Matthew calmly considered. She had no way of knowing what was going on in his head. That he was angry and afraid for her, was evident, but a calmness had come over him and she wasn't sure if it was a ruse to lull her to complacency so he could return to Sutton's manor and kill him, or if he was merely sad at the prospect of her leaving.

"I don't pretend to know the heart of a man so heartless. I do know he detests losing. That there will be action against you and your family is almost assured, but I cannot say to what extent." He went to the window and gazed out. Lillian watched him and tried to remember her vision of the changing journal, but with her body no longer soaked through with adrenaline, she could not see what would happen. Matthew started to pace, his hand over his mouth, his breathing coming hard and fast through his nose. Lillian stood, wobbly and uncertain but she could not lie still while he moved.

"What did the Colonel mean?" he asked and turned back towards her. Lillian looked up at him. That was not what she'd expected him to bring up. The man had attention to detail, even when it was unhelpful. She wasn't sure she knew how to explain it, or if it would completely upend the rational man of science.

"It's difficult to explain," she said. "I have much to explain to you, I know that. It's just that I," her body felt unsteady and she rocked where she stood trying to find a way to tell Matthew the absolute truth without causing him to think she was mad. "I don't know where to begin." Her shaking hands dropped to her side.

"Lily," he whispered and came closer. He made her sit on the bed and sank in beside her. He gently pushed back a lock of her hair. Lillian closed her eyes, from shame of her whole part in this mess. She was screwing it all up.

"None of this would have happened if I hadn't fallen down those stairs. I have made such a mess of things," her voice shook.

"You've done no such thing. You have only ever been your brilliant, albeit clumsy, self."

"If I had been kinder, if I had not—"

"Do not blame your pure and gracious heart for the actions a man of violence took." Matthew tilted her chin up to meet his gaze. "Never have I seen such bravery," he whispered. "In everything that has taken place since your fall, you have been so brave." Tears filled his eyes and Lillian's heart was lost.

Miriam arrived with hot water, cloths, the brandy, and some of her own herbs from the kitchen. She stood by, ready to help, and did not say anything when Matthew used slow and patient strokes to remove the small amount of remaining blood from around Lillian's chin and neck. He inspected her skin with his fingers. She had bruises from what he guessed were Frederick's teeth, on her chin and from his hands on her neck.

Miriam only made angry and disgusted noises as the cloth came back to her to be disposed of. They both, with regard and no dramatics, helped Lillian out of her bloodied dress and left her in only her shift. Miriam stood, like a guardian sentinel at the door, while Matthew made Lillian rinse her mouth out thoroughly with the brandy and spit into the bowl beside the bed. The liquid burned and she coughed violently after gargling with it. He soothed her, gently trailed his warm hand up and down her back as she spit out the bloody mess. He poured himself and Miriam a medicinal dose and gave Lillian a glass of water. Her head hurt, her shoulders hurt. Everything hurt. Matthew gently washed the bruise across her cheek and put salve on it.

"You must be tired of attending to my injuries," she whispered. Matthew shook his head as he pulled her hair back to inspect the scar and her eye. Matthew's hand went to her cheek, caressing the small sharp corner of her jaw and delicately trailing to the bruises on her shoulders. Frederick's fingerprints had already appeared around the white flesh of her arms. It was he who shivered then.

"When I stop to consider how close I came," he paused and swallowed, "to living in a world without my Lily, it leaves me devoid of all sense of reason." He finished the thought and pulled her gently in to kiss her. Lily leaned into the warm pressure of his lips on hers. She tilted her chin up to capture his lips with her own again. Her cold fingers trailed up the open front of his shirt, nails tracing up his chest.

Miriam cleared her throat. Matthew took a sharp inhale and broke the kiss, but stayed, nose to her cheek, nuzzling into her skin and her breath and trying to control his own breathing.

"Forgive me," he said to the both of them. Lillian put her forehead to his, willing him to understand the battle warring within her heart. To stay, to go, to leave him behind, to take him with her. He had a life, a practice, dreams and aspirations. He might have had a family he was supposed to start. Maybe he was never meant to marry her. What if she was robbing the future of some influential person, a descendant of Matthew's? What if she changed the course of history by her selfish want of him. She wavered where she sat and he placed a warm kiss on her forehead.

"Lie back," he bent low, removed her shoes and stockings, lifted her feet and tucked her into the bed.

"You must not leave me," she muttered, feeling the effects of the day. The discovery of the door, the violent assault, the confusing sway of history and truth that rattled through her neurons. Comfort was the only thing her body and mind wanted. Comfort in his arms.

"Please stay," she whispered, and her hand grasped at his forearm. Matthew looked up to where Miriam had finished her whisky without so much as a wince.

"Aye, ye best do as she says. Remove your boots if you please," she said like a mother commanding. Matthew smiled and did as he was told. Miriam went to the bed, untied the heavy curtains at its corners and sealed them safely inside, away from the world.

"I'll see to it you'll not be disturbed, so long as you let her rest and not try anything ungentlemanly."

"You have my word," he responded, taking Lillian in his arms, the dreamlike delight of his warm weight beneath her, her leg draped over his. His arm around her shoulders, holding her head against his heartbeat. Lillian made a small whine.

"Not even a little ungentlemanly?" she said into his collarbone and he smiled.

"Rest, love."

When Lillian woke, she was alone. She pushed open the heavy curtains and bolted out of bed, heart racing and covered in sweat. She found him sitting in the chair beside the bed, reading a medical journal, bare feet propped up on the bedframe, shirt open, candlelight casting a warm glow over his skin and the golden highlights in his hair.

"You left me?" She gave him her best false indignation, to

which he smiled, caressing the stubble on his jaw as he studied her messed hair and thin chemise.

"I extracted myself so that you might rest."

"Did you think I would not rest if you were in bed with me?" She lifted her skirt to get out of bed and flashed a long pale thigh, he studied her as she stood beside his feet.

"I know you would not have if I had stayed. I was nearly hysterical with wanting you." Matthew said seriously. "My hands were wandering beneath your clothes and you were responding to the questions they asked." Lillian blushed. "I did not think it was right to continue until you were fully conscious." Lillian came closer to him. He dropped his legs and she climbed brazenly into his lap, legs spread, round bottom against his thighs. Matthew grunted and sat up.

"I'm conscious now," she whispered and bent her head to kiss him just as a knock sounded on the door.

"As are other people in the house, it would seem," Matthew growled, his hands on her backside gave a squeeze and he gently lifted her off. Lillian sighed and reached for a robe. Mrs. Shaw came in with the desire-killing news that the Colonel would like a word with Miss Byrne. Presently. She added the last word with a look at the two half-clothed lovers before removing the tray of cloths and cold water. Lillian tightened the robe around her.

"It seems you have things to discuss," Matthew said.

"As do we, when I return," she responded, bent low, kissed him above his eyebrow and messed up his hair before leaving.

He watched her go, heart pounding out of his chest. Matthew wondered, perhaps, if she had been called to the Colonel's office for a negotiation. He dressed quickly, nervous and already decided where his heart resided. When she returned, if the outcome was favorable, he would ask the Colonel for her hand in marriage. Even if she needed time to think or recover, he did not mind waiting, so long as they could be together someday.

～

Lillian took a lantern through the darkened halls of Westbury Manor. No doubt Lady Mayfield had been told of the events of the day, as she had made herself reclusive. She hoped that the horrid woman felt some remorse. But it was probably not the case. At best, she probably just held simmering disappointment that she would have to go on supporting Lillian Byrne for longer, now that no good, socially acceptable man would want her after such deplorable behavior.

Well, she wouldn't have to worry about Lillian much longer. One way or another, she planned to be gone from Westbury Manor soon. She hoped, as she knocked on the Colonel's door quietly, that her father might finally have the answers.

"Come in," the Colonel called, and she opened the door. He was at his desk, standing behind it, studying charts and journals. He looked up when Lillian came in and a soft smile played over his lips.

"How are you?"

"I feel like I've been punched in the face."

"Rightly so, but if I may say, good show not letting that stop you."

"Well, I guess I'm not as fainting a damsel as I should pretend to be."

Her father looked down. "I'm sorry. I'm sorry I ever asked you to—"

"I understand the implications. But I also understand that I won't let myself be killed. There has to be another way."

"I was recruited by the Timekeepers when I was not much older than you. I've spent much of my life correcting time. Free will is never looked upon with favor in these situations."

"So they're mad at me? For fighting back?" Lillian's anger bubbled up in her chest. "Maybe if they'd do something about it, and get me home, I'd stop being such a bother."

"After your encounter this morning, I received at letter." The Colonel bent and dug into his coat pocket and withdrew a tattered and torn piece of parchment. "It's a map of time rifts. An older one. The guild rarely uses them anymore with their new technology."

"That's it? They gave you an antiquated map to help find our way home? What are time rifts?" Lillian said. Her father handed the map to her, urging her to be gentle with its frayed edges.

"They cannot risk you knowing too much. And I suspect they aren't pleased with my continued involvement. So they are giving us only the bare minimum in navigation tools."

"To navigate time rifts? What in the hell *is* a time rift?" she said and looked over the map.

"Places people have documented strange things happening, especially around celestially significant times. Like little doorways that open in the time space continuum, weak points, like threads in the cloth of time, that are pulled at by the astrological shifts all around us. Drawing different times together at coinciding points."

"And the Timekeepers use them?" she asked.

"We have more precise methods these days." The Colonel smiled and pointed to a small red mark. "See this? That's Westbury, the town and lands. I postulate that it's almost as if a stitch were sewn near this manor, so the fold tends to return, but never in exactly the right time. Sometimes years before, sometimes far too late," his voice drifted off. Lillian stared at the spot for a long time. So, perhaps Miriam had been right. There were places, like the faerie stone, that could be doorways through time. She thought hard before she spoke.

"You came here and married a completely different woman than Mom?"

"As you know, in this day and age, marriage is a matter of convenience and comfort more often than of love."

"Is that why you agreed to let me be engaged to that man?"

Lillian pointed angrily towards the northern property where no doubt Mr. Sutton was currently plotting her death.

"The line time follows is a funny thing Lil, you can never be sure what small act or how the tiniest decision may be the butterfly wings that set off the whole course of history. Now that I am assured of Mr. Sutton's intentions to you, and you have, in your own clever way, assured the engagement of your brother to Miss Darlingwood, the timeline is following the original path enough, that maybe your part will be less consequential."

Lillian's heart fell. "So," she swallowed and clutched the map close to her chest. "We'll be able to leave?"

Her father studied her face. "If it is what you still want."

When Lillian looked up at him, her eyes stung. "I thought I was so sure. But—"

"But Doctor Blackwell has thrown a wrench in the works?"

"It's silly, isn't it? I'm being ridiculous."

"My darling, love is never ridiculous," he said softly.

"But if he was not intended for me, then by staying I'm jeopardizing his future."

Her father sighed and shook his head. "I cannot say. It is quite possible he would have never married. I haven't been able to contact anyone directly about the details in play, and I hadn't inquired about Doctor Blackwell's thread before."

Lillian felt sick to her stomach and wanted to throw up. She leaned against his desk and looked at the worn map. Her father came around to sit beside her.

"You have much to consider," he smiled and took her hand gently in his. She held on and the strangest warmth crept up her arm as though she was reunited with something from her true life. "Luckily, I believe you will have some time. But not forever to decide."

Lillian's face drew into a frown. "Do we know that Sutton will not still try to kill me?"

"Time and space have a way of seeking balance. Part of what

drew Fitzwilliam and Kitty together was the tragedy of your disappearance. The man is unpredictable and violent and I fear I cannot guarantee he will not attempt something. But you are safe here, with me."

Lillian looked down and sniffed. "I do not wish to run forever from him."

"I do not wish that for you either. I've only ever wanted you to live a full and happy life, Lil."

She looked back up at him and felt her heart heal one stitch more. "Thanks, Dad." Her voice was far away in thought. She did have much to consider.

21

AN ALMOST-PROPOSAL AND
THOUGHTS OF MURDER

When Lillian returned to her room, Matthew was tying his cravat and getting ready to put his coat on.

"Where are you going?"

He smiled and looked at her slyly. "Miss Miriam may have allotted us a brief respite, but me spending an entire night in your bed would be unsuitable, unless you were my wife," he said the last phrase softly as though in question of her conversations with the Colonel. Lillian came to him, her face starting to throb with the still fresh bruise. He did not step away but his hands went to her shoulders and he studied her face.

"I'm afraid I don't look like bride material of late."

His eyes lowered. "If I had been there—"

"Then you would have done something rash, and that man has an innumerable number of guns, and no qualm in using them on animal or man," she whispered with a tremor in her voice. Her hands came up to grasp at his arms and she shook. "I fear for your safety."

Matthew huffed and looked down. "Isn't it I that should be saying that to you?"

"I wish we could leave this place," she said softly. "Disappear, never be found again," the words felt like a curse in her mouth and she leaned in to bury her face in his chest. He held her close.

"How did your conversation with the Colonel go? Were you able to come to some conclusions?" he asked softly into her hair. Lillian sighed and wrapped her arms around his middle. She did not know how to respond. How could she even begin to explain? And if she did, would he think she was mad and refuse to follow her into the future? She chose her words very carefully.

"He is afraid for me. He only wants to see me happy and well."

"As am I," Matthew whispered. "As do I," his arms went around her and he kissed her temple.

"He does not know if I will ever be safe, so long as Frederick Sutton breathes." Matthew pulled away and leveled his eyes on her. "Do not," she stopped him and put her finger on his lips. "Do not speak words that would tarnish your soul. I believe the man deserves dire consequences, but you will not be the one to exact them on him."

"Oh? And who should? You?" He looked down. "Do you not think I am also concerned with your soul?"

"Perhaps fate will step in and balance out his indiscretions."

"If fate were to find a balance to that man's cruelty, he would die in the most painful of ways," Matthew said darkly, and a shiver ran up Lillian's spine. He felt the shuddering of her body and held her closer. "I'm sorry, my darling. I did not mean to frighten you. Let us not dwell on such things tonight. I wish for you to rest, so that I may see you in the morning."

"I wish for you to stay, so that I may rest," she said softly with an expectant hope that she knew he would have to deny.

"You know I cannot," he smiled sadly. "Perhaps someday though," he whispered and took her left hand in his right one. He caressed her ring finger with the sensitive pad of his thumb and stared down at the empty space. She did the same with his and they let the moment pass between them. If only fate would only be kinder, they might never have to leave one another's side.

"Someday," she said.

Matthew pressed a kiss into her forehead and another on her cheek. She leaned up and caught his lips with hers and he fell into the sweet pressure before pulling away with a sigh.

"Lily, don't start, or I won't be able to leave you, and then Lady Mayfield would hang us both," he smiled. Lillian pouted and kept his hands in hers.

"How shall I ever feel safe if you leave?" She knew she wasn't a damsel in distress, but she was willing to play it if it meant she could have a few more kisses.

Matthew looked despondent and sighed. "The Colonel has assured me that he and your brother are taking turns on watch tonight and the servants have been alerted to Mr. Sutton's actions. No one in this house, save the horrible Lady Mayfield, would ever let harm come to you."

"Where will you be?"

"I have an important matter to discuss with my father."

"Whatever about?" Lillian scowled up at him. He shook his head and leaned in to kiss her temple.

"I will reveal all when I am assured of the outcome."

"You must promise me that you will not seek out Mr. Sutton."

"I swear it to you, Lily," he whispered softly even as his eyes turned darker with the thought. "I will not harm him on this night."

She scowled up at him. "Or any night."

"I cannot be expected to make that promise." He shook his head and she sighed.

"Then kiss me, so that you can go, so you can return all the more quickly to me," she said, even as tears sprung up in her eyes. He wiped them away and placed a kiss on her trembling lips.

"It is but a few hours," he said softly and kissed her once more before taking his coat and hat and leaving her bed chamber.

. . .

The space felt eerie without his even breathing and warmth. She sat in his chair and picked up the journal he'd been reading. She thumbed through the intricate drawings of a cadaver and the lines pointing to various signs of disease. Matthew was indeed a smart man, kind, intelligent, calm headed, and rational. She'd never been afraid of him, but the intensity of his voice and gaze made her realize that he would kill for what he loved. He had yet to speak those words to her.

Lillian was anxious with the jumble of thoughts in her head. That she wanted to go home. That she wanted to stay with Matthew. That she needed to rid the world of Sutton before he could harm anyone else, especially her or Matthew. That she was only a small cog in the giant storm of history and powerless to sway the hands of fate. She did not sleep, but tossed and turned in the bed she wished he was still occupying.

The impatient rapping on her door woke Lillian with a start and her brain seized with the violent episode of yesterday, causing her to sit up abruptly and tumble out of bed, trembling with fear, as she held the blanket to her chest. She felt the rapid beat of her heart through the fabric and before she could call a response to the knock, the door opened and her father stepped inside, still in his clothes and looking hurried.

"Lil?" His eyes searched the dark room and lit on the empty bed. "Are you here?"

"I'm here," she whispered and rose from the floor, willing herself to calm down. She came around to him. "What is it? Are you okay?"

"Earlier today you said, with much conviction that Matthew would be hanged for the murder of Sutton if he sought him out."

"I did."

"How did you come to this conclusion?"

"I—I guess I saw it? Like a hallucination? When he was talking, it was as if I were back in my time, reading Fitzwilliam's journals, only the story was different from before I left. That the great scandal of the season came from a young doctor murdering his own cousin, over a woman. It was so real, but I don't understand how it could be rational."

The Colonel smiled smally, "I've just heard from the office in Westbury."

"And?"

"How long have you had these visions?"

"Not long, just after the fight with Sutton. Why?" she asked, studying the sweat beading on her father's brow.

"The Timekeepers are highly interested."

"In me?" Lillian scoffed and wrapped the blanket around her shoulders in the chilly room. "I'm an accident," her voice drifted away.

"Perhaps there is a greater purpose for you here. Perhaps there's a reason the rift opened for you," he responded softly. "Are you able to tap into those visions?"

"Not since I was upset," she said and shook her head. "Why?"

"I am afraid that despite his vows to keep distance from his cousin, Matthew might do something rash."

"What do you mean? How do you know?"

"The guild contacted me that his thread has changed, it is undetermined yet what he intends to do. But I fear he means to act against Sutton. It would irrevocably alter the course of the timeline."

She adjusted the blanket and came closer. "No, that can't be right! He said he had a matter to attend to with his father. He—he lied," she breathed and leaned against the post of the bed. "If he does something to Sutton, they'll catch him. He'll be hanged. Where is Sutton now?"

"My sources say he is currently on his way to London. I have reason to believe that he's reaching out to some of his contacts there in order to enact some type of retribution."

"But why? Why can't he simply accept the loss and move on?" Lillian said angrily and rose to pace the room.

"He is not a man who accepts losses, I'm afraid."

"And Matthew intends to intercept him on the journey?"

"I believe so."

"And murder him?"

"I believe so."

"Idiot! Stupid, stubborn asshole!" she yelled and rushed to her armoire to grab a dress and her underclothing.

"Lillian, you mustn't. I have been up all this night, calculating the upcoming astrological alignments. If my calculations are right, you have only two days to try and return home!" The new information hit the wall of her worry for Matthew. Days were longer than the hours it would take for Matthew to seal his fate in the pages of an old journal.

"Well, I'm not going to let the man I love commit murder and be tried for it."

"And just how do you intend to stop him?" The Colonel stood between her and the door not knowing that Lillian had already snuck out the window once before and was not afraid to do it again.

"I will simply have to kill Sutton first," she said.

"You cannot, and will not. I won't allow it." Now her father was in the room with her, not just some kind and caring patriarch, but the man who had raised and risked his life to save her. "I did not come this far, through time and trials to see you hanged for murder, or worse to put a stain on your immortal soul."

"My immortal—Dad, really? That man has murdered and tortured hundreds of people. He could kill Matthew. I believe he's probably killed me before, and would gladly do so again. It's past time that the world was rid of him."

"Then let me do it," he said quietly and dropped his chin to his chest. "Killing a man is not as easy a pulling a trigger, Lil. It leaves a mark on you."

"And just how do you know that?" Lillian stopped her frantic hopping into stockings and looked up at him.

"It matters not. Even when it's in defense of your life, it will follow you for the rest of your time on earth. I won't have you carry that weight or risk getting caught and losing your chance to get back to our time."

"What about you? Aren't you going to jump with me?"

"I still have obligations to the guild. Especially for their assistance in helping to save you." Her father's face seemed pale in the night at this confession.

"But I've only just found you again," Lillian said, pausing her desperate shuffle to get dressed.

"And it won't be the last time." The Colonel nodded. "I will intercept Matthew, before he can reach Sutton. Perhaps it's time we told him the truth, he's a man of science and may be swayed. Then—" her father paused and rocked back on his heels, "you can give him the choice to follow you into the portal."

Lillian's head swam, if she were to steal the doctor from this time, then what would happen to the continuum? Who would not be born? What diseases would not be cured? What lives not saved? She thought of the young boy who may have ended up disabled for his life without the doctor setting his arm when he had.

"I can't take him from this world. It would be selfish," she said and her eyes teared up. Her father watched her face and his own features drew into sadness.

"I would not have you parted. But you cannot live in a world where Sutton lives. And he cannot die by Matthew's hand."

"You're right," she nodded softly and her hand slipped beneath the covers to the metal bed warmer buried in her sheets. "You're right." She came closer to him and smiled. "I'm sorry, Dad. This is the only way." With a swift and determined stroke, the metal pan clanged against her father's temple and he fell, unconscious, to the rug. When she'd checked, he was breathing and truly out, she kissed his forehead.

"I don't envy the headache you'll wake up with," she said, "but I don't want to be the one always running from her death. I'm taking my fate in my own hands, on this trip." With that she snuck into her dad's room and stole a pair of his breeches and a shirt, vest, and traveling cap. She tucked her hair up in the cap and tightened the belt around her waist. London was a few days' ride, and if Sutton had started out hours before, she might still be able to catch up to his coach with a good steed. She slipped a couple of knives from the kitchen into her belt.

Then there would be the problem of getting there before Matthew. She sighed. Her mother would tell her this was an idiotic and ill-thought-out plan that was doomed to fail. And she would have been right. But it was all Lillian had to cling to now, and only hours to accomplish it before her only way back home would close, possibly forever.

22

VIOLENT ENDS FOR A
VIOLENT MAN

Lillian hadn't come across Sutton, and she'd been riding like the devil for over an hour. She hadn't seen Matthew either and worry filled her heart. What if she was already too late? What if Matthew had already killed him? Or worse, what if Matthew had been caught and was now on his way to the gallows? Or even worse that Sutton had instead killed Matthew?

It wasn't in Matthew's nature to kill. Though he was strong, he was a healer and she knew how much it would hurt his soul to take a life. She, on the other hand, had no qualms about Sutton not existing in this timeline or any other for that matter. These useless and panicked thoughts ran on a loop in her head, over and over, ever increasing in intensity so that she almost missed the sound of men's voices raised in anger just up ahead, on an intersecting road, off the main route. She slowed her horse, steadied her own breath, and turned in the direction of the noise.

Fifty yards off the road, standing next to an overturned carriage, Matthew held a rifle tight against his shoulder and pointed down towards one of the broken wheels where Sutton had propped himself up. The light of the kerosene lamps from inside the carriage lent an eerie glow to the new dawn approaching.

"You'd be a fool to do this. You won't make it past the next day before they'll be after you. When I am late to my destination, they will surely send someone," Sutton bellowed. Lillian hid in the grove of trees to the south and quietly dismounted. She tied her horse to a nearby branch before she snuck around the perimeter of the carriage.

"I'll not have you harm her again," Matthew's voice shook and Lillian could tell he would not pull the trigger.

"She is not yours to defend," Sutton growled.

"She's not yours to own!" Matthew countered. Lillian's heart sped up and she tried to decide how to best interrupt without giving Sutton the leeway to hurt Matthew, in case she distract them both. She snuck to the rear side of the carriage, thankful that the low light gave her a cover of shadows. If Matthew could just keep him talking a little while longer.

She reached into the back of her belt and grasped the handle of one of the knives she'd taken from Miriam's kitchen. Just as she moved around the side of the carriage, she saw Sutton shift, grab a pistol from a holster at his back and draw it. She did not have time, she let out a harrowing cry and leapt at Sutton, knocking the shot off by mere inches. Matthew's body did not crumple from a heart wound, but rotated where the bullet entered his shoulder and he spun before falling. The surprise of her attack caught Sutton off guard and he fell to the side, the gun dislodged and tumbled into the muddy backwoods road that he'd wrecked his carriage on, no doubt trying to avoid capture by Matthew.

"Stupid boy!" he yelled and scrambled for his gun as she searched to find the knife she'd lost in the rash move. Her hands found only clumps of grass and mud, but as she rose, she saw a glint of the knife in the rising sun. In Sutton's hands. He pointed the sharpened tip at her. She raised her hands. Her hat had fallen off in the struggle and her hair had come loose.

"Not a boy at all. You idiotic girl. Seeking out trouble again? Well, now you've found it," he growled and moved towards her. "First to go will be those ridiculous pants, and you'll learn a hard lesson for such hedonistic behavior. You want to be a wildling? I shall spread you like one. Then I'll slit that pretty little throat and defile you again." He licked his lips.

Lillian stood up slowly and checked her belt for the other knife, but it must have fallen. She was defenseless, but for her wits and the fact that she was still able-bodied. Sutton limped towards her. She backed away, hands out, around the carriage and trunk, its contents spilled and scattered in the rutted road. She fell backwards in one of the deep grooves and felt her ankle twist in a sharp shock of pain. The gravel bit into her palms and scraped them raw as she scrambled away from him.

"You're making it too easy. That's a good girl, already on your back," Sutton chuckled and moved closer. A rustle sounded from behind Sutton, distracting him, as Lillian's hands closed over the thick wooden handle of something as she found her footing.

"I will kill you," Matthew growled, staggering towards Sutton, the gleam of a scalpel blade flashed in the darkness, raised above Sutton's neck.

"No!" Lillian yelled and swung the weighted stick hard into Sutton's middle. But as she tried to pull it back to take another swing, she realized that it was stuck. The axe head was buried deep into Sutton's belly. Lillian yanked it out with a sickening gush of spurting blood and the cascade of Sutton's intestines followed. Wet and glistening, purple and red as they hit his shoes and he stared at them in wonder before looking back up at her. Matthew stepped away, scalpel falling to his side.

"Lillian," he gasped.

"Whore," Sutton stuttered and stumbled, dropping his knife to clutch at the writhing red snakes that seemed to slither from the opening in a rush. Lillian backed away, stood and kept the blood-wetted axe firmly in her hands.

"I hope that hurts, you son-of-a-bitch," she gasped. "It will still never be enough pain for what you deserve." Sutton looked at her, glassy eyes still filled with anger as he reached into his coat pocket with a bloody hand and withdrew another small pistol. He trained it on her heart but then swung it madly towards Matthew, now unarmed, weak, and close enough in range to have a bullet put in his brain.

The journal's pages filled her head. Ice ran through Lillian's veins.

Fair Lillian Byrne driven into the Avon, drowning herself after violent argument between her fiancé and lover that ended in both of their deaths.

Time is a funny thing.

For Lillian, it had been a set of chains, and an opening of a new world. It had been at once an enemy and a blessing. Time had taken her father from her and taken her life. It had given her Matthew. But in the moment before Sutton's finger could fully depress the trigger, time stood still. The axe felt heavy and kinetic in her hands. As though the universe had painted the exact path it was made to take, she let the weight of the sharp blade fall, severing Sutton's hand, then looping it back up in a swift figure eight that buried itself in the crook of his shoulder and neck. She did not pull it out but let loose the handle and Sutton fell to his knees, axe stuck in his thick neck, gun and hand fallen to the ground away from him. His eyes slowly dimmed before he toppled face first into the dirt.

"Lily," Matthew croaked and stumbled towards her. The smell of iron and human insides muddied the space between them and she gagged before covering her mouth with a sob. "Lily?" he said again, his voice shaking. She stumbled towards him and felt the warmth of his body fall into hers. She pressed her face to his shoulder and the bloodied cloth stuck to her cheek.

"You're hurt," she said softly and pulled away to look, but the light was too dim. He was bleeding, and his left arm hung limply at his side, unable to move, even to hold her.

"You are alive," he gasped.

"Of course I am, just as you left me. You nearly weren't," she said, angry and tearing off her vest to fashion a sling for his arm.

"Damn fool of a girl. He could have murdered you!"

"Oh? Says the damn fool who got himself shot?" Matthew groaned as she lifted his arm and tied it securely to his chest and neck.

"We are in danger," he whispered, sweat on his brow from the pain. "We haven't long before someone comes looking for him. And then for us. I have done this; you were never a part of it."

"No, I will not let you take blame for my actions." She shook in his arms for a moment and then took in a deep breath, wiped her nose on her shirt sleeve, and nodded. "Let us be sure they never find him," she whispered and turned to the carriage. Sutton had kerosene lamps in his carriage. Which meant he also had fuel. Accidents happen. Carriages overturn. Lamps catch their fuel source on fire. Bodies are burned. Matthew stared down at his cousin as she looked through the wreckage.

"I cannot," he gagged into his good hand and stepped away from the body. "I cannot believe you felled him like a tree," he coughed.

"Surely, as a doctor you've seen the insides of a man."

"Never ones so violently obtained."

"Violent men die by violent means," Lillian said and looked back at him. She could see from his eyes, that he was debating her eternal damnation. "He meant to kill you, then rape and kill me. Then probably defile me again," she said, having found what she wanted, turned back to him. "Would you have let him?"

"No! Of course not."

"Then let God deal with the things I have done. I cannot believe a higher power would judge me for saving the man I love and myself," she said softly. Matthew caressed her cheek with his bloody fingers. She nodded. "Now, step back. Best get my horse, when this goes up, it will be startling." She spread the kerosene over the body, the bones of the carriage and unfastened Sutton's horses, whipping them until they sped away towards the rising sun. Taking the flint and steel, she stared at the mess of a history she'd effectually rewrote. It was too late to change now. She needed to get Matthew and herself to safety and dress his wound before she left. Tears stung her eyes.

Damn this. Damn all of this. She swallowed a cry and struck the flint hard. The spark lifted, arched and fell perfectly into the fuel-soaked pile and immediately took light. Lillian stumbled and fell away from it, in time for Matthew to catch her up in his good arm.

"What have we done?" he whispered.

"Survived," she said and turned to help him onto her horse, before mounting behind him. Lillian took the reins and galloped away, back towards Westbury Manor.

23
LILLIAN LEAVES WESTBURY MANOR

The ride was long and perilous. Several times, she felt Matthew sagging against her as if he lacked the strength to stay upright. He had lost blood. The shock of the encounter and possible infection were the threats she worried about most for his survival. What good was saving him for his time, and murdering Sutton, if he didn't live? She rode faster, pushed the horse harder, whispered loving commands into his back.

"Steady. You will make it." She ached to drive them both into the portal, horse and all, and cross into a different world. A world where they could wash the blood and the sin of the last hours away. A world where the plume of smoke and the smell of cooked meat wasn't wafting over the countryside behind them. A world with antibiotics, and surgeons, and painkillers. "Stay with me, love, do not falter," Lillian cried into Matthew's back as she saw the faint glow of Westbury Manor in the distance. "I will save you," she said softly. "I will save *you* this time."

The last mile seemed the longest and when she arrived on the back steps of the manor, horse lathered with sweat and breathing hard, she nearly carried Matthew on her own over the threshold into the kitchen. He groaned in pain, skin slick and cold with sweat, and muscles tremoring. He was in shock. She took him to the fireplace, where embers still glowed, and built it up into a roar. As she laid him down on the stones, he looked up at her with glassy eyes, but she did not find his smile.

"Lillian," he shook his head. "Frederick," he mumbled and turned away, as if to look back to the carnage they had left behind. Lillian sobbed, heart breaking and hating herself in so many ways. If she hadn't done what she did, they would both be dead. But to have Matthew witness her transgression was the worst. She sniffed and went to fetch water, a knife, and her sewing kit from the parlor. By the time the water had started to boil and she had threaded a needle to sanitize, Miriam shuffled in, in her bedclothes, irate and holding a lantern.

"What's all—" she stopped. "Saints, child, what's happened?" She came closer to the light where the doctor moaned in pain and threw his head in fevered dreams of violence and death.

"Dear Miriam," Lillian said in a voice much stronger than she felt. "We must clean the wound, remove the bullet, and sew him up. It must be as clean as possible. Do you have whisky? And willow bark?"

"I do child, I do at that, and I will brew it. I will also pick some comfrey and burdock root and some fine onions and garlic, they's always good for drawing out the red." Miriam did not question why a decent and good man was bleeding to death on her kitchen floor or how her young charge knew so much about bullet wounds. She just did what needed done and Lillian loved her for it. They cleaned the wound, with near to boiling water and whisky, and Lillian worked, with steady hands, even as Miriam held the lantern close, to remove the heavy lead slug from his shoulder. Matthew cried out, a horrible, pained yell and grasped onto her thigh. He opened his eyes to see Lillian holding the bullet up in the flickering light.

"Lillian," he gasped and fell back. Miriam and Lillian cleaned the wound, packed it with a poultice and gently wrapped it and secured his arm to his chest. When it was all done, they sat back and watched him breathe. Lillian counted his heart beats by the pocket watch at his waist. Even, calm, resting. He stirred, eyelids fluttering open to see her.

"Have I been shot?" he whispered before falling back to sleep.

"Well, he didn't take it so well as you did the stairs, but I suppose we can't blame him too much. He is only a man after all," Miriam said and brushed his long blond locks from his face. A chuckle formed in Lillian's throat, and it grew into a pure and hearty laugh, letting loose the tension and horror of the past few hours and the relief that at least one thing, of all of it, had turned out well. Matthew would live.

Matthew was sure he had died. The pain and nightmares that followed him into the night and early the next morning made his head swim and his body shudder. He saw his cousin, holding his own intestines before drawing a gun. The oil slick metal of its barrel staring into Matthew's face as the eye of certain death. Then the gun was gone, along with Frederick's hand. And an axe was wedged in his neck like the trunk of a tree. And Lillian, face and clothing streaked with blood, let loose the handle and stared at him, a strange and calm resignation in her eyes. He didn't remember much after that. Jostling, white hot pokers in his shoulder, Miriam, Lillian, counting his breaths, laughing in a strange maniacal way. Sometime in early morning, the Colonel, his own head bruised, helped the ladies carry him to Lillian's room, where he rested more comfortably.

And now he was awake, and she was beside him, eyes closed but not asleep. He knew because her fingers were on his wrist, counting his heartbeats. She must have sensed the difference, because her eyes opened to find him staring at her.

"You're awake," she whispered. "You should be resting." He

could not speak. He did not know the proper words to express everything in his head and heart. One moment he was certain he would marry her, take her away from the danger. The next he wondered if she wasn't the danger herself.

"Frederick," was the surprising word on his lips. Lillian's face darkened.

"I'm sorry," was all she could say. He saw her close her eyes, trying to recall the memory but her brow pulled into a pout and she shook her head. "His death was an accident and I disappeared," she said softly, as if reading it from the backs of her eyes. A tear formed at the corner—between her long lashes and her pert nose—and it slid down her cheek. He moved to wipe it away, but his arm was tightly bandaged and every muscle hurt. When he tried to sit up, a wave of dizziness overtook him and he faltered backward. She settled him back into the covers, resting his head on the pillows. She tried to kiss him, but he turned away in his confused and weakened state, and felt his body go light, floating—weightless—down a river of sleep.

He did not see Lillian sob and cover her mouth at his slight. He did not see her gather her things from the chair beside the bed. He did not see her leave Westbury Manor. And he did not know it would be the last time she would run down those perilous stairs. He was too weak to open his eyes, and in far too much pain to rise and follow. Instead he succumbed, pulled back under into dreams of fire and blood.

24

LOVE THROWS A WRENCH INTO
ESCAPE PLANS

Lillian was nearly to the door. By the time she had packed a small bag, changed out of her bloody and fire-singed clothes, kissed Miriam and gifted her a journal and pens from her desk, it was nearly mid-day. She stopped at her father's office door and knocked, but there was no answer. When she opened the door she found a note addressed to her and broke the seal.

Dearest Lillian, I'm sorry to have to disappear yet again. The Timekeepers insisted that I come at once. I won't be long. Hopefully they have an answer to your way home.
Love, Dad.

Or, much more likely, the Timekeepers knew what she'd done and there was going to be multi-dimensional hell to pay. Maybe she should have waited for his return. Or at least until night, but Lillian would not risk retribution from an unknown guild, nor could she face Matthew waking up again and looking at her with the sorrowful judgement, the horror of knowing how murderous she could be.

Plus, she couldn't face her father. Because he was right. And he was wrong. Killing a man did indeed leave a stain inside of you. But she did not regret killing Sutton, only that Matthew had seen her do it. And even in not regretting, she felt a sense of shame. What kind of person had she become? To murder a man and still not be able to embroider a simple flower?

She did not belong in this timeline. And she did not belong near the goodness of Matthew Blackwell. She penned a note on the back of his envelope, telling him what she'd done and that she couldn't stay at Westbury. She knew of the portal, and suspected it was her own father that Miriam had witnessed coming through. She expressed hope that she would see him again, in time. That she would try to right the wrong of her being here. Of surviving.

She left in haste, away from Westbury Manor and towards the gate. She could not stay.

She and Matthew were not meant to be. The sun was swallowed up, the moment the thought crossed through her brain. A dark cloud, ominous and low with the threatening grumble of thunder in its belly, warned her a storm was coming.

On the eve of the portal opening, perhaps the sky felt the impending split of time and universes. Perhaps it was bellowing and weeping at her fate. The clouds that were once over the distant fields moved in swiftly over the supple green countryside. She had planned on camping beside the gate so as to not miss any opportunity of its opening. But she hadn't counted on the rain and she didn't fancy sleeping outside in a storm.

She was muddling through how she could possibly get a room as a woman traveling by herself, especially where someone was bound to recognize her, when she heard the approaching hoofbeats behind her. The urgency of the horse's gait and its heavy breath told her its rider was after something. She ducked quickly into the tree line and scrambled for cover.

The horse passed by and she let out a breath of relief, continuing on up the small hill to keep further into the forest, and away from any future encounters. But as she came to a small clearing, the roan stallion burst through the bushes and blocked her path. Lillian's heart thrummed in her chest and she screamed before tumbling backwards.

She righted herself and drew her bag close to her body as she stared up at the man, high on his steed. Her heart didn't know who she feared to find. It took her a moment to recognize him.

"What are you doing here?" she grumbled and righted her skirts, smoothed an errant lock of hair from her forehead, and looked for a less doctor-infested path to take.

"You're running away?"

"Perhaps we should just call it a nice, long walk for the sake of any future argument and you can go about living your life with a clear conscience."

"Live my life?" His horse danced in place agitated in the same way he was.

"I do not wish to impede your future plans to set up your practice in the South of Wales. Nor do I want to darken your life with the violent nature of my presence. I am unforgivable in my actions, and you are far too—" she paused and swallowed her tears, "—far too good a man to associate with someone like me. It would be best if we went separately into the world." She stared up at him resolutely, trying to contain the catch in her voice and the tremble of her chin.

"You seem to have a very assured opinion of what is best for me."

"I do. And I very much doubt that my presence in your life is that. I have caused you to suffer, and I cannot bear the disappointment in your eyes. Not for a moment, certainly not for a lifetime." She moved past the horse with ease on nimble foot and continued along a walking path that sprung up, leading back towards the road.

"You cannot go," he yelled, desperate and mad, from behind her as he urged his horse forward. "I beg of you," the words were softer as he dismounted awkwardly, still bandaged and lacking both arms to assist him. Despite his discomfort and the evidence of weakness in his pale complexion, he strode to her in a strong and purposeful gait.

"Doctor Blackwell, please."

"I cannot stand the coldness in you now. You are cruel to suppose I would be content to know you will suffer for your actions against my cousin. You are cruel to accuse me of being complacent in a life without you."

"Without me?" she said weakly and stopped walking. "Doctor Blackwell, if I am cruel, it is only because, I cannot ascertain your true feelings for me after last night."

"My true feelings?" he said achingly and came closer to her. "How could you even question my heart? When it has been yours since the very start."

Lillian hesitated, her heart stopping at his confession. Her face fell in confusion and pain. Matthew dropped the reins and allowed his horse to graze complacently beside him. He leaned close and whispered with equal intensity.

"However, if any doubt should remain in your heart of your feelings for me, tell me now, so that I may begin the mourning that shall own me until I am buried beneath the ground." Matthew took her hands in his. Her cold fingers folded into the warmth and strength of his. "I will not force you to love that which you do not. Put me out of my misery or curse me to it, but tell me now, in truth, what lies in your heart."

Lillian sighed out a cry and her fingers wove tightly into his as the words melted the resolve and doubt in her heart into nothing more than pathetic excuses. She bowed her forehead to touch his and her eyes clouded over. How could she leave him now? How could she have ever thought she could leave him before? Whether by oceans of salt, or oceans of time, the chances of them falling in love, of finding one another, was once in twenty lifetimes. The rain pattered through the canopy of trees and soaked into their clothing.

"As our pact of honesty would request, please, tell me now in truth, do I mean all or nothing to you?" he whispered.

"All," she returned softly. "By truth, there is no other answer but all." He sobbed and took her in his arms holding her close while she laughed and cried and clung to him as if he were the rock in the storm of the future yet to come. His arms shook and he breathed in gasps against her neck. Relieved and invigorated. She knew this happiness was incomplete while so much of the truth still lay hidden between them.

His hands were warm even as the cold afternoon shifted around them. The sky's haze began to gather into tight-knit clouds. The winds howled in the forests to the south, where she had been headed, and she could feel the energy in the air change as though every particle was beginning to charge, preparing for something big.

"I desperately need to tell you something," she said into his neck. "But I do not know how."

"Start at the beginning," Matthew said and kissed her temple. One hand came up to smooth away the loose strands of hair that danced around her face in the shifting, tempest winds.

"I am not from here," she said.

"I am aware, darling. You came from Sussex, wasn't it? Or Berkshire? I can't—I can't seem to recall right now."

"I'm from Illinois," she said. "Parker, Illinois to be exact."

"Illinois? I am unfamiliar with that township."

"In the United States," she said and leveled her eyes on him. Matthew drew away but kept his hands around hers. He looked quizzically at her, as though he was trying to determine if she'd had a relapse in cognition from the head injury.

"Of America," she elongated. He smiled and shook his head.

"Lily, that's impossible. You could not be from any part of that barbaric and rebellious—" he stopped and his eyes took on a strange light. She could feel it, as though all of their conversations were replaying in his mind and he was calculating every dropped word, every strange intonation, every mistaken phrase or brash use of language.

"I time traveled. I fell down the stairs in 2023 and woke up here, in 1812."

Matthew chuckled. "I don't know what kind of strange story you are attempting to weave but this is—" the thunder cut through his words and the winds assailed them with so much force that her bonnet was torn from her hands and her cloak whipped around them both. "We must get to shelter," he said and looked to the skies that had taken on a darker hue.

"But Matthew—"

"I assure you we will talk, my darling, but I will not risk losing you to the rising water of a swollen river in the face of such a threatening storm. I'll not have you drown on my watch," he said, and an eerie shiver shot up Lillian's spine. She wondered if she would ever be safe. She allowed him to take her hand and they ran back to where his stallion waited, nervous at the approaching storm. It pulled against the reins when Matthew took them up. After coaxing him to calm, Matthew allowed her up first, then he pulled himself up behind her. She assisted him with his wounded shoulder and once settled, he held her close to his chest.

"Seems we were here recently," he whispered in her ear. Lillian shivered and hung her head but Matthew only held tighter. "You promised to save me, and so you did," his warm lips touched her temple. "My strong and beautiful Lily, you have saved me," he said softly. The warmth he gave through her soaked clothes made her want to sink into his bones and never leave him.

Not far down the road was the small town of Westbury for

which the manor was named, with a pub, lodging and several small merchants as it was a crossroad for travelers. They entrusted the horse to the stable hands of the inn and Matthew escorted her inside, still clinging to her small satchel as if she were a child who had tried to run away but only made it as far as the gas station down the street.

Matthew left her beside the warmth of the fire in the front room of the quiet inn, and went to find her accommodations for the night. The storm raged outside, to a degree that she did not think it safe to leave for fear she might actually drown from the rain itself. She could not be but a league from the stone, less than an hour's walk. She had almost made it, but fate had chosen to throw him into her path once more.

And the truth was that she did not wish to leave him.

When it was all settled, he came back for her, took her small and drenched satchel and helped her climb the narrow wooden staircase to the room at the far end of the hall, away from the noise of the street. A fire had been prepared but not started in the small grate by the bed. They both stopped upon entering the room and stared at the clean covers and welcoming softness of it. Matthew's hand intertwined with hers, warm fingers delicately caressing her sensitive palm.

"Matthew, what I said earlier, where I come from—"

"Lily," he started, fingers flexing into hers. "I don't pretend to know all of which exists in the universe. I do not understand what you've told me, but I've never known you to lie, so I am having a difficult time. All I know is that you are real, and here with me now. Safe. When I woke to find you gone, my heart would not be still. Miriam was reluctant to tell me where you had gone but I assured her that I meant to find you."

"Matthew—"

"And marry you."

Lillian was struck speechless. Her eyes fell to the bed and then back to him. His features flashed in the brilliance of the lightning strikes outside and his gaze seemed to mirror her own need. Suddenly time travel was the furthest thing from her mind and she couldn't imagine running away from a destiny that included his body against hers beneath those sheets.

"You would marry me? Even after everything?"

"*Because* of everything. Everything you are, and mean to me. Your brilliance, your fire. I would marry you for the selfish purpose of simply being able to bask in the glow of your presence for the rest of our days."

"You make it so difficult," she said, lips trembling even as she stared at his.

"What do I make difficult?"

"To act a lady, and not want to reward such beautiful words," she said and pressed her body against his. How he could be so warm, even after being soaked through? Her skin ached to crawl inside of him, the quiet only heightened her sense of awareness of everything about him. Her breathing quickened.

"I confess my thoughts are turning to similar conclusions. Only it's I that want to reward you," Matthew said softly, looking at her and then to the large bed in the small room. Lily turned her face up to him, eyes searching as her fingers caressed his.

"Even for running away?" she said and brought his hand to her lips. Matthew tore his eyes away from the large and plush bed and back to her.

"And did I not thwart your brave plans to save my soul and reputation?"

"I—" she paused to swallow, tears gathered and crowded in her eyes. "Matthew, I want for so many beautiful things that I fear we cannot have." Matthew pulled away and studied her. She was shaking, her shoulders shivering so violently in moments that her whole body seemed to convulse. Her bottom lip trembled and she felt her cheeks blush as he watched her. Another round of shivering shook her body.

"You are cold," he whispered and kissed her hand sweetly. "Let me build us a fire, so that you may compose your thoughts," he said, and she wished he would just pull her into his arms and keep her safe from the uncertainty of what would happen next. She only had a few hours until the sunrise would strike across the stone. Only a few hours to decide the course of her life.

"Once the room is quite warmed, I will see to it that they find me alternate lodging, even if it be in the stables, as long as I am close to you," he said and looked back at her from his crouch beside the slowly budding fire.

The events of the past two days and the confusion of want and love in her heart caused every neuron and physical cell to collapse into itself. She wanted to faint but her body was too excited.

"Be closer," she whispered hoarsely. "Please, do not go. I beg of you—please stay. Here with me."

A QUIET MARRIAGE AND A NOT-SO-QUIET CONSUMMATION (FINALLY)

"Miss Byrne—"

"Please, Matthew, call me Lily, or Angel, or Lillian, or stubborn girl. Anything but Miss Byrne."

"Anything?" he asked and stalked closer at the sound of her voice pleading with him. The flames behind him sprung to life and the room was lit with a warm glow that moved from her frozen feet all the way up her legs and between.

"Yes," she whispered as he stood before her.

"Seeing you in this light, safe with me, all I can think to call you is my love," he whispered. The crackle of the fire and the quiet falling of rain outside the room leant to the magical sense of destiny and desire that wound around them. She reached up to kiss his chin, the line of his jaw. She nuzzled into the skin of his neck and inhaled the scent of him. His hands trailed down her arms and his fingers dug gently into her skin, even as he pulled away.

"I know I should try to advise you against this," he gasped but her tongue had traced its way up the delicate line of the pulse in his neck and her teeth tugged at his earlobe and he seemed to lose all sense of being sensible. He pulled her up, close to his hard and straining body, and kissed her fully, his tongue delving into the warmth of her mouth. His hands came around her back, threaded through her free hair and pulled her head back as he began to kiss his way down her jaw, her throat, tenderly caressing the skin before kissing and biting at her delicate collarbones, below to the swell of her breasts, grunting with hard and desperate sounds.

Lillian took in gasping breaths and felt her whole body light with fire. Her fingers threaded through his hair as nuzzled between her breasts and sighed longingly into them.

"Lily, my beautiful angel. I want to taste each tender inch, worship you in a thousand different ways. Every ounce of your cream and sweetness," he whispered and his teeth found the hard bud of her breast beneath the fabric. He sucked and nipped at it and Lillian gasped in pleased surprise. His head snapped up quickly, blue eyes dark with desire and want.

"Please, if you need to stop me, do not fear to do so. You may tell me to leave and we will not speak of this moment again for the remainder of our days."

"What a sad life I would have if I should never relive this moment, if I should never remind myself over and over again, how your hands and mouth felt in praise of my body? What cause would I have to live at all without this? Without you?" she whispered.

"Lily, you speak words like spells that ensnared my heart and body. But the tender treatments from the secluded garden would not compare to the scandalous cures now in my mind. We are not wed, and this is a public establishment. To stay would be a risk to your reputation. It simply—"

"Isn't done?" she questioned and looked at him, with his breath running in waves, trying to catch up with the feelings they both shared in their mutual desire.

"You know this, Lily. You know it would mean the ruin of us both should we lay together and you would feel it more acutely than me. And I would not have the woman I love set upon with a life of shame and remorse for—"

"Then marry me," she said simply. Matthew pulled away to look at her with a frown. "Here on this night, swear your heart to me."

"We simply cannot just be married."

"Why not? Why not just be my husband, and spend the rest of our days trying to tell me what to do, and love me all the more when I refuse to do it?" she said, kissing him and caressing his jaw. She nudged his chin with her nose.

"You *would* refuse to obey me, I fear," he said with a smile from the corner of his mouth that she kissed and her breathy laugh tickled the skin of his neck.

"I would. But I'm sure you would find ways to persuade me," she said breathlessly as he returned her kisses, and pressed his body against hers. His hot tongue found the wet skin of her cleavage. Strong hands went around her slender waist and trailed down to cup her bottom with firm fingers pressing. Lillian gasped and felt her hips move to their own accord pressing closer to his thigh between hers. Her fingers ran down the length of his chest, over the broad expanse of his shoulders, down to the clasp of his trousers. She'd never had to undo this kind of fastener before and even her nimble fingers seemed to struggle. He grunted and pulled his hips away.

"Lily," he paced away, tugged his hands through his hair. "Before God and the Devil both, I fear I may lose my mind." He took in a gasping breath. "I cannot marry you. We've no priest and the hour is late."

"Marriage is between two souls and the eyes of God," she said desperate to be close. He held out his hands to stop her but she unfastened the buttons on the bodice of her dress and Matthew's resolve faded. The desperation of wanting him drove her across the floor. "So kiss me, now. Under the eyes of heaven and where my soul yearns so desperately for you and let us seal the promise.

I love you, Matthew. There can never be another, now that my heart knows yours. Please be mine, for always." Her breath was a gasp, her proposal a prayer. She took his hands in hers.

Matthew looked down to where she had taken his hand and was kissing every finger, every knuckle, turning it over to kiss the wide and strong plane of his palm before placing it against her breast through the delicate thinness of her chemise. The tip was hard against his touch. He sighed and closed his eyes.

"Lillian Byrne," he said quietly and opened his eyes to meet hers. "My darling, my angel, I would marry you on this night, here before the eyes of all the heavens. I would take you into my heart and home and never allow you to be anything more than desperately happy for all of your days. I love you." He paused to stare into her eyes. "You are the only woman I want. Even though you are stubborn and headstrong, with a total lack of regard for decorum. Your supple strength and your kindness—" Lillian kissed him but he continued.

"The way you believe in me and make me feel I could do anything in the world as long as you stood at my side. That you should always question me and make me yearn to be better, do better, always. I am talking far too much," he said shakily dipped his head low to kiss her, fully and warm with his tongue tasting her, his arms went around her and lifted her from the ground, spinning, spinning until she was breathless and dizzy. When he fell into the bed with her, she laughed out loud and he followed suit.

"You would laugh at your husband?" he teased, and his fingers ran the length of her neck to caress her breast.

"I would laugh with my husband, because he has brought me back from the brink of death and his laughter lifts my heart as bird taking flight," she whispered, and her fingers guided his head to take what he wanted so desperately.

He pushed away the fabric of her chemise and took the taut peak of her breast in between his teeth. His tongue flicked across it until she arched off the bed against him. His hand traced up under her skirt, around her legs, and gently to her inner thigh that trembled at his touch, until his long fingers pushed away her frilly underclothing and found her wet and hot core.

She cried out suddenly with the sweet pressure of his touch and he pulled his hand away, glancing at her with worry. She directed his hand back down.

"No please, whatever delicious magic you are weaving, do not stop."

He smiled up at her and shifted so that he could kiss her, while his hand went back down between her legs, his long finger slipping inside while his thumb gently teased her sensitive core.

Lillian's world was on fire, the room seemed to spin in waves of heat and need, and she threaded her hands into his hair while he kissed her breathless and swallowed her cries.

She was so close, she pressed into his skillful hand, gifted with such precision and patience, pushing her ever closer to the crest. Suddenly Matthew broke the kiss and pulled away to look at her, his hand stilled.

"Please," she gasped. "Please." Her hands clung to his shirt, nails scratching his chest.

"I did not want to continue, unless you were fully," he paused and kissed her chin and lips lovingly. "Prepared."

Lillian had never been a prepared person. Not in life, not in school. She was always a little underwhelming and awkward. But tonight, while the storm raged outside and a storm of equal measure pulsed between them, she had never felt more ready.

"I cannot wait, Matthew, please," she whispered and emboldened by her desire and the truth of her words ringing out in her heart, her hands traced down his taut and muscled stomach to slide his breeches from his hips. His proud and hard cock sprung loose and pulsed like velvet steel against her palm. Her eyes searched his downturned face and he pushed into her hand, wanting, as a wild animal might.

"God," he whispered and inhaled. "Let me undress you, fully. Let there be no barriers between you and I. No interrupting parties, or clever chaperones. Only you, and I and this night." At this he pulled away and stripped his shirt off over his head. She watched, fascinated by the sprinkle of blond hair that ran down his chest and stomach.

Her experiences were limited to the bare-chested boys of her high school days and the summertime romances that were far too superficial. They had no merit when compared to the virile and stunning man that Matthew was. She fumbled with shaking fingers to untether herself from the chemise. As long and wet as it was, the task was quite cumbersome and she found herself breathless with the struggle. He smiled to see her toiling so frantically and came quickly to her aid, tearing off the under layers where they were frayed.

"Let us not waste time in the error of trying to save this shift," he said with a wicked smile and discarded the pieces as they came off. It was Lillian's dream come true to watch the restrictive and impractical garment laid to waste by his strong hands.

In the warm glow of the fire, he deftly stripped away every layer of her clothing then stood briefly to discard his breeches. She sat up, knees to chest in uncertain modesty and watched in rapt awe as the fire lit his strong legs and backside, his broad chest still heaving with excitement. She looked down and felt her cheeks grow warm.

"Does it frighten you?" he said softly. "I should not have been so bold," he said and moved to cover himself but she sat up on her knees, reached her hands out to him and drew him close to her. When the skin of their naked bodies met, she sighed and shook as his arms went around her. "You do not have to. Please never feel as though it is your duty or that I am owed, especially not when it comes to your own body, Lily. You can always say no, and I will but love you all the more for your honesty."

"You are a gift," she said and nibbled at his ear. "I want all of you. I want to feel you inside of me," she whispered in his ear and he groaned with the desire to have the same thing. He guided her back down to the soft bed, arms still wrapped around her and he gently spread her legs.

"At any time, please know we can stop," he said, connecting his gaze to hers in a moment of patient pause. Lillian ran her hand down his cheek and brushed a golden lock from his forehead. With her other hand she caressed his back, down to his trim waist, and cupped his strong backside in her palm, pulling him in close to her spread legs.

Matthew shook beneath her touch and she could feel his control. She sighed against his cheek as she felt the gentle pressure of his hard head push between her wet folds.

"Please, my love. My husband. My only," she whispered, and her nails dug softly into the hard flesh of his backside. Matthew shivered and grunted as he thrust into her. Lillian's body contracted with excited relief and her legs went round his hips to clutch him closer, pulling him deeper as she gasped with delight. "Yes," she said, deep and guttural as she felt him fill her completely.

Matthew held still, barely moving but shaking from above her on strong arms. He did not attempt to even move until she began undulating her hips and drawing him deeper inside.

"Lily, my love," he gasped, and threaded his fingers into her lose, wet hair, kissing her neck, her chin, capturing her mouth with deep and full kisses as he drove into her again. The delicious tension and cresting happened so much faster than she expected, but his thickness and the pace of deep, slow strokes built every wave of desire until she felt a whirlwind inside of her and couldn't bear the pressure of it any longer. She felt her whole body break apart, her heart and soul explode into a million new and bright stars as she cried out his name.

He caught her, on the way down from heaven and pulsed inside of her calmly with his gasping breath in her ear until her world settled, then he continued, lightly drawing out and pushing in again. This time he pulled back to watch her face, her long fingers trailed down his chest, as she fought for breath. Shivers ran through her body.

"God, your eyes, Lily. Look at me," he whispered and tipped her chin up as he continued his pace. "So dark, and deep, like the night turning from dusk." He grunted in ecstasy and his words shuddered through her. Poetry, even as his heated and hard body drove into her and caused her to sweat and ache for more. "Your lips, your perfect—" he paused to kiss them even as he gasped for breath, "pink lips." He shuddered and she dug her nails into his back. "God you're so tight and hot, Lily. I cannot—" she felt his body swell, and wrapped her legs around him, pulling him ever deeper, ever more up and over the peak of his desire. He seethed and grunted as he came, a cry and surprising laugh as the explosion rocked through him and he could bear no more to be apart from her kiss. She swallowed the surprised and animalistic groans that filled his throat.

With shaking wet skin, limbs entangled and breaths coming in labored gasps, he fell into the bed with her, her legs still wrapped around his waist, her kisses still trailing down his throat and shoulder. He nuzzled her forehead, the scar that had brought them together. The fall that had landed them in each other's arms. He placed a gentle kiss on the pink line.

"My darling wife, you have upended me I fear," he whispered through smiling lips. "I am quite unable to move," he chuckled, his whole body melted against her, warm flesh to warm flesh. Lillian took all of the weight with divine grace. She ran her fingers through his hair, down his back, lightly scratching until she felt shivers roll through his body.

"Then stay with me," she whispered softly into the crook of his neck. "Please let's just stay this way." Tears pushed from the corners of her eyes and she clung to him more tightly than before. He felt the change in her hold, the warmth of liquid on her cheek and pressed back to look at her.

"Have I upset you? Was it not adequate?"

At this Lillian burst out into a laughing cry and pulled him into her arms. "Oh you, idiot," she sniffed. "I have never known such a beautiful and earth-shattering storm. It's just that I—I cannot, I cannot imagine how life would ever go on without you." At the confession she quieted again, lost in thought.

"Then, let's not think of life without one another, not this night. Not any night," he whispered, leaned up on his arm and kissed her tears until they dried. He folded her into his arms and held her closely against his chest. The beating of his heart in its steady rhythm pressed her to sleep though she knew she should remain awake. Still, maybe she owed it to herself, to her happiness and his, no matter how brief a time in their lives, to press her cheek to the sound of his heart and lose herself in the love it spoke.

A VISION, A DECISION, AND
A DOOR

Sometime in the night, while Matthew's even breath gently blew against her cheek and neck, the nightmare struck Lillian. It felt real; less a dream and more a premonition. Traveling through space and time could do things to one's senses and affect one's neurons. It broke free of the culturally-construed boundaries of the mind to see life and time as a singular line, it allowed for the instinctual, unconscious mind to see how timelines would loop and swerve as different tracks were laid down and torn back up again.

The track they were on had torn out the original. Instead of drowning at Sutton's hands and being mourned, she was a girl runaway. A girl, possibly involved in the killing of Frederick Sutton. The track that led them to their passionate marriage bed would also lead to them being found at dawn by a constable with questions about Mr. Sutton's untimely demise. With him were other gentlemen, for surely the horror of what had been found must have been caused by multiple bandits.

The Colonel was nowhere to be found, as an ally or as her father. And so no one stood up to help dissuade further violence. Matthew would scramble from the bed, protecting her at all costs. The state of her seen by so many of the men, would dishonor them both and give cause for his motive in the murder. He would be arrested and executed for the gruesome murder of his cousin and the defilement of a young lady.

Lillian would never return home again. She would miss the opportunity of the portal opening by hours while she begged and clawed at the men to let Matthew go, trying to convince him it was she and not him. The tears felt real in her throat and her cries echoed in the space between her skull. The vision went dark as though the horror of it had struck out all light completely and Lillian bolted upright, sweat and tears running down her neck. His hand reached out.

"It's alright, my angel," Matthew mumbled incoherently.

But it was not alright. It would never be right again. Her father had said she'd possessed his same power, to step through time, to be connected to the threads of life, woven in different tracks. But more than that, she could see the future threads, before decisions were made. And she knew this thread to be true in her bones. As long as she stayed here, in this time, as long he was in any way connected to her, he would never be safe. Matthew would die within the next month. She knew it as certainly as she knew the sound of her own heartbeat loud in her ears. She caressed his back and ran her hands through his hair, memorizing every detail she could and putting him solidly back to sleep.

When his quiet snores filled the room, she wrote a note warning him of the impending arrival of the group. Writing that he should confess only that he was on his way out of town, South to Wales and away from his father, as he had been planning for months. That he knew nothing of her absence and had not seen her. That was all he must tell the men. Then he must burn the note. Lillian stole a pair of his pants from his satchel, as well as one of his shirts. She threw her torn dress into the fire and built it up to consume the evidence of her ever being there. She threw her traveling cloak on still wet from last night's downpour and felt her body shiver as she stood at the doorway to look back.

No time, whispered the universe. *No time unless you intend to stay with him forever, in death.* Lillian could never come back to him if they were both dead. Her father had warned her that she only had days. The time was too quickly approaching. She still stood a chance if she left now. She closed her eyes, steeled her heart, and silently crept from the room. Without thinking of who might see her, she kept her hood up over her hair and made great haste towards the Avon, following the fence line towards the arch.

The early light of dawn came in slow undulations over the green horizon and the grass was wet with the summer dew. It soaked through Lillian's shoes and the breeches she had borrowed, sending a chill up her legs and through her body. She shivered and pulled her cloak tighter around her while she trudged onward. Her tears would not stop though she reasoned with her heart, over and over, that this was the only option.

All she had was a thin veil of hope that the gateway would lead her home. All she had was hope that this was the right and only course to take, in order to save them both. Even if they fled together, the community would find out what they'd done and he would be ruined; he would lose his good reputation, his clinic, his life's work. Kitty's father may not allow her to marry Fitzwilliam. She might never be born. And her father? All of his efforts to save her life would have been in vain.

Each step brought her closer to choosing her survival and the better course for the future over the love she so desperately wanted to save. Sobs wracked her so fully that she fell to her knees in the tall grass and cried up to the early morning sky.

"I wish there another way," she whispered to the universe. A butterfly flitted in front of her and her swollen eyes followed its haphazard flight towards the grove of trees.

A flap of butterfly wings could save a universe, she thought distractedly. *Or ruin it.*

She had no reasoning to follow it like she did, only that she was desperate for a sign. When she arrived at the grove, the dark shadows of trees enveloped her. The whisper of voices met her like a curtain of silken spider webs, covered in the crystalline droplets of dew.

There the granite slab sat, perched between the archway and beckoning.

"Is this my only way?" she asked it softly, looking to the butterfly now perched on a patch of daisies beneath the arch in the rising dawn. Flapping its wings. Possibly changing the universe forever. As the sun rose, the light from its rays touched the stone and illuminated the ancient symbols in a soft blue. She looked around, listened for hoofbeats, footsteps, anything at all that could give her pause before walking slowly to the arch and taking in a deep breath of the earthen smell of decaying leaves and new growth.

Quickly before the last symbol could be illuminated, she took out the notebook and drawing charcoal from the pocket of the cloak, and scrawled out as much an explanation as she could.

I am traveling through Time
  tell the Colonel I'm going home. He will explain all.
  I will find my way back. I will find my way back to you.
  The only truth you need believe is that I love you,
  Your Lily

The last symbol lit at the top of the arch and a great rushing wind began to pull her towards the doorway. She held on to the cloak, securing her note beneath a rock before feeling the inescapable desire, tugging at every atom in her body, to go back to where she came from. She looked over her shoulder, as the suffocating pressure started to envelop her and saw a dark shape moving quickly along the fence line in the underbrush, hand outstretched. She saw Matthew's face, pain and fear etched in his perfect features. She reached back desperately.

"Come with me," she tried to say as their fingers gently touched. Her hand grabbed on to his, but the pull was too great and it tore them apart. She wanted to tell him she loved him but her breath was gone and the pressure inside and around her felt as though she would be crushed to death.

Then all light went dark.

TIME TRAVEL BREAKS HEARTS

Matthew watched as the glowing doorway swallowed her whole, breaking her hand from his. The last vision of her shaking her head, desperate, crying, torn between going forward and staying with him burned itself into his memory. When the portal had closed, he was left in the muck and mire of the forest floor, the silence a creature in itself after the deafening sound of the witchery that had stolen his love. He came to his knees, shuffled over to the now-cooled stone doorway and pushed at it, clawed at it, tried to dig beneath but found only more stone buried over a foot deep. He stopped to listen; certain he could hear her voice on the other side of the gateway. When he searched behind it, he only found the expansive forest continued on.

He swiped at his tears and nose as he called out for her in the dense darkness, swallowing his cries. There came no response and his eyes and head fell in defeat. Then he caught sight of her note. He stumbled to it, sat in the dirt and opened it. He read it, again and again, over and over until the words blurred before his eyes. *Time travel*, the phrase didn't make sense to him, though she had spoken of it only yesterday before the storm. *Time travel*. She said she came from a different time. From a future where maybe she knew the outcomes of their love already. She had to go. They weren't safe. He wasn't safe with her, in this time. Matthew reluctantly burned her note of warning in the fire, and made sure to clear the room of any evidence. He made the bed and dressed as though he was about to begin his journey.

The men had come, and burst into his room. They found him alone.

He said he was on his way to Wales, just as he had been planning and as all the county knew. No, he did not know where his cousin was. No, he had not seen Lillian since two days before when he'd assisted her after a brutal attack. They seemed at ease and continued on. They'd been muttering about bandits and thieves and that maybe the young lady was taken from the scene.

Matthew waited until they had left to continue their search further into town. His heart did not feel a part of his chest. It was somewhere else, gone away. His beloved wife had run away to save him. He pulled out her last note, and held it between his shaking hands.

She loved him. There was no other truth but this. Matthew tucked the note into his breast pocket and sat beside the portal, searching his weathered and pained mind for the next path to take. No path without her seemed the right one.

After the men had left, the boy in the stables had told him which direction he thought the 'young man' who'd left on foot had gone. Still, he'd been far too late to reach her. Matthew sniffed, and looked to the note again and read it, tracing over her writing.

Perhaps he could start with her list. Tell the Colonel that she'd gone home. What home could she have had besides one with him? Matthew's head spun and he tried to focus. Had she really traveled through time? How could such a thing be possible? He had to admit that he knew very little of the universe and that perhaps more magic was at work than he could ever understand.

He was a man of science. He was a man of honor. His wife had made requests of him. And since he had very little else to do, he would follow her bread crumbs and hope that someday, they would find their way back to one another. He had to believe this was the only and right path.

28

THE LION OF THE LIBRARY

Lillian sat, feet tucked beneath her as she curled into the well-worn armchair of the Oxford Library. The study groups around her were a horrid distraction, with their loose tongues spewing slang and their bright little screens giving them the answers to questions once only answered by real research...in books. She frowned and looked back down at the book she was reading now. Curling up like this, reminded her of quiet mornings in the parlor. She never realized how loud the future was. Between all the whirring machines constantly running to provide people with the modern conveniences they'd become accustomed to, to the traffic, and even the jet engines high above. Even electric lights, she had discovered upon her return, made noise.

And then there were the people. Rude and annoyed. Constantly looking at their phones or screens instead of your face. There were no formal greetings, no attention to the details of conversation and body language. But the worst of it was that in everyone's face she looked for Matthew. She had not been able to trace his lineage. She'd been researching it for the past week, having secured a special pass to the library through her mother's company.

She hadn't heard about or from her father either. She tried to think back, to remember if he had said he'd see her again before she'd left, but the memories were fuzzy now. She knew she had a father, and remembered him, in come-and-go flashes. She remembered the time she was with him in 1812, everything between seemed a horrible gray mess. She rubbed the scar on her forehead.

With no one to talk to, to research with, to help her find her way back, and no history of what had happened to Matthew, she was starting to feel at a loss. She put her hand into her pocket absentmindedly. She had tucked his handkerchief carefully inside and sought it out in her need for comfort. She was surprised that anything came with her through the portal, but the things close to her body made the journey.

She looked out on the rainy, green landscape and sighed. What would she do? She didn't know if that portal would ever open again. After all, that's where they'd found her a day after she'd come through. She'd spent the day crying, clawing, and begging the stone to let her go back. Spent the night sleeping at the base of the gateway, clutching his favor tightly to her chest, hoping the universe would recognize that it had made a mistake and drop her back into his arms. The whole rain-filled, bone-chilling day, before a sheep farmer had come across her and called the authorities. She'd been nearly unconscious from dehydration and delusional from the cold and wet. Her mother and brother had been contacted. Apparently, she'd been missing from Westbury Manor, for just a day. The gateway had deposited her right back into the moment she'd left, slightly off kilter from the manor. As if time had not passed at all.

As if she'd never met Doctor Matthew Blackwell, changed the course of history, or altered her own life and ended the life of Frederick Sutton. As if Lillian Byrne had, once again, disappeared from history.

Alone at the library, Lillian thought back to the last two

weeks. She had been brought to the hospital, she had tried to tell her mother about how she had disappeared, and reappeared six miles to the north. But words were jumbled and confused and when her once brilliant mind tried to explain, nothing came. For days she was in and out of sleep and her head and heart were on a strange rhythm, as though the time-jumping had affected her ability to tell what was real, what time it was, what she had been doing before she'd been transported back. When she was coherent enough, she'd asked her mother about Lillian. What had happened to her? Did she marry a doctor?

"You know this story, Lil! Come on! Don't tease me, you've heard it nearly every night since you were a little kid."

"But she's in the journal and there was nothing about a Doctor Blackwell?"

"Lil, come on. Seriously? The whole amnesia thing is overdone." Will rolled his eyes as he came back in from the food court.

"I think you should really rest."

"Surely there must have been something. She ran away but then came back or, or maybe Matthew found her again—"

"Lillian, that's enough for the day. I get it, I want to be a romantic too, but you hit your head and wandered off. Now you need to rest." Her mom's voice faded away as she saw Will held up two pudding cups from the cafeteria, which he ate both of while giving Lillian a shit-eating grin. She looked away. If Lillian never reappeared in the journals, then that meant she'd never found her way back. She had not married Matthew. She'd simply disappeared.

But Lillian knew the record could be changed. Her father had done it. She had done it. There was a whole society of secret Timekeepers whose entire job it was. She just had to figure out how to do it again. Looking at her mother's stern brow she decided she wouldn't push. If she did, they might make her stay for a psych evaluation and she'd never find a way back.

She played her part well, telling them she'd fallen down the stairs and gone wandering to the stone where she'd passed out. It was the most normal explanation she could come up with. Now she'd convinced her mother to let her stay an extra two weeks at Oxford, while she and Will had to return to work and school. Lillian's mother had pulled a few strings through her investment company and the Dean of Oxford had allowed her access to their records for what she claimed was research for a book she was writing.

More like a history she was trying to rewrite.

Seeing her mom again was wonderful. Even seeing Will, who had been slightly more affectionate after having thought she'd fallen into the Avon herself and drowned, was good in some respects, for her heart. But the life she'd fought so hard to get back to, the life she'd tried so hard to escape, the two timelines she couldn't be both a part of, pulled her in different directions and she found that what was once good for the pre-fall Lillian, would never do for the after-fall one.

She looked out the window, at the approaching weather and wondered if she could get an extended visa until the next celestial event.

Perhaps the portal would open and allow her back. But in what time would she return? Would it be moments? Would it be years? Would it be even before they met? Had she already messed too much up? There was no guaranteeing any of her ideas and research would work. And short of getting her doctorate in Quantum Physics, there would be no way to plan.

She wished her father would find her. She wished that Matthew had found him, and that they were working on a way to reunite her with Matthew. She bit her lip. Her father should have been able to meet her in this time, but he had not. Maybe something had gone wrong. Maybe he was hurt. Maybe worse. *Maybes* were all she had and Lillian hated it.

She closed "South Wales: A History 1750 to 1850" with a huff and resisted the urge to throw it into the middle of the bad-mouthed group of entitled students. She didn't know if she'd ever see Matthew again and her heart seemed to squeeze itself into a tight ball in her chest. Why had she ever left? Tear stung her eyes and she stood to walk the stacks impatiently.

She wandered into the section that was curated by a special librarian. These books you could only check out if you wore the gloves and remained under the watchful eye of the burly man in his dark beard who liked to look over his spectacles at you whenever it was necessary to turn a page, she stopped to look at the titles inside the case.

Most of them were original editions, protected in their little vacuum-sealed world, away from light and moisture and all those things that destroy the fragile words and ideas from centuries long gone. Her eyes fell on a beautiful bound book of poetry, late seventeenth century if she had to guess. She'd seen Fitzwilliam carrying similarly covered books in and out of the library whilst wooing Miss Darlingwood. She looked back at the boys taking selfies and sending them to some poor, disinterested girl, as if that were the kind of thing that could turn them on. Maybe it did. Did it ever for her? She furrowed her brow.

Love in her time seemed so shallow and impermanent now. The kind of hook ups and fluidity was fine for someone with a short attention span and the need for instant gratification, but now that she'd known different, she couldn't stomach less.

Immediately Lillian's eyes welled up and she began to cry. There in front of the books, sniffing and trying to hold back the audible sobs, she disturbed the great lion behind the restricted section shelves and he looked up from his book at her. His eyes, penetrating and no nonsense, felt strangely familiar to Lillian.

"What *are* you on about?" he said and rose from his seat. Lillian had never heard him even speak before, except the occasional grunt when she lingered too long or blocked his path back to his sterilized den of solitude.

"My apologies, I was just reminded of someone very dear to me," she said and nodded to the poetry book.

"Really?" he said with an air of disbelief and handed her a tissue over the glass barrier that separated the common people from his desk. She took it gratefully.

"Thank you."

"This young suitor read a lot of seventeenth century poetry, did he?"

Lillian laughed and sobbed and then quickly contained herself, clearing her voice. "At times. Though, truth be told, he was probably much more interested in The Philosophical Transactions of the Royal Society of London to amuse him in his quiet hours. But occasionally—" her eyes went far away, "he would call me Angel and be inspired to wax poetic," she said softly, and her finger touched the glass above the book. Rather than wipe away the fingerprint and give her a scathing lecture, the librarian's brow fell. Lillian looked up at him and saw in his features that same familiarity, though she couldn't place it. "I'm sorry, sometimes I get a little too Austeny," she said, trying to fall back into the language of the century.

"The Philosophical Transactions of the Royal Society of London predate the British Medical Journal by at least fifty years. And they're very rare indeed. What kind of man would have access to such a treasure? And how do *you* know about them?"

"I saw it once in his possession, he liked to read it with his feet up by the fire."

"Aside from the fact he should not have had such a precious book so close to open flame, let alone without two feet on the ground, that's quite impossible. Wait," the librarian paused. His gears visibly turning. "What did you say he called you?"

"I don't—"

"Angel?" The librarian said suddenly followed with the cynical harshness of "he was a doctor and he called you Angel?"

"Well, yes, among other, less flattering things."

"Look what kind of game are you playing at?"

"I'm sorry?"

"There's no way you could have known about that journal or the notes inside its margins. It's in the most highly secured vault and only five people have ever, in its history since coming to this facility, been able to view it."

"I don't understand what you're saying."

"Was it Hopkins? Did he send you to pull one over on me? Is this another one of his asinine jokes?"

"I don't know what you're talking about! Why are you yelling at me?" she shouted back, defensively. The heads at all the tables turned their way and the librarian took a deep breath, straightened his vest over his plaid shirt and bow tie, and huffed.

"You. Come with me," he said. He pointed to the vault door to the side of the glass room and she looked warily at him. She opened her mouth to protest, but he seethed. "Saints, child. Now."

29

THE DOCTOR'S JOURNAL

"Fine, sheesh, alright," Lillian said and walked with her arms crossed to the door. The buzzer sounded and she heard the click of the lock. The librarian swung the door open, admitted her and then handed her a sterile white coat and acid-free gloves.

"Oh, is this all?" she snorted. "Shouldn't I have a sneeze guard too?"

"Kindly, do shut up," he said crisply without turning back to her.

"Rude. And not very proper," she stammered and held up her gloved hands.

"Well, we can't all be Austeny," he said as they passed through yet another locked door, this one in the back, where the wall was still stone and the wood of the door was burnished a deep mahogany. They descended a small stairwell into a dark and lesser antechamber off of the library. The hairs on Lillian's neck quivered.

"Where are we going? Is this a dungeon? Who are you exactly?" She straightened her spine and stopped in the doorway, keeping the stairs easily accessible. The librarian turned towards her and rolled his eyes.

"You Americans are so barbaric. I would never," he looked her over with no sign of sexual appreciation. "You're not my preferred gender." He flipped on a switch beside the arched doorway and the room illuminated all the way back as if each light were a step upward through a giant hall. It wasn't an antechamber after all. It was nearly the length of the library and along its walls were uniform glass cases housing books, artifacts, newspapers from first printings. Things so rare and delicate that they couldn't afford to have them mingle with the common people upstairs.

"Now, you wonder who I am," he said and stared down at her as though studying her face more closely. He reached up to turn her cheek one way, to expose her scar, and Lillian pulled away with a glare. The light of recognition flashed in his hazel irises. "But I think the more fitting question, my dear, is who are you?"

He walked straight to the third case on the left, which held a leather-bound journal. "In this case we have one of the most interesting journals of the early and into the late eighteen-hundreds. Meticulously kept and the strangest mix of poetry, scientific theory, sketches, human anatomy and history. It was as if the author were trying to puzzle through a mystery, find his way back to something."

Lillian scowled at the librarian and he gestured for her to come closer. She stood over the case and looked down at one of them. There was nothing particularly special about it. Except the color. It was a beautiful lavender blue.

"That's a strange color for a journal of the time." She bent down to look closer.

"The first inscription explains that the author had them specially made to match the color of his wife's eyes. Even he admitted that nothing could do such a color justice."

Lillian's head snapped up and she looked at the librarian who looked back at her just as intensely. Not just at her, but into her eyes. A visible shiver ran through his spine and he reached for his keys. Lillian's heart raced. Lavender, Angel, doctor, wife, scientific theory. Her gloved hands broke out into a sweat and she rubbed them nervously against each other.

"I scarcely want to hope," she whispered. "May I see it, please?"

The librarian stooped to gently pick up the journal and carried it to the special holder at the center of the room, beneath the soft and carefully measured glow of appropriate lighting.

"What do you know of Edward Page Mitchell?" he asked her. Lillian shivered now. She'd been skimming through his works, one of the first authors to write on the possibility of time travel, even before Einstein and Rosen. Sometime in the late eighteen-hundreds.

"The Clock That Ran Backward?" she whispered. A memory flashed of her father reading her that book. Her father who traveled through time. She shook her head trying to focus on the journal.

"Now, some would argue that the author was suffering from some late term and undiagnosable brain tumor or opium addiction, but I've heard a different legend that says he got some of his ideas from this very journal. Conversing with the author, a man of science, who he'd met in the South of Wales."

"Pray tell, sir," Lillian's voice shook, tears brimming. "Who was this man? Who wrote the journal?"

"Pray tell, sir? My name is Richard." His voice was softer, kinder and he shook his head as she tried to keep her tears from falling. "My but you are giving yourself away, dear Lillian with the lavender eyes and the tongue like sharp honey."

"How did you know—" Lillian pushed him aside and pulled open the cover to his astonished protest. "The Road Back," she read the beautifully penned title. "By the humble and faithful Dr. Matthew Edward Blackwell." Lillian collapsed onto the floor, taking the book with her and clasping it to her chest with her breath heaving in and out.

"No," she whispered and clung to the old journal, sobbing.

"Madam, please! You mustn't handle the books in this manner."

She scrambled away from Richard while still holding it ever so carefully, tears in her eyes, begging him not to take it from her. A small hint of sympathy lit his eyes and he sighed.

"It will tear and we'll never get a chance to find out what the good doctor said or if he ever found a way to get back to you."

"He hasn't!" she sobbed and touched the book through the gloves, knowing that sometime, hundreds of years ago, he touched it. His hands, his long fingers, that only days ago to her had graced her skin, were long gone now. What if he had lived his entire life without her? Hoping. Pining. Looking for a way, to no avail? She broke down into a fresh set of tears for the life they had lost.

"Does this go to his death? Did he live without me? Die without me? Alone? Oh God? How long? How long?"

"Miss Lillian, please!" Richard held out his hand and his rich voice aimed to soothe. "I don't know. I've yet to read the whole thing. We won't be able to read it at all if it's damaged."

"I can't," she lost her breath. "I don't know if I can read it. The truth might be too painful to bear."

Richard knelt down beside her, his deep voice lowering to a compassionate purr. "If you found your way to him once. You can find your way back. The universe does not tear apart what is meant to be," Richard said softly and offered him her hand. Lillian stared at it through her cloudy eyes.

Surely, if their story could melt the heart of the abominable librarian, there must be something worth fighting for. Lillian sniffed and then slowly nodded. She allowed him to help her up and, together, they placed the journal on the stand and turned the first page. Her gloved finger traced over the likeness of her he'd drawn, a soft charcoal sketch of her dark hair, up and her sly smile on him, deep eyes seeking, scar visible.

Richard looked once more at her face, delicately touching the pink mark. Lillian looked at him, more trust in a person than she had felt since she'd left Westbury Manor. There it was again, that odd familiarity of Richard's face, his eyes. The kindness.

"Stairs of that time were wicked narrow and treacherous," she smiled slyly.

"Especially for his Lillian," Richard agreed. They both faced the book again and seemed to hold their collective breath as they turned the next page.

30
DOCTOR SHAW MAKES EXCELLENT SCONES

Matthew's penmanship was impeccable. At least, to today's standards. Scarcely a present-day student could read such careful calligraphy. He had written a forward that began in this way:

To my Angel, Lily,
My wife, my love, my partner and honest confidante. Should I find you again, in time or in heaven, I shall never again let your hand leave mine. I will always remain, yours and yours alone faithfully,
Matthew

Lillian cried, covered her mouth at the outburst, and looked at Richard to see if this was real or if she'd somehow been transported to an alternate reality. Richard touched her hand gently and motioned for her to continue. She pored over every beautifully angled word.

The first three pages of the journal were an account of how they had met, the fateful day of her fall, and how, he had not been expected down the road beside Westbury Manor, as he'd forgotten some paperwork of great import and it had led him back to his father's estate. He continued on, the feelings of first meeting her, the desperation of sadness at learning this woman was to be his cousin's wife. That he could not love her, and yet every day and every moment in her presence, he fell steadily and hopelessly for every stubborn and beautiful thing about her. Her strange speech, her lack of decorum, her honesty, and her breasts. Lillian blushed and looked quickly over at Richard whose eyebrows raised,

"Well, I suppose if you're into them," he shrugged. Lillian smiled, despite the pain of reading her love's words, now long gone from the earth. Next he recounted, in horrifying detail, the continued abuse and disgusting things Sutton said and done and the increasing level of anger that had built in Matthew's chest. Despite his oath to do no harm, he very much intended to kill the man the night of the carriage fire. Instead, his darling Lillian had taken the weight of the violent man from the world.

He wrote of the days following the investigation into his cousin's death. Not enough evidence had remained, and it was ruled a robbery gone wrong. Even his business partners were glad to be rid of his nefarious practices. It seemed the whole world wished for his death, but only Lillian was brave enough to follow through with it.

Richard paused to sit up and look at her. "How did you do it?" he asked. Lillian stared back at him and felt her cheeks get hot. "The statute of limitations is well passed and after hearing about what he did to you, you'll get no judgement from me."

"An axe," she said and felt her stomach turn remembering the gory episode. Richard pushed up his glasses with one finger and let out a whoosh of breath.

"Savage."

"He was going to kill Matthew. He would have killed me. I would have used a cleaner means, but that's all I had on hand."

"Good show, Lizzy Borden. Or should I say Lily Borden?" Richard said with a slight smile.

"Can we just," she shook off a shiver. "Please, not talk about it, ever again?" Richard nodded and they turned back to the book.

Matthew had taken her last words to heart and, with confusion as to how she'd disappeared before him and the scant explanation, had gone to the Colonel and told him all that had transpired. Despite expecting a harsh reprimand, Matthew was surprised to find that the Colonel was not only not angry at him for impugning her honor, but pleased that they had finally come to their senses and made the match, giving him his belated blessing to marry, not his niece, but his daughter. He had then confessed to Matthew, that he himself, was a traveler through time, and had come to Westbury Manor to save Lillian. When he'd told the Colonel about how she had disappeared through a magical fairy door, the Colonel's happy demeanor changed and he began to pull charts and notes from his desk drawer, shaking his head and muttering it was 'impossible'.

"Fairy door?" Richard interrupted. Lillian placed her gloved finger on the narrow line where she'd stopped and looked up.

"Miriam told me about it. She said she'd seen a man pass through it when she was younger. It was a portal, a thin space in the time fabric if you will. It's where they found me in this time. I don't remember much, except that I tried to hold on to him," she stopped, gasped and felt her hands clench, nails cutting into her palms through the gloves. "I tried to bring him with me, but it wouldn't let him through."

"Only one shall pass, eh?" At this Lillian's lip quivered and Richard sighed. "You mentioned a Miriam? What can you tell me about her?" Richard cocked his head at her curiously. Lillian had to rouse herself from the feeling and frustration of Matthew's hand slipping from hers.

"Miriam? She was the head housekeeper. She was my friend," Lillian's voice shook. "She was tough and kind, she was mischievous and believed in young love and fairies, and she didn't put up with meanness or deceit. She covered for me, and conspired with me. She was a heroine." Lillian finished and sniffed as the tears came. She missed so much of that world. When she looked up into Richard's eyes, she swore the memories of the kindly woman were blurring into her present day. Lillian's brow pulled in, the jump, the head wound, the trauma and hope mixing from the day made her head feel like it was stuffed with cotton.

Lillian's eyes fell to Richard's lanyard, his picture. His name.

Dr. Richard Shaw.

She took a sharp intake of breath and let loose with an excited squeal. "You're her family!" She took her hands from the book and grabbed him around the shoulders as though she could hug Miriam through the ages.

Richard leaned back at the uproar and held up his hands. "A few generations ago, yes. I actually inherited this journal from my great-great-great grandmother's belongings. She'd worked many years at Westbury Manor."

"This is the best surprise I've had since falling down those stairs." She sniffed and looked back to the book. "What happened to him after he gave her the journal?"

Richard sighed, the sigh of a man that didn't want to say what was next on his mind. "Lillian, I don't know for certain." Richard nodded to the pages. "Everyone who's looked it, Hopkins for instance, believe that the young man was touched with madness. Time travels, affairs with a murderous man's fiancée, erotic musings, magic, fairy doors? One of the first works of fantasy fiction if anything, but written in such a way as to not be published. It hasn't been taken seriously and is more of a curiosity. Apparently it just ends, with no resolution whatsoever. I haven't even read it all myself. I stopped after the erotic wedding night recount he writes of in such detail."

Lillian slumped down to the floor, gently taking the book

with her. Richard did not protest. Lillian stared at Matthew's writing and put a hand to her forehead.

"Do you think he gave up?" she asked, not wanting to get to the last page in fear that the hopelessness would be too great to bear. Richard, with a groan and no small amount of effort, lowered himself down to the stone floor beside her and sat.

"I'm not sure where on the journey he stopped recording. Or when he decided to pass it along to my great-times-eight grandmother."

"Probably when he remarried?" she sobbed.

"Don't be dramatic, a man who writes like he does of you, doesn't pick up another wife in less than a year."

Before she could open the journal again to skip to the end, the lights dimmed and the call for the closure of the library came through the speaker. Lillian looked at Richard. He was a puzzle piece the universe saw fit to send to her. She searched the familiar stare with sad and pleading eyes. He cleared his throat. He took the journal from her and patted it softly.

"The restricted section locks down with or without people in it at closing time." Lillian's lip trembled and he sighed. "Tomorrow we can be rested to face what's next and I will be here first thing. We will read through the last pages and see if there are any clues as to where your Matthew went. We will find out how to get you back, my dear."

"We?"

"I simply cannot just leave this mystery unsolved. Gracious no. What would my grandmother say if I did not help you?" He smiled at her and put the journal safely back.

"Do you think it's impossible, Richard? He's already dead."

"Here he is," Richard looked around the silent repository of books, a tomb in the recent light of events. "But somewhere in time he is waiting for you. We just have to take what he knew, what we know, and—" he shook his head and took a breath as though he'd forgotten to do so for the last two hours.

"And?"

"And have faith, fair Lillian." He said softly and gave her cheek a pat. Lillian, unaccustomed to the warmth of human touch in days, sprung into his giant bearlike arms and hugged him tight. "Oh! Oh my," he whispered, and his large frame stiffened before he resigned himself to her hug. "Go on now and get some rest. I'll see you promptly at seven."

"Thank you," she said and pecked his cheek before hurrying from the room. If she didn't leave the journal now, she might be tempted to stay there all night and she couldn't let Richard lose his job over her heartache. She rushed from the library and back to her room, too overwhelmed to eat or sleep. She just lay on the small twin bed by the shabby lamp and stared up at the crumbling plaster on the ceiling. She had awoken that morning with so little hope. Now she feared the very real possibility that Matthew had died alone might drown it.

3 1

THE FINE THREADS OF HOPE

When Lillian arrived the next morning, earlier than she had for anything in her life, Richard was waiting with a to go cup of tea and a bag of warm scones.

"You are Miriam's kin," Lillian smiled to him and the hardened librarian smiled back.

"She did have the best recipe. Passed down to every generation. But you need to finish it all before we go down into the vault."

"What? These aren't archive-safe scones?" She smiled and looked into the bag. Richard rolled his eyes.

"Any ideas last night?"

Lillian took a big bite despite her stomach rolling at the question. "No. No sleep and no ideas," she said around the buttery goodness. Richard motioned for her to follow him into the library.

"Well, luckily for you I'm not stupid with young love." The library was quiet this time of the morning and Lillian brushed off her crumby fingers before entering the back room. "You still need to wash your hands. Our pants are not napkins," he said, in a very Miriam-like fashion. Lillian rolled her eyes but complied and scrubbed her hands thoroughly before returning to the door of the vault.

"So? What ideas do you have?" she asked as they put on their gloves.

"I think it would best if we were to read the section after the wedding night. According to Hopkins, it's supposed to contain more discussion about the theories of time travel that Matthew heard about from the Colonel. My hope is that therein lies the clue to help you get back to him." They approached the case and Richard took out the journal. He started to read while Lillian listened, eyes closed and world still spinning.

Matthew had met with the Colonel, who was not at all surprised about Lillian's insistence she had traveled through time. He was, however, impressed that she had confided in Matthew. The Colonel confessed that he himself had traveled several times, but only through a sanctioned society of Timekeepers. The existence of the fairy door that Miriam had told her of was an unsanctioned and unmarked portal. Much like the stairs themselves.

Lillian listened and her brow furrowed. The reason her father had taken so long to find them a way home, was due to the Timekeepers not realizing how she'd found a portal to begin with. He himself had traveled through the fairy door on his non-approved trip to save his daughter. It seemed, as the Colonel told Matthew, that the Byrnes had an uncanny ability to open portals on their own, if the veil was thin enough. But they would not admit others through if it weren't meant to be.

Lillian's eyes filled with tears. Had she and Matthew not been meant to be together? He couldn't be pulled through the portal.

"So we were not meant to be?" Lillian asked, teary gaze on Richard. He shook his head.

"I do not know, I would not think such a thing as dividing you should be possible." Richard gently closed the book.

"Perhaps I should stop this foolishness," she whispered, and a tear fell down her nose. Richard sighed.

"Perhaps the door did not allow him through because it was not the right time." He cleared his throat and looked once more at the book. "You said your father spoke to you of these 'Timekeepers'?"

"Yes, apparently, it was why he was gone so much during my childhood. His job was to keep the timeline on track. But he sort of went off the books to find me."

"And they are ... everywhere?" Richard looked carefully around them in the quiet and secure vault.

"He said they had an office in Westbury. Apparently they keep maps there, though they are old and unreliable. Though I suppose if one could find such a map, they could use them to travel."

"What a dangerous idea," Richard said and shivered.

"In the wrong hands." Lillian looked at him and wiped her eyes.

Richard went back through the last few entries and read them aloud. One entry, probably written in the dark of night as Matthew's writing was less perfected and wax dotted the page where he had shifted the candle to find the best light, was in apology to her. How scared she must have been, how strange and lonely a world where she knew nothing of the people or customs. Where she was used to having autonomy and had to resign herself instead to layers of propriety. Did she wear pants, those long legs of her always in some way visible to the men of her day? Did she wear her hair down or work as a professional? Could she have become a physician? A surgeon?

What wonderous world had she lost to come to his? It was no wonder she was eager to go back to where she had so many more opportunities and conveniences. All the past held for her was the trauma from Mr. Sutton and the simple doctor who had wed her in a makeshift ceremony. Would she even want to return to him?

Lillian could feel the fading hope in his words.

"Matthew," she whispered and hugged herself around the middle. She leaned into Richard. "Keep reading."

It was clear that Matthew was losing rational thought to his grief. The writing became messier, the ink fading in and out. He ended the second to last entry in lament, splotches of tears on the page blurred the ink. Hopeless and hurt in missing her. Richard sighed and closed the journal.

"I just don't know if my heart can take more of this," he said softly.

"Your heart? Think of mine," Lillian said and rested her head on his shoulder. "What's left?"

"Just a couple of lines," he said. "Nearly illegible."

"Let me see," she took the journal and swung it closer to the light. The lines were messy, separated from the last paragraph and on the bottom of the page. Written not with ink but charcoal. They looked hurried, as though he didn't have much time. Lillian gasped as she read them out loud.

Westbury Manor, Stairs, March 24th. I will catch you this time.

Richard shrieked, took the book from her, and read the words again.

"There it is," Richard said and held up the journal. "He's told us. He and the Colonel must have calculated the date the veil would be thin."

"What are you talking about?"

"The stairs. He's telling you that there's a chance the veil will be thin on March twenty-fourth, that there may be a way to cross back over at that time."

"I don't understand."

"There still may be one good trip—god strike me down for

the pun—left in those stairs," Richard said, and Lillian took the journal back, opened the last page and read it again.

Lillian felt the blood drain from her face and took in a deep breath. "Richard, what day is it today?"

"March," he paused and went pale too. "It's March twenty-fourth."

"That's today, this happens today. Can we make it?"

Richard glanced up at the clock in the archive. "We will try."

ON THE OTHER SIDE OF TIME

Matthew was a man with a mind for science. And a man with a heart intent on romantic folly. He'd never known the latter until he had been fated to meet Lillian Byrne. He was most determined, up until that fateful day to be a happy bachelor, content in his work and purpose. Until she had fallen from the stars, destined to meet him, charm him, challenge him and love him. Then his universe changed.

From the moment she had stepped through the stone portal, a traveler of time, and her hand had slipped from his, he'd been trying to find his way back.

When the ash and consequence had settled from his cousin's demise, Matthew began in earnest to set his brilliant mind to finding his way back to Lillian. This of course meant spending honest and wild conversations with The Colonel, whose name was John Hawthorne Byrne, and who himself had been pulled through time on the quest to save his daughter. The man was empathetic to Matthew's plight and wanted them to be reunited as well. But he was charged with returning to his missions with the Timekeepers as he'd traded any future freedom to save his daughter. He gave Matthew all the knowledge he had and wished him well, vowing to help as soon as he was able. Matthew, arriving one morning to John's office to find his journals, notes, maps and personal effects missing, knew that the 'Colonel' would not return.

Matthew traveled to the South of Wales consulting writers, philosophers, scientists, and theologians for over a year. He became a man obsessed. He traveled to the sites on the map that he could remember before John had taken it, asked questions of the locals, wrote countless pages of theories and mapped out possible astrological events that might have influence over the passages through time. His own father berated him for not following through with his plans to set up a practice, nor to be committed to the family's clinical legacy. He was a man adrift, his head too full of romanticism and the dramatic trappings of youth, to ever provide for a family.

But there was only one family he was concerned for, and it was Lillian. Matthew returned to Westbury Manor, visited Fitzwilliam and the new Mrs. Byrne offering his support and care in the tragic disappearance of their cousin. He tried to give them reassurances that she was quite well and he had it on good authority that she had traveled to America. Kitty was, of course, beset with worry, as she'd just learned of the impending arrival of their first child the next summer and wanted Lillian to be there. Matthew smiled at her sadly, wanting the same thing.

"Whatever shall we do to get her to come back?" Kitty said, tears in her eyes and a hand over her waist. Fitzwilliam put his arm protectively around her and looked to his friend.

"You must find her. Please, Matthew. You must bring her back."

"You needn't beg me, dear friend, it is all that is on my mind." Matthew bowed, shook Fitzwilliam's hand and gave a reassuring kiss to Kitty's forehead. He didn't know how it would come to pass. He didn't know where she might come back through or when. He didn't know anything. Which for a man of science was a very poor place to be indeed. He made his way through the empty halls of Westbury Manor, so much quieter now for the months of her absence. He passed by the kitchen where Miriam was starting preparations for dinner.

"I still cannot puzzle through it, Doctor Blackwell," she said and stopped his progress. He came into the kitchen.

"What is that, Madam?"

"How you could have let her go." The severity in the woman's face and downturn of her mouth made Matthew hang his head and run the brim of his hat between his hands.

"I tried to hold on to her, but the portal would not let me through."

"She's supposed to be with you. With us."

"Dear lady, if I knew a way to reach her, I surely would. But the expanse of time lies between us. And I have not yet solved the puzzle of how to reunite our two souls."

"Saints, child," she said, exasperated. "Do you wish to know what I think?" Miriam said and punched the bread dough down so a great puff of flour rose up in the kitchen and dispersed in the afternoon light coming in from the windows. The smell of it reminded Matthew of Lillian's neck and sitting before that very fire with her in his arms. The ache swelled and grew within him so his eyes filled with tears.

"Yes, madam, I do. I am a desperate man, drowning for any hand in the dark to pull me up."

"I think for all of your science, and charts, and maps you are forgetting that love is written in the stars. And dust that was parted at the beginning of time will always seek ways back to itself."

"I'm afraid I don't understand."

"Sit," she said harshly to him, and he obeyed, perching on the side of the fireplace with a sigh and closing his eyes to still the memories that played of her warm body in his arms. "I know you don't hold much creed to the stories of my land, but I know the legends like my own blood and I know one thing to be true. In the beginning of time the brightest, most beautiful star became so heavy, and so huge that the universe could no longer hold on to it. It burst into a million pieces and scattered itself to the far reaches of the sky.

Every life, from the smallest fish to the largest tree carries a piece of stardust in its soul. And we are forever seeking the one that's closest to where we started. You and she, you are of the same star dust."

"I don't understand."

"Why were you passing by Westbury Manor that day, Doctor?"

"I don't know. I had this strange urge that I'd forgotten something. That I'd left something behind."

"I believe that Lillian was traveling through space and your stardust knew it. It wanted to be close to her."

"That's a beautiful sentiment but if that were true why would we have been torn apart at the doorway?" Miriam continued to knead the bread and shrugged.

"Maybe that was not the right time. Maybe in order to preserve your love through the fire that had taken place, it needed to keep you apart. Sort of like hiding a heart from a world intent on stealing it." Matthew stood and paced with frustration.

"So how will I know it's the right time? How will I know when to find her? And where? You're talking me in circles."

"You've been writing in that journal?"

"Yes," he blushed. "Not that it will do much good. No telling where she is, or if she'll ever find it."

"If she's looking as hard for you as you are for her, I know she will."

Matthew scowled. "How will she ever come by it after two hundred years? It could be destroyed or thrown away."

"If you leave it with me, I will keep it safe." Matthew stopped and looked at Miriam. "The Universe doesn't tear apart what's meant to be together. And you two strange and headstrong gypsies belong in each other's arms. I believe it to be true. If you write to her, the vast darkness will carve a path to light her way back."

"But how? How will it carve a way?"

"There is no harm in asking the universe for what you want. So what is it you want?"

"I want her here! Here with me today, this very hour," Matthew choked and dropped his hat to his side.

"So ask." Miriam gestured towards the journal in his hand. He scowled, knowing it was folly and ridiculous. "Now boy! Don't waste another minute." She took up a piece of charcoal from the cold fireplace and put it in his hand. Matthew stared up at her, opened the last page where his desperate entry from the previous week still threatened to drain him of hope.

"Dear Miriam, what is the date?"

"The twenty-fourth. Write it down. Time waits for no man."

33

RETURN TO WESTBURY MANOR

Richard was able to find a suitable replacement to take over his job at the valuable collections desk, telling them it was a family emergency. Which, to the credit of his ancestors, was not a complete lie.

"Are you sure? You needn't trouble yourself, Richard. Do not allow me to simply take over your life."

"Oh, Lillian, kindly shut up," he rolled his eyes and sighed as they left the library and he searched his phone for the train schedule. "This is the most adventure I've ever had and probably more than I will ever have again," he said and put his arm across her shoulder to keep her from walking into traffic. "Besides, if you're really going to toss yourself off a set of stairs, someone should be there to call the paramedics in the event it doesn't work."

"Your vote of confidence is comforting," she grumbled, and he nudged her. Together they crossed to the nearest train station. While on the long ride, Richard drilled her on any details she could remember about her father's experience and particularly the map.

"Why are you so interested in it?" she said smiling.

"I just think a map like that would be useful to have."

"Doctor Richard Shaw, I know you're not contemplating messing up the timeline."

"Of course not! I have nothing but impeccable respect for the historical record." He paused and looked out at the countryside as it sped by. Lillian's leg twitched up and down nervously and she started to cry. Hadn't she messed up the timeline? Richard sighed.

"Here," he grunted and bent over to retrieve his leather satchel. He withdrew a linen-covered bundle. "Busy yourself with this and stop crying." Lillian grabbed the package and carefully unwrapped it to find the journal.

"Doctor Shaw, you are a rebel at heart," she gasped and kissed his bearded cheek. He promptly wiped his face and waved her off.

"Yes, yes, well don't tell anyone. I filled out a 'In Repair' form at the front desk to avoid any questions."

"Will it disintegrate in the common air?" she teased as she carefully opened it in her lap, keeping the cloth around its cover.

"Just don't put your prawn crisp fingers all over it," he said gruffly but she watched him smile as he turned to once more stare out the window.

"You know Lillian, I don't think I've ever been so deeply in love," he said softly. Lillian looked up from the journal, her mind and heart distracted. She stared at Richard's far away gaze, his pretty hazel eyes, the sheer size of the man. She smiled and put her hand on his bearded cheek to turn his face to hers.

"Somewhere, out there, is a very special man, just waiting for you. I know it."

Richard's eyes went soft before he shook it off and went back to his phone to see what their next stop would be.

It took two hours for the train to Westbury and the short Lyft ride to the manor. Lillian was agitated and constantly checked the last page to see if anything changed. She willed her brain to send her a flashback, a warning, anything to tell her if this was the right way. Nothing came. After what was the thirtieth time of opening the journal, Richard confiscated it from her.

"Enough." He scowled and tucked it safely back in his bag. "The date has not changed. We're nearly there."

When they arrived, Richard paid the driver and they both stood at the long driveway, much changed from the manor that Lillian had lived in.

When faced with the door of the ostentatious house that had served as her home for those months, she could barely draw breath or strength to enter. It was afternoon, on the twenty-fourth. He hadn't given her a time of day. She'd wait the whole of it, and walk the length of those stairs on repeat, no matter what the current owner of the house thought. What would she even find? Would the portal just sense her desperation and take pity? Open itself to the world where her darling Matthew sat waiting, frozen in time in memory, but long gone in reality?

"Deep breaths, Lillian," Richard said from her side, still there despite this being a strange and delusional quest. She looked up at him. He was a testament to romanticism and hope existing in the world. If she went back through, she would miss him greatly.

The thought of going back through chilled her. Of course she wanted to go back, but she also knew that her father said the Timekeepers were not pleased with her traipsing around the timeline. If she went back, would there be retribution from them? Even against her father? She stifled a cry into her hand and turned away. Wouldn't it be worth taking that chance to find Matthew again? Hadn't her father wanted her to be happy?

Richard patted her shoulder in an awkward caring way.

"Look. Maybe this isn't the best time. I mean maybe we can come back this evening when you're not so," Lillian wiped her nose on her sleeve to his visible disgust, "moist."

"No," she responded, shakily. "No, I need to be here. I need to go in and wait. And if nothing should come of it, then I maybe I can at least try to say goodbye."

"Goodbye?" Richard whispered and looked down at her. "What do you mean goodbye?"

"My father's life was one of constant leaving. The Timekeepers may not look kindly to me throwing myself back in time. What if it messes up the timeline? What if something terrible comes of it?" she whispered and clutched at the scrap of linen in her hands like a lifeline as they climbed up the stairs to the manor. Richard sighed, perturbed, and rang the bell.

"I had something beautiful and I should be grateful for that, not asking for more. Who gets—" she sobbed and choked the sadness back. "Who gets to have a love like that? Even for a day?" Richard turned to her.

"Lillian Byrne, I do not believe that. That last line was written for a reason. The journal entries stopped for a reason. If the Timekeepers would not allow it, it would not have been there."

"But what if—"

"You are tired and hungry, and not in the best of moods. Chin up girl!"

Lillian scowled and was about to lay into him about not being a cranky toddler when the door of Westbury Manor opened and interrupted their quiet disagreement. A very proper lady answered, in a sweater set and pearls, British to a proverbial T.

"Good morning, may I help you?"

Lillian stood, feet stuck to the stone steps and unable to breathe.

Richard looked from her to the woman and cleared his throat. "Uh, yes, quite right. Good afternoon. My name is Doctor Richard Shaw, this is my friend Lillian Byrne."

"Aren't you the young woman who disappeared after falling down my stairs?" she interrupted, hard eyes boring into Lillian's.

"Yes."

"No," Richard argued at the same time.

"I am, Lillian Byrne. I was here, with my mother Jane and brother Fitz—Will," she stuttered. "I disappeared and caused a great deal of unnecessary worry. I came to apologize and try to retrace my steps. My friend Richard came with me to assist."

The woman stared at them incredulously. "Richard? *Doctor* Richard Shaw? What is this? Is he some kind of lawyer? I'm not liable for you wandering off."

"No, my darling lady, you aren't. I assure you. Doctor Shaw is here to help me remember only." Lillian leaned in conspiratorially, "If you'll pardon me, madam, he's my psychologist and it was his idea to help me relive the moment and understand what had happened and help me with a bit of amnesia I'm suffering. I understand if you don't want to allow us access."

The woman stared at the two of them, at the teary eyes of Lillian and the uncomfortable lion of a man beside her.

"Sometimes, with these kinds of cases, amnesia that is, it helps the patient to go back to the places where the episodes have occurred in order to jar the memory," Richard said, trying to sound as though he knew what he was talking about. The haughty air of his demeanor was just enough to push the owner to nod.

"Fine then, but no more than twenty minutes. I've got a tour coming through this afternoon, and I don't want them being bothered."

"Yes, ma'am, thank you," Lillian said, head bowed in a curtsey, a recount of her time in a more genteel era. Richard lifted her by the elbow, lest the woman might find her truly mad and call the white-coat wagon to cart her away to a nice, safe, padded room. He nudged her forward, and they followed the woman inside.

"Wipe your feet," she commanded, and Lillian and Richard obeyed. Though the updates to the foyer were minimal, the décor seemed gaudy, even in its staunch, traditional British style. Sounds were more muted with the carpeting and new draperies. It was the house she had visited with her mom. But it was not the home she'd come to love in a different time.

Richard walked beside her and nudged her arm with his as he nodded to the drawing room door. She stopped in the doorway of the present-day gift shop and stared at the fireplace, flanked by the tall windows facing the gardens. Before that fireplace she had argued with Mr. Sutton. She had confessed to Miriam. She had bowed before Matthew and felt her hand tremble in his. In this room she had sat still as he had stitched her wound closed once more. She had listened to Kitty about Fitzwilliam's secret proposal. She had lived and loved, been frightened and comforted. It was her home and yet still the place she could never return to.

The tears fell full and slow down her cheeks and belied the calm demeanor she kept. Richard stood behind her and waited, a patient lion at her back.

"How do I go on living if this doesn't work?" she said softly. "When this was more my life than anything I had before?"

He touched her shoulder lightly before the squawking call of the housekeeper echoed down the hall. "I haven't got all day, you two, hurry along."

Lillian took in a deep breath. "What do I do?" she whispered.

"Whatever she says, I dare say, that woman is frightful." Richard muttered to the staunch woman's back as she once again led them to the stairwell in the back of the manor.

"Here we are, you've got about fifteen minutes to make your peace with your mental issue." She nodded with finality towards the stairs and turned to busy herself with preparations for the next tour.

"Fifteen minutes? But that's not nearly enough time." Lillian tried to argue but the woman was already in the kitchen. Lillian looked up to the sun streaming down the ornate and curved stairway from the topmost windows. Dust motes filtered down and she felt the softness of the space fill her heart.

She closed her eyes, her hand fumbled to find the banister. She listened.

34

A BREATH AND A UNIVERSE APART

Matthew stood in the garden. Sunlight streamed down and the quiet early morning settled around him with its muted sounds, wet-earth smells and the delicate rays warming his shoulders. How he wanted to believe he could bring her back. How he wanted to believe that Miriam Shaw's universal postulating was true. She seemed one to believe in fairies, so there was no accounting for her rationality. But if Lillian could step through the veil, and had gotten his message in time, perhaps there was hope. Tears formed on his long lashes and dripped onto the thick page between his hands. All he could really do was ask.

"How do I go on living if she does not come back?" he whispered to the journal. He stared so hard at the words that he was almost certain he'd imagined the way they flickered and shimmered on the page. He dried his eyes quickly with the back of his hand, sniffed and brought the page closer. The words faded away and returned.

Westbury Manor, Stairs, March 24th. I will catch you this time.

. . .

Curse it all, what if he missed her? What if she'd gotten the message and was about to fall again? He wanted too badly to believe. Matthew turned quickly, his heart racing, his breath shallow and fast, and he raced into the manor and down the hall. The stairs were near the front and he hated the twisting maze that stole time as he tried to get there. Miriam, alerted by his heavy footfalls through the quiet house, followed.

"What is it? Are you well? What's happened?" she said and paused only briefly to wipe her hands on her apron. Fitzwilliam and Kitty, who were in the conservatory, watched as Matthew flashed by them.

"What on earth is vexing him so?" Kitty said, and put her embroidery delicately down. Fitzwilliam helped her to her feet and they followed, nearly bumping into Miriam on her way after Matthew.

He slid to a halt at the base of the stairs and waited, hands clutched around the journal, for any kind of sign, any slight waver in the air or crackling energy. The fairy door had been a very clear portal, glowing and rushing with wind and energy. But the hall was quiet. The lazy drifts of dust motes floated in the air as he stared up at the light coming in from the highest windows.

"Is everything well, Doctor Blackwell?" Fitzwilliam asked, as Matthew stood at the base of the stairs, gasping for breath.

"Today, today, sometime, on these stairs," he said, incoherent and hopeful.

"Whatever does that mean?" Kitty said and looked to Fitzwilliam for answers.

"If you fall, I will catch you," he whispered to no one in the room. "If you fall, Lillian. If you fall."

"'Tis a shame, such a brilliant mind." Fitzwilliam whispered under his breath to Kitty. "I fear he's quite gone mad."

"He's not mad. This is where she came through. And so she shall return." Miriam said.

"Who?"

"Lillian," Matthew said softly, closing his eyes, clenching his hands at his sides and praying to every god, every deity, every power in the universe. "Lillian, please."

∼

Richard looked behind them, checking for the housekeeper and any other guests that may have arrived early for the tour.

"What now? Do you want to go upstairs? See the rooms? Look for a portal?" Richard ruffled some nearby draperies and dust billowed up.

"Stop touching things! You're going to get us in trouble," Lillian whispered over her shoulder at him, still staring up at the empty stairwell.

"Well, excuse me! I'm looking for a time and space door," he grumbled back.

"I don't think it's upstairs. I think it *is* the stairs. When I fell, I was in one time and—poof, suddenly into the other."

"Does that mean you have to fall again? What if it doesn't work and you break your neck?"

"Well, I don't know how it works," she yelled back, feeling tumultuous and confused inside. "I don't even know *if* this works that I'll end up in his time."

"Maybe you could show up in a time before Frau Clutch-My-Pearls buys the manor, and scoop it up for yourself," Richard muttered at the sound of pots and pans banging in the kitchen.

Lillian worried her lip between her teeth. "What if I muck up the universe?"

"If anyone could, it would be you." Richard said over the tops of his glasses. They heard the housekeeper down the hall talking to herself about the tea going to be late. "How long do you think I could distract her?"

"She seems non-distractable."

"A woman with a schedule and a purpose."

"I've a purpose too." Lillian. said.

"You do," Richard said quietly. He came up closer to her and put his hands on her shoulders, making her meet his eyes. "You need to fall down some stairs."

"What if I do break my neck?"

"I will be here to catch you." Richard said. Lillian's eyes filled with tears. "If you don't fall into his time, then we will try something new, together."

"How did I ever get so lucky?" she said and kissed his cheek. He feigned disgust.

"Ew, girl cooties."

"Are you two about done?" came the sharp voice from the kitchen. "Tour arrives in five minutes, unless you want to pay the fee."

"Go on, Lily with the sharp tongue. Take a leap of faith." Richard whispered and pushed her towards the stairs. Lillian's heart raced in her chest as she climbed. She took every step slowly, as if she were afraid to miss the hole in the universe that would lead her back to him.

Matthew climbed the first few steps, eyes closed and attuned to the smallest changes. The drafts of the house, the shaft of sunlight that spilled over half the wooden stairs. Every footfall, he stopped, sank into the step to see if this was the way. One hand remained on the banister. He breathed softly. Pictured her face, smiling and lavender eyes meeting his, her soft cheek against his lips, her body close against his chest. The smell of her hair, the safety of holding her once more. He stopped on the stairs. Felt a strange pressure, like a pane of glass, unmoving, halting his progress.

"Lillian, please. I'm here. I'm here."

35

JOURNEYS END IN LOVERS' MEETING

Lillian reached the top of the first landing. The place where her shoe had first caught in the carpet and she had felt the frightening and unavoidable loss of weight, and the hard points of stairs that battered her body. Her palms erupted in sweat, her heart pounded so hard that it hurt. She rubbed her temples and stared at Richard, at the base of the stairs, the light reflecting off his glasses, a man blind with faith.

"I don't know, I don't know, I don't know," she whispered over and over even as her breath quickened to panicked speed.

"Lillian, breathe," Richard tried to say but Lillian froze before pressing her hand to the scar above her eye.

A sudden and painful pressure filled her head. Her hand tightened on the wooden post, she closed her eyes tighter and felt a strange echo ripple through her. His voice. His pleading. His sadness. Matthew's words, muffled, centuries away but cut through the fabric of space that was stretched thin in this place. She could feel him, smell him, the very essence of him in this space, this moment.

"Lillian?" Richard's voice was far away,

"Matthew," she said his name. "Matthew?" louder and cutting

287

through the blocks of time and stone and wood. Matthew's voice paused, a rustle, the pounding of feet and heartbeats, her name shouted down corridors, long-empty and devoid of the people she loved, echoing through the present-day house like a ghost rambling through the halls.

"Matthew!" she shouted again and the world stood still. Lillian closed her eyes to the sunlit space.

"What's the matter with you two? You can't just come in here raising a ruckus!" The housekeeper's voice was a whisper in Lillian's ears, far away, by eons and universes.

"Lillian, we should go," Richard yelled, strained with fear of the housekeeper's wrath.

"No, I hear him! Don't you hear him?"

"Lillian, I don't—"

"It's him. Matthew!"

"You two need to leave now!"

Lillian saw Matthew's face, gaunt and eyes pleading with sadness, fractured and disappearing through a sudden veil of light and reflection. God how she'd missed him. She'd gladly tumble to her death just for the chance to be in his arms again. Lillian launched herself from the top stair and into the thin and murky sheet of time.

A horrid tumbling sound ripped through the space, the wood of the stairwell shook and the stone halls seemed to echo with the cry of surprise as she tumbled into strong arms that caught her before falling, a crashing mess, to the ground at the base of the stairs.

The housekeeper squawked in surprise as the light of the hall first intensified then settled to a low, dusty hum. Lillian's head throbbed, and her chest felt heavy as though she could not breathe. The smell of electricity mingled with the earthy notes and she felt the scratchy fabric below her cheek.

"Richard, are you hurt?" she gasped.

"How is it you've already forgotten my name," he groaned. She felt the man below her move, and the smell of pipe tobacco and linen came into her senses. The light scent of lavender fields and rain, and though she was frightened to open her eyes and thereby end the dream, she steeled her nerve and sat up, teary-eyed and speechless, to stare into Doctor Matthew Blackwell's eyes.

"We must stop meeting this way," he whispered, and Lillian cried in surprise, wrapping her arms and body around him. He groaned and sighed.

"My love, you are injured," she said and tried to retreat from their embrace. But he held her fast in his arms, every muscle shaking. His hands ran up her back, down her jean-clad legs and every square inch of her as if assessing the reality of her warm body against him.

"I assure you, dear Lily, as long as you are in my arms, no further harm can come to me," he whispered and began raining kisses against her cheek and neck, pressing the softness of them to her lips, tongue tasting, tears mingling. "My dear, sweet Lily. How is it possible? Am I dead?"

"If you are dead, then I am happy to be perished with you," she whispered and for the first time in hundreds of years, they kissed. His mouth warm and soft against hers, his breath ragged and happy as he couldn't contain the laughter and cries between kisses and caresses.

"Saints, child, it is good to see you again. There's a good lass," Miriam said from behind them, tears in her eyes and as Lillian disengaged to look up at her, she saw the faithful librarian's eyes in hers. "I knew you'd find your way back home."

"I've you to thank for that," she said and nodded to the year-old journal that she'd picked up from the floor when Matthew fell. "Keep that safe, I'll need it later to come home," She turned her attention back to Matthew, "and to you."

"Lillian, my angel," he said, his eyes and hands never leaving her body. "It has been torture."

She kissed him again, and again and the couple heard nothing, saw nothing, felt nothing except each other's quickened breaths, lips pressed after centuries apart, arms reaching, touching, feeling to make the improbable dream real.

"You're here, you're really here," he whispered between kisses. "Please say it is not a dream. Please tell me my eyes and body are not deceiving me. You are really here."

"I am in your arms, my darling. Where I am, I cannot be certain nor do I care beyond that," she whispered, pulling back to look at him and smiling in the rays of sunshine that filtered in around them.

"How did you get here?" he whispered.

"I fell, my love. As I'm prone to do." He smiled and kissed her. Lillian threw her arms tight around him and felt him shiver and wince. "You are hurt."

"I will heal," he said softly and looked over every inch of her. The knitted sweater, the jeans, her Converse, he shook his head in wonder. "This garment," he pressed the fine weave between his fingers. Lillian smiled.

"Wait until you see what's beneath it," she whispered against his chin and his fingers held her tighter.

"I do not wish to wait," he groaned, and his hands slipped under the fabric to caress her bare skin "It would seem there is not much but the most delectable flesh I've ever tasted." Matthew smiled on her lips.

Miriam cleared her throat. "Tea will be served soon."

"I have missed a good tea," Lillian said breathlessly as his hands wandered beneath her sweater and their breaths came quickly. He was kissing and biting her neck. It was decadent and scandalous, and she pulled away to rest her forehead against his. "But I've missed you more. I'm sorry it took me so long."

"I would have waited until the end of my days."

"I would have searched for you until the end of mine."

He kissed her and smiled. "Whatever shall we do then, with this lifetime together? No quests to follow."

"I'm sure we will find something to match our passions and keep us busy."

"I have a brilliant idea of where to start," he gasped, and she felt his body respond to their position.

36

KITTY IS A KILLJOY AND MATTHEW IS A REBEL

"Can you stand?" Lillian asked.

"You are here, my sweet wife, I can fly if you ask," he said. She helped him up and he pulled her into his arms quickly. Her nose pressed into his chest and she smiled. His hands ran through her hair and he sighed into her forehead. "If it does not vex you to climb the stairs once more, I think it would be wise of you to lay down."

"Only if I'm doing so naked in your arms."

Matthew gasped in agreement and tipped her chin up to kiss her. A loud clearing of throat pulled them apart in a propriety Lillian felt deep in her bones. She was elated, even to see the displeased pout on Kitty's glowing face. Before she could rush into a hug, Kitty straightened and spoke.

"I have been informed that you eloped, which is quite scandalous and simply will not do. Even though Lady Mayfield herself is staying for an undetermined time in Bath with her cousin, the Duchess, and no longer resides at Westbury Manor, it is my duty as the lady of the house to right ruinous wrongs. As such, I've already made arrangements for a proper ceremony to take place, the moment you found your way home."

Lillian scowled, but it lacked the true annoyance she once held. Kitty was her dearest friend and knowing that the horrible Lady Mayfield would not be around to torture her, made the bright day even more glorious. Matthew's hand slipped into hers.

"How did you know I would be back?" she asked Kitty.

Kitty looked at her as though she'd hit her head again. "Because you belong here, dearest. With us. Colonel Mayfield, before he left on his extended scientific study, was most assured of that fact."

"Colonel Mayfield?" Lillian looked to Matthew who stared back at her knowingly. "He is gone? For how long? Will he return?"

Matthew took her hand. "I have not heard from him in over six months. He assured me that he would check in, as his work allowed him." Lillian's brow drew up. She'd hoped to see her father again. But it wasn't unlike him to disappear either. Matthew kissed her cheek and she was brought back to the happy present.

"In any case, I knew you were smart enough to find your way home. Though those clothes—" Kitty looked at Lillian. "I dare say, they will not do."

"Perhaps my husband can help me remove them," she said with a smile up at Matthew and he blushed. Kitty cleared her throat.

"As there has been no formal ceremony, he is not technically your husband and he will do no such thing," Kitty reprimanded.

Lillian's brow lowered and she pulled her hand from Matthew's. "Wait, are you serious?" Her cheeks felt hot even as Matthew shrugged and blushed.

"It is a minor detail. Only a week away with my efficient manner. You will surely survive the brief period of time apart."

"Brief period of time?" Lillian fumed.

"It has already been over a year!" Matthew argued. Lillian

looked up at him. Mere days for her, had been a year for him. Her eyes filled. Never again would she let them part.

"All the same, tea is in a few minutes. Please, do go to your quarters and find something proper to wear, I have joyous news." Kitty said, gave her a peck on the cheek, thereby finalizing the matter entirely and turning to retire to the parlor. Fitzwilliam pulled Lillian in for a brief hug.

"It's good to see you again. My heart has been filled with much worry." He kissed her forehead and nodded to Matthew. Lillian sighed angrily as they watched them go and heard Kitty calling for the doctor to join them. Matthew turned to Lillian, kissed her gently on the tip of her nose.

"A week is not so long."

"A week is a lifetime," she argued hotly and stomped up the stairs, no longer afraid she might disappear.

"Lillian, please," he said after her, but she rushed to her room and slammed the door. Once inside she slid down the wood and sat in the quiet. The lovely quiet. The quiet of her home, the taste of her soon-to-be-husband on her lips, the smell of him on her clothes. She stood, went to her armoire and opened the doors to find her dresses, untouched. Kitty and Fitzwilliam had believed. And she had them and Miriam. Perhaps one day her father again. But most of all, she had Matthew. A man who believed in her, loved her, and kept her mind and body open and excited to all the possibilities of the life ahead of them. She nearly cried and touched the soft linen. With a giddy amount of happiness, she shed her clothes and had just stepped into a fine, light blue gown when the window to her bedroom opened abruptly and Matthew tumbled into the room, breathless and red-faced.

Lillian let out a surprised cry that she stifled with her hand and Kitty's voice came up through the floor. "Is everything alright?"

"Perfectly wonderful! I merely tripped on all these skirts, dear sister," she called back, even as Matthew rushed her.

"Do you think I would honestly let you out of my sight or hands for even a moment?" he growled and came to her, stripping his own coat and taking her face in his hands to kiss her. The dress, not yet fastened fell from her shoulders and he pushed it the rest of the way down with a pleased grunt. "You are my wife and I will not stand being parted from you, even if I have to climb the damn drain pipe every night for a week," he grumbled against her lips and began unfastening his breeches.

"I love the rebel you've become," she gasped and stepped out of her dress and chemise. "But do we have time?"

Matthew locked the door with a smile. "We have all the time in the world," he whispered as he returned to her. She was still wearing her modern underclothing. He stared at it with wonder and a smile. "Is this all women in your time wear beneath their clothes?" Lillian looked down at the simple lace bra and panties.

"Scandalous?"

"Delicious," he breathed and pulled her into the bed. "The moments, the hours I have missed you, Lily. I thought I would never see you again," he kissed her face, her neck her chin and Lillian could not stop smiling as she untucked his shirt and pulled it up over his head.

"I thought you'd be lost to me forever," she whispered back, and the sudden onslaught of tears came quickly.

"Do not weep," he said, kissing the tears down her cheeks. "You are here now, we are safe. I shall never let you go, unless I can follow." Matthew laid her on the bed, and she removed the small scraps of clothing to feel the warmth of his skin against hers. As he pressed his body to hers he sighed and nearly sobbed. "I fear I've died and gone to heaven." Lillian wrapped her legs around his hips and bit his chin.

"Let's go there together," she whispered in his ear and he kissed her, swallowing their pleased gasps as his body joined hers. Shocks of electric pleasure swept up her spine and she dug her fingers into his back. Matthew grunted and seethed, muffling his excitement in her neck. Sweat erupted between them and over his shoulders in his relentless need to fill her and the lonely space of time between them.

"My Lily, my angel," he gasped, propping himself up on strong arms to watch her face. Lillian's hands went to his firm backside as she felt herself cresting. She cried out and he silenced her with a kiss, climaxing along with her in a shaking, sweaty tumble of skin. He fell to her chest with a pleased moan and wept into her hair. Lillian clung to him, hands gently caressing his back as her breath pulled and sighed with relief.

"I love you Matthew," she whispered. "With all my heart, through all time."

Matthew lifted himself up on one arm to stare down at her. He traced her lips with his fingers and smiled before kissing her.

"And I love you, hopelessly, without an end in sight." They kissed and he fell back into the bed, pleased. He held her close against his chest.

"Do we really have to go through with a ceremony?" she said and looked up from drawing hearts on the tight skin of his stomach. Matthew raised an elegant blond brow at her.

"As though you wouldn't like to be fretted over, showered with gifts and gowns?"

She stuck out her tongue. "You know how I feel about gowns."

"I much prefer you without them as well." He smiled and shifted below her.

"What will we tell people? Where have I been?"

"Do not let this worry plague your mind, I will take care of all the questions and details. All you merely must do is show up."

"That, Doctor Blackwell, I will most certainly do," she smiled at Matthew and they fell into a laughing pile of kisses and playful caresses before Kitty called up the stairs that they weren't fooling anyone.

37

SWEET ENDINGS OR EXCITING
BEGINNINGS?

The bump in the night woke Lillian from a dead sleep.

Matthew, curled around her protectively, snorted and sat up next to her, before pulling her naked body back into the bed. Moonlight splashed across the room in a soft gray hue and all was quiet again. But Lillian's body stayed tense.

"What is it my love?" he said groggily. He caressed her bare thigh, fingers trailing up the soft skin and back down again. He gave a pleased sigh and Lillian fell under the spell of his comfort.

Her eyes drifted closed in the dark room, where their wedding garments had been strewn about unceremoniously, in their fervor to properly consummate their vows. And how fervently they did, a few times over. They were to leave tomorrow on their honeymoon, both deciding to opt for an extended stay away in Scotland. Matthew's fingers were magical as he began to massage the flesh of her thigh, her ass, to her low back. She held the blankets to her bare chest and was about to make sleepy, slow love to her husband when the door to their bed chamber opened.

They both sat up. Matthew quickly reached for the silver

candle stick beside the bed. He held it over his head menacingly and growled into the darkness. "Who dares to—"

"Save your breath, Romeo," the strange and raspy voice came out of the darkness, followed by the muffled sound of crystals tinkling as if beneath a thick curtain. "I'm glad I caught you in a happy mood because the honeymoon is officially over."

"What are you talking about? Who are you?" Matthew asked again and moved to stand, eyes still searching in the darkness.

Lillian squinted into the shadows and the strike of a match exploded the darkness. Matches didn't exist in this time. Lillian's heart rate rose as she climbed from the bed and draped a blanket over her body. Matthew, not bothering to cover himself, stood between the intruder and her. The flame lit a candle in the gnarled hand of an old woman, draped in dark red, and looking rather unhappy. Lillian's eyes narrowed and she moved to stand in front of Matthew.

"Who are you? What are you doing here?"

"Who are you?" Matthew said at the same time.

"Not that it's important to know, but, I'm an official member of the Timekeeper's Guild." She looked annoyed as she stared at the two of them, disheveled and covered in love bites. She moved to the mantel, lit more candles from hers and turned back to them. "I hate to break it to you, Lillian Byrne, oh, I suppose it's Blackwell now?"

"It is."

"Well, Lillian Blackwell, I'm afraid, you have some work yet to do; on the timeline." The Timekeeper took an appreciative once-over of Matthew, who then donned his pants, but still looked at her suspiciously.

"What in the hell does that mean?" Lillian asked. "What about my father?"

"In the wind," she said curtly. "He has not been seen or tracked since last he left this home."

Lillian's brow drew together. "Surely, that cannot be right—"

"As such, you will now acquire the debt he owes us."

"Lillian what madness is this?" Matthew asked.

"A madness of her and her father's doing, I'm afraid. Though I suppose you're also somewhat to blame, Doctor Blackwell."

"What's happened to the timeline? Was Matthew meant to do something?" Lillian asked.

"Indeed, he was."

"I don't understand," Lillian began, shaking her head. "We've done nothing but be married in a quiet and simple ceremony. His journals ended and I was able to pass through. So time must have wanted us to find each other, we intend to continue his life of helping others," she said and took Matthew's hand in her own.

The Timekeeper shook her head. "Be that as it may, before you two created your story, he had a purpose to serve, which he did not. So in a way, it's both your faults. You may not have intended to cause damage, but Matthew by your side means he did not play his necessary part. Because we lost your father, our best field agent, we were not able to intervene before, that damn brute got it into his head to 'help' and found the damn map. Oh the mess," the Timekeeper sighed.

"What are you talking about? Which brute?" Lillian said, perturbed.

"Why your troublesome librarian, of course. Doctor Richard Shaw."

RATE AND REVIEW

We hope you enjoyed *Time to Byrne* by S.E. Reichert. If you did, we would ask that you please rate and review this title. Every review helps our authors.

Rate and Review: Time to Byrne

MEET THE AUTHOR

Sarah Reichert (S.E. Reichert) is a novelist, poet and mentor. She is the author of The Sweet Valley Series; *Raising Elle, Granting Katelyn,* and *Composing Laney,* and two 80s themed sweet romances; *Rewriting Christmas, Back to the 80s* from 5 Prince Publishing. Her most recent novel, *No Words After I Love You* was published in May 2025.

Reichert is the Director of Writing Heights Writers Association, a local organization dedicated to the education and success of writers at every level, and is on the board of Wyoming Writers, Inc. Her work has been featured in several publications both in the U.S. and abroad. Reichert lives in Fort Collins with her family. In her non-writing hours, she is the mother to two teenage girls, loves being outdoors, and is working towards her third degree Black Belt in Kenpo Karate JuJitsu.

www.ingramcontent.com/pod-product-compliance
Lightning Source LLC
Chambersburg PA
CBHW030246030726
47493CB00023B/608